ALSO BY ANDREW PYPER

The Demonologist
The Guardians
The Killing Circle
The Wildfire Season
The Trade Mission
Lost Girls
Kiss Me (Stories)

THE
DAMNED

ANDREW
PYPER

Simon & Schuster

New York • London • Toronto • Sydney • New Delhi

Simon & Schuster
1230 Avenue of the Americas
New York, NY 10020

First Simon & Schuster export edition February 2015

SIMON & SCHUSTER and colophon are registered trademarks
of Simon & Schuster, Inc.

For information about special discounts for bulk purchases,
please contact Simon & Schuster Special Sales at 1-800-268-3216
or CustomerService@simonandschuster.ca.

Jacket design by Jaya Miceli
Jacket photograph by quavando/Getty Images

Manufactured in the United States of America

10 9 8 7 6 5 4 3 2 1

ISBN 978-1-4767-5514-4
ISBN 978-1-4767-5519-9 (ebook)

To Heidi, Maude, and Ford

I've died more than once in my life.

Some can spin plates on sticks, some can go around Pebble Beach at even par, but few have as many stamps in their afterlife passport as me. It's a gift, I suppose, though not one I'd wish on anyone.

There will be one more crossing over for me, just as there is for all of us. But most can't tell you what awaits you there, and even I can only report on what I've seen myself, because whether you're meant for the penthouse or the boiler room, it's a place of your own making. Paradise or Hades, heaven or hell—they're custom made.

I know because I've been to both.

—*The Damned*, by Danny Orchard

PART I

The After

I

My name is Danny Orchard. It might ring a bell. I wrote a book a while back, a memoir of my near-death experience. A surprise, top-of-the-list bestseller from the moment it first appeared. Twenty-seven languages and fourteen years later, I still catch people reading it on the subway. I never introduce myself to tell them the story's mine.

It's made me an authority of a sort. A death expert. One of those third-tier celebrities who is invited to give after-dinner speeches at dentists' conventions and service club fundraisers, a public figure who comes cheaper than a Super Bowl quarterback and has a more interesting story than a retired senator. Everyone remembers that spot I did on 60 Minutes when I showed my mother's Omega watch—the book's evidence that heaven is real—and Morley Safer's eyes seemed to well up.

My book can make one other claim, namely its inspiring the formation of the Afterlifers, a community for those who've traveled to the other side and returned. You'd never guess how many of us there are out there. The last time I checked there were a dozen chapters across North America and a handful in Europe and Asia, too, each group meeting on a monthly basis to discuss the effect of NDEs on members' lives, marriages, beliefs, work. They get together in the usual cheap, disheartening venues: church basements, HoJo conference rooms, linoleumed community centers. It's like AA, except with booze.

I used to get asked all the time to be a guest at one of their gatherings in Miami or Toronto or Amsterdam or L.A., and sometimes I'd accept if they paid my way, but mostly I claimed to be too busy "working on something new." A lie. The fact is, I'd had more than my fill of tearful recollections of angels taking the form of beloved first-grade teachers or the feelings of joy someone had in seeing their dearly departed, haloed and at peace, telling them not to be afraid.

Because it's not always like that.

Sometimes, you should be afraid.

Still, it was a habit I couldn't shake, like putting on a tie and going to church on Sunday, and for years I attended the monthly meetings of the local Boston chapter. I sat at the back and almost never spoke to the group, a priestly figure the other Afterlifers tended not to bother once they'd had their dog-eared copy of my book signed.

"So why do you come?" the chapter's leader, Lyle Kirk, once asked me as he tossed a twenty onto the bar for the beers we often found ourselves drinking after a meeting. "Why show up if you've got nothing to say?"

I surprised myself by telling him the truth.

"Because you're the only friends I have," I said.

Followed by a thought I didn't say.

And you're not even really friends.

Lyle was a good guy, though, a Revere contractor who specialized in eaves troughs, manageably alcoholic, his nose a burst kernel of popcorn in the center of his face. His heaven was a bit unusual. An eternity spent rolling around on the grass, a diapered infant being tickled by the family dog as it licked spilled applesauce off his belly.

"To each his own," he'd said with a shrug at the end of his presentation.

One night, four months ago, I sat in the corner of the banquet room of a Cambodian restaurant on Beacon Street. Maybe a dozen or so Afterlifers in the chairs in front of a lectern with crackly speakers built into its base, the mic unnecessarily on, so that every voice was turned to ground sand. And what did the voices talk about? Heaven stuff, for the most part. Repeating their tales of a glimpsed Forever. The sailboat trip with Mom. The hand-holding walk on the beach with a dead husband. The football game where the Hail Mary pass is caught every time. When Lyle asked if I'd like to speak I declined as usual, saying I was just there to offer support. But these people didn't need support. They needed to get on with their lives before life was taken away from them and that walk on the beach was all they were left with.

Lyle was about to close the meeting when an arm went up.

An elderly woman smelling of clothes left too long in airless closets, sitting directly in front of me. She asked if there was time to tell her story. Lyle told her there was always time for someone who "knows what you know, sweetheart."

It took her a while to make her way to the front. Not just the coaxing of an arthritic hip slowing her down but some deeper reluctance. When she turned we saw it wasn't shyness. It was everything she could do to make the crossing from her fold-out chair to stand before us because she was quite plainly terrified.

"My name is Violet Grieg. My experience is a bit different from yours," she said.

Her skin lost all its color in the time it took to speak these two sentences, the circles of rouge on her cheeks standing out like welts.

"Our father," she started after a full minute, then paused again. I thought she was about to recite the Lord's Prayer. I even lowered my eyes to join her in it. "When he was alive, our father was what everyone called 'a good man.' He had that kind of face, that kind of laugh. A family doctor up in Skowhegan where we grew up—delivered babies, doled out the pills. 'Your father's a good man,' they'd say. But what in the good goddamn did they know?"

She shouted this last part. A furious blast into the mic that turned into a shriek of feedback.

"How can you tell a good man from bad if you don't live with him, if you don't have to trust him?" she went on when the noise had retreated. "*A good man.* It was an act! 'I'll just go upstairs to *say goodnight to the girls,*' he'd say. Our mother never stopped him. It was just my sister and I who . . . knew what he really was."

She made what I thought was a move to return to her seat, but it was only a step back to shake her head. A dizzy spell, or sudden chill. When she spoke again her voice had lowered to an unsettling growl.

"I tried to kill myself a year ago. But suicide—that's a *sin*. That's what the good book says. It's a *law*."

One of the Afterlifers got up and left, gesturing at his watch as if he had somewhere else to be.

"I was dead and gone," Violet Grieg went on, her eyes fixed over our heads at the room's back door, as if expecting someone to enter. "Taken to a place where the most terrible things I'd known happened over and over. It would've been like that forever except this world decided it wasn't through with me yet. I came back. And now I see him all the time. Hear him, too. Coming up the stairs to wherever I try to hide. Wherever I go, he follows."

Her forehead shone with sweat. The skin over the knuckles gripped to the lectern's sides so thin I expected it to tear open, easy as tissue paper.

"I'll stick a chair under the doorknob, lay pillows against the crack under the door so I don't have to see the shadow of his shoes. I'm like a kid again. Lying in bed. Trying not to move, not to breathe. Watching him walking back and forth like he's looking for a key to open the door. Sometimes he does."

Lyle glanced back at the rest of the room with a seasick grin of apology. One of the fluorescent lights near the front started flickering. A strobe that lent Violet Grieg's face the waxy stiffness of an antique doll.

"'Only a ghost,' my sister said, but I told her no, it isn't that. It's different. It's more," she said, her hands shaking the lectern so badly the woman sitting directly in front of her slid her chair back a foot.

Then the shaking stopped. Her eyes fixed on something at the door behind me. Something I didn't see when I turned to look.

"When I died and came back I brought my father with me," she whispered. "Unlike you people, when I passed, I went the other way. I went *down*. And that man . . . that filthy sonofabitch put his arms around my neck and hitched a ride all the way up!"

That's when she fell.

Even though I was the farthest away, I was the first to reach her. Throwing some chairs aside, jumping over others.

By the time I knelt next to her and slipped a hand under her head she was already coming around. When her eyes rolled back into focus I could see how all the rage had drained out of her, leaving her trembling and boneless.

"You're going to be okay, Violet," I told her. "Just a little fall, that's all. You're going to be fine."

She looked up at me and I knew that she'd come here as a last hope, and that hope was now gone.

I felt I knew something else, too.

It was her father she'd seen at the back of the room.

After the paramedics came and she held my hand all the way on the gurney ride into the ambulance, Lyle and I headed down the street to O'Leary's, where he ordered a round of Jameson shots.

"Thanks for coming tonight," he said as we clinked glasses, the whiskey dribbling over our fingertips. "Sorry about that one at the end, though. Jesus."

"Not her fault."

" 'Course not. Just, *those* ones—I think of them as Underworlders more than Afterlifers, y'know? They tend to bring the mood down a few notches."

"Demons will do that."

"Holy shit, Danny. You believed her?"

"I'm speaking figuratively."

"Yeah? Well, she sure as hell wasn't."

Lyle raised an index finger to the bartender to signal more of the same.

"What about you? You're the expert," he went on. "You're the *guy*. What do you know about that stuff?"

"Nothing, really. But I've thought about it more than a few times. Who hasn't?"

"I suppose," Lyle said, not liking where this was going all of a sudden.

"Just follow me for a second here. Most people's NDEs are positive experiences, right? Or maybe mysterious. A little troubling at worst. 'Go toward the light!' versus 'Don't go toward the light!' At the end of the day, what difference does it make?"

"The light's going to take us eventually."

"That's right. For most of us, the good light is waiting. But there are those—not many, but some, like Violet there tonight—who don't have a lovely little visit over there."

"Because they go to the Other Place."

"You tell me. How do they describe it?"

"It's different for every one of them. Each of us has to find our own place."

"Except in those cases, the places are bad."

"The worst," he said. "The moment when shit went south on them and they started on a different path. From *being* harmed to *doing* harm."

"Have you noticed any other pattern about them?"

"Let me think." He put a thumb to his chin, but it slipped off and he returned his hand to the top of the bar. "Almost always something to do with where they grew up. The place they were scared of most. The hallways of their school, their uncle's basement, a night swim with their mom where the mom didn't make it back. Most of the time, they can't even talk about it."

"And I'm guessing there's not a lot of them coming to the meetings."

"If they *do* come, they stop after one or two times. I can pretty much guarantee you we won't be seeing Violet Grieg next month."

"Why?"

This time, Lyle bent to take a sip from his glass without picking it up.

"People like that, what they've seen—it's too much," he said, giving his head a shake as the whiskey burned its way down. "And they can see they don't fit in with the rest of the group. I mean, we *try* to include them. But there's only so much including we can do. We're all 'Heaven is great and wonderful and waiting for all of us! Oh, sorry, except for . . . *you*. You're just *fucked*.' It's not real uplifting, y'know?"

I pretended to take an interest in the Celtics game that was winding down on the TV.

"Why're you asking about all this?" Lyle put to me after a time. "You know someone you think might have gone where Violet went?"

"No, it's nothing like that," I lie. "Just keeping some things in mind for my next book."

Lyle Kirk is a semiemployed drunk and one rung down from a full-blown crackpot, but he isn't stupid.

"Can't wait to read it," he said.

2

My sister and I both died on our sixteenth birthdays.

We were fraternal twins, though you wouldn't necessarily know it from a first glance. Ash had the posture of a dancer and a confidence readable in every gesture, as if all her actions were part of a subtle but commanding performance, a summoning to gather round and watch. I, on the other hand, tried to hide behind hair grown long over my eyes, a boy who sought the nearest corner upon entering a room and let his sister take the center of the floor. If you'd met the two of us back then you would have said life had given its clear vote to one over the other. And yet when death came for us it chose her over me, holding her in its grasp and tossing me back to a world I barely recognized without my sister in it.

Before the day we turned sixteen we lived the whole of our lives in the same house. The nicest house on one of Royal Oak's nicest streets, though in both cases only marginally so. The Royal (as we called it, "Be Loyal to the Royal!" the slogan of local businesses) was pleasant but consistent in its modesty, having none of the monster renos or brand-name designer shops of Grosse Pointe or the newer suburbs miles farther from the city of Detroit. Most families we grew up with were in the middle of the middle class, professionals on their way up or down, a smattering of tradesmen who'd borrowed all they could to move north of 8 Mile. By comparison to most of our neighbors, we were exceptional. Not because of money, but because of Ash. The girl everyone said could be a model, an actress, a President of the United States one day.

Ashleigh Orchard was Royal royalty.

Ashleigh on straight-A report cards and graduation Honors Lists and the *Detroit Free Press* Metro section review of a "stunning turn" by the star of Dondero High's production of *South Pacific*. But in the real, living world, she was only ever Ash.

Beautiful Ash. Though it is the sort of beauty that comes with an asterisk.

Beautiful in the way our own father once called "uglybeautiful," her features so excessively lovely taken on their own that, in their assembly, she suggested the alien, the genetically modified—too-blue eyes set too far apart, limbs and fingers too extraterrestrially long.

By looking at our family—at her—you would almost certainly mistake us for lucky. But inside the walls of our house on Farnum Avenue there was a secret. My father, mother, and I were aware that a monster lived with us, however photogenic, however scholarship-guaranteed. And because she was only a girl, because she was one of us by name, because we feared her, there was nothing we could do about it.

So we tried to manage, in our ways. Dad retreated into work, leaving earlier in the mornings, returning later and later at night. He was an in-house "liability man" at General Motors with an office in the middle tower of the Renaissance Center, where the company leased space from the hotel that occupied the other floors. His windows on the forty-second floor overlooked the Detroit River, so high up he could look across to Canada and the flat tobacco fields beyond. In the year before Ash died, he spent a couple nights a week sleeping on the sofa there. Hiding.

Our mother was a self-described homemaker, but in reality she was an earplugged sleep-inner, a noontime sherry drinker, a Chardonnay zombie by the time we came in the door from school. Sometimes I'd find her passed out in a flower bed with gardener's gloves still on, keeping their grip on pruning shears and trickling hose. Once, I discovered her in the tub, the water cold. She was still alive, though barely so. Her naked body surprisingly heavy as I attempted the impossible: heaving her out while trying not to touch her at the same time. We both ended up in a pile on the bathmat.

"Thank you, Danny," she said when she could find the words, using the walls for balance as she tried to bring some dignity to the walk back to her room. "That was *gentlemanly* of you."

She died there, in that same bathroom, two years before Ash did. A "domestic accident," which is what they call falling asleep drunk and drowning in the tub, so that you don't have to use a different word for it. Dad found her after coming home late from work, his wife's eyes looking through him from six inches under the surface.

It wasn't the usual suburban strain of depression that plagued her, but a terror she did what she could to quiet. A knowledge of what lies on the other side, waiting for us to call out to it, open a door for it to pass through.

And guilt, too, I think. The regret of being the one to bring Ash into the world.

WHAT SORT OF THINGS DID ASH DO? WHY WAS SHE A GIRL WHOSE own mother might wish was never born?

Let me tell you a story. A short, terrible little story.

In the winter when Ash and I were twelve, there was a day of sun that followed a cold snap, a melting of snow that left slicked streets and dripping eaves. The very next morning, the cold returned. Sidewalks and driveways turned to ice rinks. And hanging from every roof, icicles as long and sharp as spears.

"Monster teeth," Ash said when she saw them.

When we got home from school that day, the icicles were still there, though the forecast called for higher temperatures later in the week.

"We need to save one," Ash said. "They're too pretty to just *die*."

She made me get a stepladder. When I returned, she directed me to the icicle she'd chosen, and that I had to climb to the ladder's top to pull away.

"Be *careful!*" Ash said, a real concern for the ice that I'd never heard her genuinely express for another human being before.

When I handed it over to her she cradled it like a baby as she carried it to the garage and hid it under a bag of pork chops at the bottom of the freezer chest.

Months passed. At some point in the spring we both watched a TV show, a police procedural where the killer used ice bullets to shoot his victim through the skull. Only a trace of water was found in the pool of blood left on the floor, puzzling the detectives. "Ice! Completely undetectable!" the prosecutor declared during the trial.

That night Ash repeated the line, like a song lyric, on her way up to bed.

From the day I pulled it down for her she never mentioned the icicle, and neither did I. There wasn't one of those days when I didn't think about it, though. Imagining the electrocuting pain of it driven into the back of my neck as I slept. Waiting to open my eyes in the night and find her standing over me, the icicle held in both hands like a stake, her face set in the blank mask she wore when she wasn't acting and was her perfectly hollow self.

Summer came. Long, unstructured days of waiting for something to happen.

And then it did.

I went out into the yard to look for something in the garage and found the dog instead. We'd only gotten him a few weeks earlier, a yellow Lab stray Dad brought home from Animal Services. Another gesture at normalcy.

Ash was listening to the Sex Pistols a lot at the time. She named it Sid.

The day was hot and the flies were already buzzing around Sid's body as if looking for a way in. It was the blood that had drawn them. Red and glossy, still wet. All coming from its eye socket. The eye itself missing.

The dog appeared to be smiling. As if it had been trained to Lie Down and Be Dead and was waiting for the command to rise.

A puddle of pinkened water spread out around its head. I knelt down and touched it.

Still cold.

And at this touch, a thought. Spoken not in my voice, but Ash's.

This will never stop, it said.

THEY TRIED SENDING HER AWAY.

Not that they sold it to Ash that way. They called it an opportunity.

We couldn't really afford the prep school tuition and boarding fees at Cranbrook, but Dad said it was worth it no matter the cost. He told her it was a chance for her to "change course."

This was when we were thirteen.

I remember driving with her and Dad up to Bloomfield Hills to drop her off. Me sitting in the front passenger seat, Ash in the back. She didn't resist, didn't argue. There were no tears from her or any one of us. She just looked out the window as our suburb greened into a fancier, more distant suburb, a trace of a smile at the corners of her mouth. As if it were all her idea.

After she was shown her room she closed the door on us both without a word. I could feel Dad fighting the urge to turn his solemn walk into a run to the car.

Dad took me to his office. A drive down Woodward Avenue and into Detroit all the way to the Ren Center. He said he wanted to get some things from his desk, but it was really an unacknowledged celebration. Just the two of us, trying out jokes on each other, Dad telling stories I'd never heard before about when he was young. The city crumbling and beautiful all around us.

I'm not sure anyone really thought it would work. But for the three months Ash was out of the house and up the road in Bloom-field Hills something like peace visited our house. A quiet, anyway. The recuperative stillness of a veterans' rehab ward, the three of us wounded but on the mend, shuffling around, feeling a little stronger every day. I cut my hair so that anyone could see my eyes. Mom even dialed back on the drinking. Tried out a recipe for Beef Wellington she found in a never-touched Julia Child cookbook. It remains the most delicious meal of my life.

Sometimes I thought of Ash and was reminded that my sister had never done me any direct harm. Threats, manipulations, frights, yes. But with me, she never carried all the way through in the way she did with others. I was the only one she spared, the one she kept close even if she didn't know how to love, and in recalling this my happi-ness was momentarily grounded by shame. Yet soon the horizon of a life without her would come into view again and I wished only to see more of it.

And then I came home after school to find my father standing in the kitchen, red-faced, silently reading a letter torn from a Cranbrook envelope, and I knew Ash was home, that we would never try to ship her off again, that we would be punished for the attempt we'd made.

She'd been expelled. That's all my father would say about it, though the letter contained more information than that. A naming of specific, unspeakable crimes. I could tell by the way his face changed as he read it. His features not just falling but going slack, a deaden-ing.

When he was finished he folded the letter up into a rectangle the size of a business card. Left the house with it clenched in his fist.

Ash's door was open when I went upstairs. A rare invitation to look inside and find her sitting on the edge of her bed, calmly writing in her journal.

When she sensed me standing there she looked up. Pouted. Blinked her eyes, the lids darkened by makeup the color of a bruise.

"Miss me?" she said.

3

After the failed Cranbrook experiment, our family carried on as it had before, or tried to, which is to say we lived in even sharper anticipation of the Truly Bad Thing we knew was coming.

Over the months that Ash and I moved deeper into teenagerhood our distinctions became more exaggerated. My friendlessness graduated into a kind of sustained performance art, a survival stunt like the swami we watched fold himself into a plastic box on TV and remain for days, silent and unmoving. As for Ash, her public charms grew even more assured, her private cruelties more disturbing. It wasn't any side effect of puberty, either. She wasn't "maturing." She was becoming *something else*. And though my father, mother, and I never spoke openly of what that might be, I think we could imagine, with looming individual horror, the inhuman shapes she might choose.

It only got worse after Mom died.

Within days of our father coming home from work to find her in the bathtub, drunk and drowned—the very afternoon that followed the morning of our mother's funeral—Ash asked if I would come to the house of the boy she was seeing at the time, Brendan Oliver, and walk her home. It was an odd request on several fronts, considering we'd stood by a hole in the ground of Woodlawn Cemetery and watched our mother be lowered into it just two hours earlier. But this was Ash. Free of grief, of boundaries. It was all she could do to keep the trembly-cheeked "near tears" look fixed to her face at the graveside as long as she did before bursting out of the rented limo and running into the house to call Brendan and see if he was around and wanted to see her.

He was. He did.

"Could you come by Brendan's later, Danny? I need to talk to you about something," Ash said before she swiped her lips with strawberry gloss and headed out the door. It wasn't a request. And I knew it wasn't something she wanted to talk to me about, but something she wanted to show me.

I made it to the Oliver house on Derby Avenue shortly after five and tried the front doorbell though I figured there was little chance of anyone answering. At seventeen, Brendan was even older than the other older boys Ash was moving between, a wide-jawed senior on the basketball team known for his success with girls. He was the sort of aggressive, taunting, self-certain kid who went unquestioned in his actions, a towering collection of physical gifts set to play for Ohio the next year, not so much above the law but, in our world, the law itself.

All of this, along with the absence of his parents' car in the driveway, meant that he probably had Ash to himself somewhere inside. He would be murmuring his commands in one of the curtained rooms. He would ignore the doorbell until he was through.

It made me wonder what Ash wanted me here for. And as I thought about that, in an instant, the first real grief of the day arrived. The realization that my mother was gone forever came over me in a blanket that left me gasping and blind, reaching for the porch railing and blinking out at the street until its trees and awnings returned to focus. And when they did, I glanced back at the Olivers' door to see the hall light behind the pane of decorative glass dim and brighten. A sound, too. The low hum of machinery.

Ash had said something about Brendan's dad having a workshop in the garage behind their house. Even as I started up the driveway toward it I was thinking, *If I know there's a workshop back here, she wanted me to know it.* The conclusion that followed—*If I'm going to look through the window, she wants me to*—didn't stop me from lifting my nose over the splintered window frame to peer inside.

At first, it seemed like they were dancing.

Wrapped close and swaying to a slow song I couldn't hear, the side of Ash's face held against his chest and Brendan folded over her like a question mark. But it wasn't a dance. His shirt was off, for one thing. And their movements were a single-bodied negotiation: he trying to get her to the floor, where his Dondero High hoodie lay as a makeshift bedsheet, and she keeping him up, nuzzling her cheek against his ribs, directing his lips down to hers with a hand.

Without turning her head Ash glanced over to the window. Found me.

She related a couple of facts through her eyes alone. The first was that she'd been waiting for me to get there, had worked to situate herself and Brendan where they were at that moment, and now, finally, she could begin.

The second was that the standing bandsaw behind Ash was on.

It looks so sharp! Like teeth!

I could hear her voice, her very words from moments ago, like the trace of an echo in the air. She would have gasped after speaking them so that he could feel the heat of her breath. Mock-scared, mock-aroused. But the excitement real.

Could you turn it on, Brendan?

I watched him kiss her as she arched to meet him. Her eyes closed. His wide as an owl's bearing down on something small and doomed in the grass. Eyes that watched as Ash took his hand in hers and guided it toward the smooth table of the bandsaw. The blade a steady blur of motion.

It happened fast, though not that fast.

There was time for Brendan to see what was about to take place and stop it before it did. He could have pulled his hand away, jumped back from her touch, demanded to know what the hell she thought she was doing. Instead, he watched as I did as Ash placed his hand on the table and slid his splayed fingers into the spinning saw's gray teeth.

If he screamed, I don't remember the sound of it. What I remember, before running down the driveway to the street, before I voiced a scream of my own, was Ash opening her eyes. Making sure that I saw.

What was important for me to see wasn't the violence, the seductive ease with which the bandsaw parted two of Brendan Oliver's fingers from the rest of him or the neat jet of blood that left what could have been an attempt at a valentine's heart on the plank wall, but how she'd made him do it to himself. He hadn't fought her, hadn't protested. He'd been as interested in seeing what she had planned for him as I was. And it would only be later, after telling his parents it was an accident and the revocation of his invitation to play for Ohio and the new, hollow resignation that haunted his face whenever I saw him, usually alone, on the streets of Royal Oak over the years afterward, that he realized the beautiful girl in his father's workshop hadn't stolen a part of him but the whole thing.

4

If you ask the Detroit police today where they keep her file, they'll tell you Ashleigh Orchard is a cold case. A girl who bicycled off with some friends to watch a matinee of *Dead Poets Society* at the Main Art Theatre to celebrate her sixteenth birthday, but instead led them down Woodward Avenue toward downtown.

All four of them would have understood the audacity of a bike ride into Detroit. It would take them into the world they normally viewed from behind the windows of their parents' cars, the doors locked. Homes abandoned and burned each year on Devil's Night. The gangs of Hamtramck and Highland Park left to themselves by police. Whole blocks returning to weedy fields, bricks piled here and there like funeral mounds.

Ash's friends wanted to know why. Why was she making them do this?

"I want to show you something," she said.

Ash didn't slow. She pedaled on shining ballet-class legs, her long, yellow-blond hair waving against her back like a farewell.

It was Lisa Goodale who finally turned them around. Lisa

Goodale, pretty in the kittenish way that never ages well and who was doing ninth-grade math over for the third time in summer school and who taught blow job techniques to other girls (I came downstairs into our basement once to find her holding a banana before her puckered lips), who shouted, "Ash! *Seriously!*" and pulled over to the curb at the corner of Woodward and Webb.

Ash carried on for a moment. It seemed she hadn't heard. But then she, too, stopped. Gave them one of her killer smiles.

"Aren't you *curious?*" she said.

"No," Lisa called back. It wasn't true.

Ash went on smiling and smiling. And though I wasn't there, hadn't yet been called upon to rescue her, I can see her face as clearly as if I stood on the same corner with those girls. Possibly even clearer, as it's a smile I've seen since. A look that says something like *You couldn't possibly know what I know.* Or *One day, I'll show you all the things I can do.* Or *I always win. You know that, right?*

What she said in words was, "Don't tell."

Then she stood on her pedals, working up to cruising speed before sitting on the saddle once more. The three girls watched her shrink into the shimmering waves of heat over the pavement, her hair now a finger tut-tutting them, reminding them of an oath to secrecy they never made.

It was only after none of them could see her anymore that they started back.

AFTER THE GIRLS TURNED AROUND ASH CYCLED ON TO (OR WAS carried to, driven to, dragged to) an abandoned house on Alfred Street. That's where she was burned alive. Down in the same cellar where the remains of Meg Clemens, a classmate of ours who had gone missing ten days earlier, were also found. Two girls, same age. Two bodies almost erased forever by fire, except something went wrong the second time around. Whoever did it, whoever knows, left Ash unfinished. Screaming in a pit at the bottom of a house nobody had lived in for longer than she and I had been alive.

There are even fewer witnesses, even less known about what Meg Clemens did or where she went after her mother gave her a ten-dollar bill and watched her walk out the door of her house on Frederick Street, a block and a half from where we lived. Meg wrote for the school paper, publishing "investigative reports" about the nutritional atrocities of the cafeteria. She wore glasses, tortoiseshell frames a little too big for her face that slid, charmingly, down her nose. She regularly declined invitations to go out with boys, so that she bore an unfair reputation for being stuck-up. That was all anybody knew about her. Or all that I knew about her.

Two girls, both raised on the same playgrounds and schoolyards and in the family rooms of Royal Oak homes with the Stars and Stripes hanging over one of every three front doors. It naturally gave rise to fears of a connection, despite the police's reminders of a lack of evidence. In the Holiday Market aisles and standing at the video store's New Releases wall our parents allowed themselves to whisper about the possibility of a monster living among us, plucking their children off the street.

Meg Clemens's disappearance was a mystery that started our minds down paths that led to private horrors, our own individually imagined outcomes, none of them good. But it was, for ten days, still only what the authorities were orchestrated in calling an "isolated incident." Then Ashleigh Orchard disappeared, too, and they had to stop calling it that. Two girls old enough to be referred to as "young women," an acknowledgment of their knowing looks in the photos that appeared on the news. "Young women" meaning the enjoyment of independence, of mysterious, troublemaking time spent outside their parents' view.

And sex. "Young women" meant *sex*, where "girls" did not.

AFTER THE FIRE, WHEN I WAS IN THE HOSPITAL, THE INVESTIGA-tors asked if my sister had any reason to entertain suicide, and I told them there was no chance of that. It was impossible to think of Ash leaving behind all she'd claimed for herself in Royal Oak, the school

5

When you're dead, you know that's what you are.

You always hear about the other ones, the souls who need help "crossing over," the confused loved ones in those paranormal reality TV shows who ghost around at the foot of the bed, needing to be told it's time to go. But in my experience there's no mistaking it with being alive, because where I went after the fire was something *better* than being alive. Heaven, you'd have to call it. A slightly altered replay of the happiest day of my life.

I was thirteen. Sitting next to my father in the Buick Riviera he drove then, floating down Woodward Avenue toward the round, black towers of the Renaissance Center, where he worked. A drive through inner-city Detroit on a sunny day, the pawnshops and cinder-block motels passing by through tinted windows.

It was the day we took Ash to Cranbrook. The day I let myself imagine it was possible for her to be left behind.

What did we talk about? I can't really remember all that much.

she half ran and the "best friends" she'd anoint and abruptly exile for no apparent reason and the older boys who literally threw themselves off rooftops into backyard pools and streetside snowbanks to win a flicker of her attention. She would never abandon me, the brother she wished dead most of the time but also needed in a way neither of us could begin to describe.

I know because I went into the house to save her.

It was a mansion once. When that part of town was more than ruins, more than brick and glass returning to meadow. A stately home for some doctor or city-builder, then deserted, the windows wide and black as dilated pupils. All of them billowing smoke when I drove over the curb in my mother's car and sprinted for the open door.

I ran inside. Because that's where she was, holding on. For me.

Not that I saw her through the choking dark. Not that I heard her voice. I knew she was there because we're twins, and twins know things. They know even when they don't want to, wordless and instant as pain.

I found her at the foot of the cellar stairs. Except the cellar stairs weren't there anymore, so that only her face and raised hands were visible in the swirling black. A girl drowning at the bottom of a well.

"Danny!"

She was still standing. Her hair curling into charred buds.

"Don't leave me here! *DANNY!*"

She wasn't speaking of the fire or the house. It was death. She pleaded with me to not leave her alone in whatever came after this.

And I didn't.

Even knowing what she'd done, knowing what she was, I lay against the floor's buckled wood and threw my hand down to pull her up. But she was too far. I told her to jump—or wanted to, tried to—but the heat seared my throat closed against a scream.

I reached down to my sister, and she reached up. But the only thing we touched was fire.

She didn't want to die. But the flames took her anyway.

Just like they took me, too.

We laughed a lot, anyway. Dad telling stories of his teenaged years upstate in Saginaw. His life before us revealed as a series of exciting or ridiculous but ultimately blameless crimes. Throwing rocks at a wasps' nest and suffering the worst stings on his butt after a bunch of them got trapped in his shorts. Falling through ice and having to walk home without pants on because they froze hard as cement. Driving a Beetle down the main hallway of his high school only to be given a congratulatory slap on the shoulder and told not to try *that* again by the cop who met him at the other end.

It was a memory of a day that had actually happened, though it was more vivid than any memory or dream. In fact it felt more real than the first time I lived it, sharpened by my awareness of how special it was to hear the untroubled version of my father's voice. All of it colored by the knowledge that none of it would last long.

Heaven was driving down Woodward with my dad, pretending we were just like other fathers and sons. A family without an Ash in it.

We parked in the lot next to the black towers. Paused to look across the milky tea of the Detroit River.

"There's a border in the middle," my father told me, just as he had in the living world. "An invisible line."

It was a pairing of concepts—invisible/border—that gripped my young mind as we walked through the revolving doors and into the building's broad atrium. Cars and trucks, all "solid GM product" as my father invariably called them, sat shining on the floor below us, while a couple flashier models, a Corvette and a Fiero, turned slowly in midair, suspended by wires on cast-iron pads.

We proceeded around to the glass elevators that would take us up to his office. He stepped in and guided me with him, the weight of his hand on my shoulder igniting a current of warmth within me.

The doors closed. We began to rise.

The elevator drifted up through the open stories of the atrium and then we popped through, climbing the outside of the main tower. An endless view that improved the higher we went. Below us the river and the stubby skyline of Windsor on the opposite shore and, beyond its limits, the rest of Canada. Vast and flat, fading out before reaching the horizon as though a landscape painting abandoned for lack of a subject.

"That's forever, Tiger," Dad said, and slipped something into the palm of my right hand. Closed my fingers around it to prevent me from seeing what it was.

The elevator slowed as it approached the forty-second floor. I didn't want it to stop. Not that I dreaded whatever awaited me on the other side of the doors, but because I wanted my father to stay with me and knew that he couldn't.

I knew that, if I turned away from the window and looked, he'd already be gone.

DING!

The elevator doors opened.

I stepped away from the window. A dizzy rush like butterflies trying to escape the inside of my skull. I tried to blink it away.

It worked.

"HE'S BACK," A WOMAN SAID. SHE LOOKED PLEASED. IT MADE ME wonder who "he" was.

Despite all the bright lights, the room was duller than the Detroit morning I'd just come from. And with this came the information—the strangers standing around me, the chemicalized air, the first flare of pain—that told me this wasn't the happiest day of my life anymore.

"So he is," a man said. He looked more amazed than pleased.

IN AND OUT. IN AND OUT.

Every time I was in, I asked the same thing. *Where's my sister?* And every time, the same answer, no matter who the question was asked of.

"Let me get your dad. Okay, Danny?"

Which was an answer in itself.

◆ ◆ ◆

AND THEN MY DAD WAS THE ONE STANDING THERE.

There was relief in his face, there was gratitude. But more than this, he looked baffled.

"Danny? How you doing, Tiger?"

Tiger? He hadn't called me that since I was a little kid. After we went to the old Tiger Stadium and watched my one and only big-league game.

He hadn't called me that since I was dead.

"Ash is gone," I said. "Isn't she?"

"Yes. She is."

He let this sink in. Then: "Danny, do you know what this is?"

He pulled something out of his pocket and held it in front of my eyes.

"A watch," I said, squinting. "Mom's watch. The one Granddad gave her."

"That's right. Know how you got it?"

"What do you mean?"

"After the fire. When the doctors—when they saved you. They opened up your hand and you were holding it."

He looked like he might cry. I couldn't tell if it was because he was angry, or grief-stricken, or impatient to know what he wanted to know. More than anything it looked like he was afraid.

"You gave it to me," I said. "Going up in the elevator."

"Elevator?"

"In the Ren Center. When I was—"

"No, *no*—"

"—wherever I was when I was gone."

"No. I couldn't have."

"But you *did*."

He pulled the watch away as though it were a gift he'd suddenly reconsidered giving. And then the tears fell. A reddening, unshaved face of frightened tears.

"I *couldn't* have given it to you, Danny. I *couldn't*," he said. "Because your mother was buried wearing it."

27

6

When I was feeling well enough for them to dial down the drugs after the skin grafts on the backs of my legs (the only place where the burns were severe) healed, I started talking about the After to whoever happened to be in my room. *Heaven is real! You know what happened? When I was dead, after the ceiling came down and all the air was sucked out of my lungs? I relived the best moment of my life! And it's not fluffy clouds or tunnels of light, it's not cheesy angels playing harps, it's part of your past! The afterlife is* inside *you already! You're living it now!*

It would have been easy for the doctors and nurses to write these declarations off as postshock nonsense or morphine ramblings were it not for the watch. My grandfather's gold Omega that my mother cherished and wore most of her life and always told me would be mine one day. The watch that my father, as witnessed by a circle of mourners, slipped around her wrist in the moment before her coffin was shut for the last time and was lowered into the ground at Wood-lawn Cemetery across from the State Fairgrounds.

The watch made me something of a burn-ward celebrity. For those inclined to believe—or persuaded by the evidence—I was Detroit's own seer, whisked to heaven and back again to bring the news that eternity is the best day of your life.

Not that everyone was convinced. More than once, my visions were patiently explained away as nothing more than a trick of the brain as it fizzled its way to the end. And the watch? That earned me knowing winks and *you-can-tell-me* looks. For the doubters, the Omega was only a ghoulish bit of sleight of hand. Nobody suggested how it might have been done, though.

The homicide detectives who visited were interested, too, and listened intently, jotting notes, when I spoke of what I'd come to call the After. They asked if I *wanted* to go to heaven. If I did, wouldn't I want to bring my twin sister with me, too? And how well did I know Meg Clemens, Ash's friend who went missing? The girl whose teeth were found next to Ash's at the fire site?

"What were you doing there, Danny?"

This is what they asked more than anything else. Though even through the haze of painkillers I heard it for what it was.

Did you kill your sister and that other girl, Mr. Heaven-and-Back?

I told them the truth.

It was my birthday, too, but I wasn't asked along to the movies, and Dad wouldn't be home until dinner, so when Michelle Wynn called our house from a pay phone at the Detroit Zoo after riding back from leaving Ash behind, I was the one to pick up. The minute she said that my sister was headed downtown, I dropped the phone and took my mom's car—which had sat in our driveway for a year, waiting for us to graduate from bicycles—and drove down Woodward to find Ash.

Other than circling parking lots a couple times with my dad, I'd never driven before, and I remember weaving between the lanes, fighting the steering wheel. When I passed the zoo I glanced over at the entrance, trying to see if Michelle, Lisa, and Winona were still there.

"And were they?" the detective asked.

"Not that I saw."

"So you kept driving. To save your sister."

"Yeah. But right then I was thinking about something else."

"What's that?"

"The birthday party I had at the zoo once. The year I turned six. The only party I can remember that was just for me. My parents got a magician and everything."

"What else?"

"He was a little weird."

"Who?"

"The magician. Creepy in a you're-standing-too-close way. And he wore way too much makeup," I told the detective, his pen held still over his notebook, waiting for me to get to where he wanted me to go.

The next thing I remember was seeing black smoke rising from somewhere just north of the downtown core. The half dozen blocks where the big houses used to be.

I knew that's where she was. That she was in trouble.

"How'd you know?"

"We're twins."

"So?"

"Twins know things."

"Help us with that."

"I'm half her, and she's half me."

Then they asked the question I didn't have the answer to. They asked why Ash would go to that house in the first place.

"Maybe somebody made her go," the detective suggested, like the idea just occurred to him.

I'd thought of this, too. It was impossible to imagine there *not* being people who'd want to kill my sister. If not for explicit revenge or some indulgence of poisoned desire, then only to be close to her, to be the one to see, finally, who she really was.

"Why?" I said.

"To hurt her. Like they hurt Meg Clemens."

"Who would do that?"

"I don't know. *You*, maybe?"

"Me? Drag Ash somewhere to—?" I almost laughed. "You obviously didn't know her."

And then I did laugh. Or maybe I was crying.

I GOT BETTER.

When my legs healed enough that I could walk without wincing every time my pants touched my skin, they let me go home. Though *home* was a word that could only be used for lack of any other. It was the same address, the same rooms, but now at once empty and claustrophobic, dark with all the lights on. Dad worked even longer hours than before and left more money than I needed on the kitchen counter every morning. There wasn't a delivery pizza in the greater Detroit area I hadn't tried. I knew all the Royal Oak 7-Eleven staff by name. Blockbuster gave me a T-shirt at Christmas for being a Most Valued Customer.

I didn't mourn Ash, but I felt her absence at every moment. It struck me as impossible that she was gone, that she could do so human a thing as die and not come back.

And it was impossible. Because she did come back.

7

I knew she was dead, that she wasn't there in the way the sofa she sat next to me on or the TV remote I dropped to the floor were there, yet the first time Ash appeared to me after the fire she seemed more real than anything I'd seen since she was alive.

It was just me alone in the living room, watching the Red Wings lose a midweek game to New York. Dad asleep upstairs. And then, from out of the clustered shadows of the fake potted fern and front window curtains, she stepped forward. Stood there until I turned my head to acknowledge her. Once she had my attention, she moved into the dim lamplight to take her place next to me, feigning interest in the game on the screen.

What's the score? she asked, but didn't say aloud. Her voice in my head just as I'd heard it at least once every day since she died, except now her body had come along with it.

"You're not here," I tried to say, but it came out in a sob.

And she *wasn't* there. Not completely. Not yet.

I was unable to move any part of myself other than my eyes,

darting from the TV to her and back again. It was impossible to see all of her at once. As if she could only manifest herself in framed bits—a bare knee through a rip in her jeans, the reddened knuckles of her hands—like some kind of photographic trick, a clever patchwork of memory and shade.

But then there was her smell. The sound of her breathing. The aura of cold radiating from her that told me I was more wrong than right.

I'm wherever I want to be, she said without saying.

WHEN THE TIME CAME I CHOSE MICHIGAN STATE OVER ANY OF the liberal arts colleges I might have gone to because I thought it would be easier to hide there. And I was right. But it's probably easy to hide, no matter where you are, when nobody is looking for you.

There were classes, more or less randomly chosen, and decent grades for the first term. But soon all I could think of was how arbitrary the "life decisions" I might make were (there seemed little difference to me between pre-law and pre-cabdriver) and I was adrift. I started skipping lectures more and submitting essays less. My dorm room cramped by towers of take-out boxes. The sound of students horsing around outside my window like a TV I wished I could ask to have turned down.

I wanted a friend but hadn't a clue how to go about finding one. I wanted a girlfriend, but this was so far beyond my grasp, so fantastical, I felt foolish even entertaining the thought, like a kid old enough to know he'll never be Spiderman or play for the Pistons but who can still vividly imagine both.

They were moot points in any case. Friend or girlfriend, Ash would never let it happen. She guarded my solitude without sleep. Once, she followed behind me an entire afternoon, a presence that chuckled into my ear whenever I glanced at a pretty girl passing in the hall. Another time I sat on the lawn with a study group from my class, and when I looked to my right she was beside me, pretending to be fascinated by the opened pages of *A Brief Introduction to Sociology.* Her appearances seemed intended to remind me that all this—the whispered jokes over study hall tables and long kisses in the quad—wasn't meant for me.

My sister made sure I remained alone. Alive, but not free to live. Still, it wasn't a depressive idleness she pushed me into, it wasn't a dope-smoking stupor. Because the thing is, I was busy. Working from morning into the night, overcaffeinated, smelling weird.

I was writing a book.

Not that I knew it was a book when I started. There was no idea of how many pages it might end up being, or what I wanted it to mean, let alone consideration of having anyone else read it once it was finished. It was just something I had to do.

It was the story of how I died and came back on my sixteenth birthday. My journey down Woodward Avenue and up an elevator with my father. The watch. A case for heaven being real.

Not being a proper book it didn't need a title, but I gave it one anyway.

I called it *The After*.

I DROPPED OUT BEFORE THEY COULD ASK ME TO LEAVE. THERE was nowhere else to go so I moved back to Royal Oak, tried to take care of Dad and pretend that, if you didn't look forward or back, time would leave you alone.

It was a while before Dad asked why I left college. I showed him the book I wrote and he read it in one sitting.

"Why was I with you? In the After?" he asked. "How could I be there if I'm still here? Still alive?"

"I don't know. Maybe I carried you with me. Things, feelings, people. Souls. Maybe they can go back and forth more than we think."

"And you didn't see Mom? Why did I give you the watch and not her?"

"She wasn't able to, I guess. Or it was something you were meant to do, because she asked you to."

He nodded at this. A look on his face like someone who'd eaten something less than fresh for lunch.

"I see your sister sometimes," he said.

"Me, too."

"She's lonely, where she is."

He touched my face. His hand was cold.

"Don't let her stop you from living," he said.

How? I wanted to ask. *Where can I go where she won't follow?*

But I didn't say anything. He let his hand fall away knowing he didn't have the answer because there wasn't one.

HE WAS SITTING AT HIS DESK WHEN HE DIED. WORKING LATE. A heart attack at fifty-two. The Orchard men being of weak hearts down the line. The kind of sudden passing you illustrate with a finger snap when you describe it to others.

One of the cleaning ladies who worked the floors of the Ren Center overnight found him. Slumped over tidily arranged files, his head on his arms, the not uncommon sight of a white-collar man against a deadline catching forty winks. She might have just pulled his door closed and carried on with her vacuuming if it wasn't for the picture frame on the middle of his office carpet. Photo-side down, so she had to tiptoe to turn it over and find the tempered glass shattered with such violence a mere fall off the edge of the desk could never have caused it.

She went to my dad, put her hand by his nose to feel for air passing in or out. Her skin registered how cold he was without touching him.

After she called 911 she pulled the photo out from the frame and laid it on the desk. She assumed he'd thrown it. Stress, trouble at home, who knew? A moment of anger he might regret from wherever his spirit lived now.

But she was wrong about that. The coroner, too. Everyone who assumed my father was alone in his office when he died.

Because it wasn't his rage that smashed the picture of him holding Ash and me as swaddled newborns, miracle babies, one blue blanket, one pink.

It was hers.

8

I have a talent for dying. It's the one thing it seems I can do, not just once like everyone but over again. Because the fire in the house on Alfred Street wasn't the only time I've died and come back. The first was right at the very beginning. The day Ash and I were born.

It was a difficult birth. Difficult in the medieval sense, in that it nearly cost our mother's life, and for the first several minutes following our appearance, it *had* taken both Ash's and mine. The umbilical cord. Noosed around our throats so when we came out we were purple and silent. Stillborn.

My mother told my father—and later, in certain boozy moods, she told me, too—how she was so terrified by the idea of losing both of us she did what she'd only half pretended to do in church. She said a prayer. An appeal to any god or devil who might be listening.

Save my babies and you can take me. I'm yours.

The doctors and nurses continued to swim around her, wheeling in new machines, the faint-hope instruments of revival. Ash and I on either side of her being taped and prodded. My mother hadn't been heard. Even though she felt her lips moving, the words passing through like warm bubbles, none of the white-smocked professionals in the surgery room paused to look her way. Other than two flat lines on a pair of screens, her babies unseen behind a raised sheet.

That was when she added something new to her offer.

If you do this, you can take whatever you want.

Almost instantly the lead surgeon—Dr. Noland, a name my mother cited with a kind of nervous awe—stopped and looked down into her face. All the others on the medical team continued to obliviously circle him. For a stretch of seconds my mother and the doctor had been yanked out of the ongoing scene-in-progress, as if one of them had declared *Time out!* and, for once, the universe had listened. This was how my mother described the moment, anyway. A strange pause that might have been what she'd heard out-of-body experiences felt like except she was lying on a surgery table, not afloat or transported but *still there.*

That's why, when the doctor's eyes turned from a cloudy green to red, narrowing into two bright pinholes of blood, she didn't see it as a dream or side effect of the anesthetics but as real as the time that came before and after.

The doctor looked at her with his red eyes and my mother instantly knew two things. The first was that, right then, Dr. Noland *wasn't* Dr. Noland. The second was that she'd made a mistake, one she couldn't yet guess the consequences of, and nothing could reverse her error, not even her own death.

Then it was over.

The doctor's eyes dulled. Returned to the placid green that, over his mask, had for years watched life come and go.

He went back to the hustle of needles and tubes, the ordering of dosages and reading out of numbers that is the hospital version of last rites. Just as my mother noticed the first sign of slowing in their efforts, the recognition that there was nothing more to be done that would soon be acknowledged aloud, the lines on the two screens jumped.

Heartbeats.

To their surprise the tubes and needles had brought us back. But my mother knew a third thing now. The doctors and nurses had nothing to do with it.

We were out a long time without oxygen, so there were concerns about brain damage or physical handicaps of some kind. Yet other than a slightly weakened left leg that, combined with my height, would leave me with an irregular gait, we were both fine. Ash fared even better than me. To all appearances, she was completely untouched. Both of us, miracles.

Yet Ash's superiority was established right from the beginning. My twin possessively attached to her mother's breast, me with rotating nurses in the corner, sucking on a bottle, as I was judged "too weak to latch" and thus exiled. They lined up to admire her ("So sweet! So *alert*!") and shower me with pity ("Poor little guy!").

Twins. So unequal in gifts, so set upon different courses from the first moments of life, we were rarely described as such as children, even by our parents. By the time we entered kindergarten only the teachers knew we were from the same family. Sometimes, when a grown-up would nod at me, the boy standing behind her for no apparent reason, and ask, "Now who is this?" I would have no reply when Ash answered, "I'm not sure. Who *are* you?"

When faced by the same question over the years she was alive as well as the years she wasn't, my first answer never had anything to do with me, nothing I'd built or accomplished, other than my relation to her.

I'm Ashleigh Orchard's brother.

If this was difficult to believe, what followed was usually taken as an outright lie.

Her twin.

IT WAS AROUND WHEN WE ENTERED THE MIDDLE GRADES THAT Ash first told me how she remembered her "time away" at our birth. I had no memory of it myself, and found it hard to accept that she could recall something as a newborn. It might have only been a fiction inspired by the story of our mother's prayer and the red-eyed doctor except that she told it to me *before* we knew about any of that. And she always described it the same way, the details consistent and clear. Over time, given the way things turned out, I've come to believe her.

In her tellings, she never called it heaven. Because it wasn't.

She stood barefoot on a frozen river. Somewhere off to one side, a huge tanker was nosed through the ice, its stern raised in the air, the rotors rusted the color of dried blood. Nothing on the far side of the river but a row of gray, uninhabited houses. But turning around to face the shore behind her she found a city. Older, Art Deco buildings with graffitied water tanks tilted on their rooftops. Five round, black-glassed towers almost touching the ice. The skyline of Detroit.

Along with a solitary figure standing on the bank at the base of the Ren Cen buildings. Squinting, she could see it was a grown-up me. Making the first steps down to the ice to join her.

That's when she heard the thuds.

A spasmodic drumroll, low as far-off thunder. As soon as she registered it the banging grew louder. More and more bass notes beneath her feet. So strong the vibrations made it hard to keep her balance.

Along with the sound of cracking ice. A spiderweb of fissures radiating out across the river's surface. Spits of oily water coming up through the gaps.

She looked down. Saw the thuds were coming from a million human fists.

All of them punching up against the ice from below. Scratching, too. Fighting to find a way up to the air. To her.

Ash glanced to the shore. I was at the ice's edge now, testing it with my foot, about to step onto its marbled surface.

NO!

She tried to shout but little more than a rattled breath came out.

STAY THERE!

Her arms raised, waving me off. I saw her and paused. A look of bafflement on my face that changed to horror when I heard the pounding from under the ice as well.

The fists stopped at the same time.

Pulled their hands away to let their faces float up. All different. Black, white, mothers, men. Staring at her through the river's mottled window.

"Like they wanted to see who the new one was," Ash said. "And they were surprised to see it was me."

"Because they thought it would be someone else?"

"Because I was a *child*."

The ice opened up beneath her. Their hands grasping at her feet, ankles, her legs. Pulling her down into the cold.

"I was dead but it wasn't the light I went to," she'd say. "It was the other place. That's where I'm going. Where I belong."

"Then I belong there, too."

"No. Because I saved you."

"Why would—?"

"I *saved* you, Danny."

Ash believed that this dream of the one and only decision she made while in possession of a soul—preventing her brother from going to the darkest place one could go after death—was proof of her fate, and that it was determined before she was an hour old. It meant that while she appeared more outwardly blessed than her brother, her self-sacrifice gave him the capacity to feel and live where she could not. It explained why she could *act* alive without being alive.

The only way she came close was when she caused other people to feel something. Desire, envy, hate.

Pain.

GROWING UP, A VEIL OF SHYNESS SEEMED TO NUDGE ME TO THE sides of crowds and the back rows of seats, wondering what to do with my hands. Not that I was regarded as unappealing. I was tall, my hair a shining black, "a handsome boy if you only lifted your chin so people could give you a look" if my mother was to be believed. She may have been right. All through school, girls of a certain kind—the bookish, the secret-holders, the looking-for-something-elsers—would seek me out. I may be a bit gangly, they told me, but I was still cute, sexy even. More than this, there was *something about me* they wanted to get closer to, a puzzle to be figured out.

And I wanted to get closer to them, too. Not that Ash ever allowed it.

However unsettled she made me, whatever she did to others, I saw Ash as my sister, but she only saw me as *hers*: less a brother than an embarrassing appendage, a withered limb that reminded her of something and could therefore never be parted with.

But why possess someone you didn't love?

This was the question I worried at for our lives together, and for a long time after I was the lone Orchard survivor. Why did my sister hover over me all the years of my adult life, preventing me from reaching out to another? I'm convinced it has to do with the logic of twins. I was Ash's sole connection to the human, the person she might have been if she'd been born whole.

When she begged me to stay with her in the house on Alfred Street, I was meant to burn in the fire, too, to complete her in death as I had in life. And for a brief moment, when the firefighters pulled me out, I *was* dead. But then the paramedics performed their emergency CPR and I coughed the ash out of my chest and I was back.

It was the first time she hadn't had me with her. And it was lonely where she was. So she vowed to make it lonely for me, too.

She's told me this herself, in her midnight whispers. A voice audible just under the white noise of the shower stall, a singsong that followed me through the streets on my long, pointless walks.

You're not supposed to be here, Danny. But as long as you are, you'll live like you're dead. Like me.

She was most threatening on the two occasions over the last twenty years when I asked a woman out to share a meal with me. The first time my date asked who the blond girl standing behind my chair in the restaurant was, and left before the main courses arrived. The second time the woman herself called to say she'd be unable to make it out as she'd fallen ill, though I could tell from the quaver in her voice that Ash had come to see her.

Jealousy is the one emotion my sister has never had to fake.

41

So I closed the door on the world, on the fantasy of companionship, of family. Heeded her warnings. It seemed to have worked.

Over the past year or so, Ash's visits became less frequent. I even tried to convince myself that, maybe, she was nothing more than a ghost among ghosts. Distracting, yes, even a little frightening. But essentially just another thing one could learn to manage. Ghosts are the dead that can make themselves visible, but once you see there's nothing they can *do* they lose their power.

But I was wrong about that.

Ghosts *can* do things. They can speak, they can touch, they can hold their face over yours so they're the first thing you see when you wake.

And if they find a bridge that can carry enough of them from their side to ours, they can kill.

SOMETHING ABOUT BEING TRULY ALONE IN THE WORLD GAVE ME the idea of seeing if I could get *The After* published.

With my father gone there wasn't anyone, not a living soul, who I might want to ask if it was a good idea, or confide in, or protect. It wasn't money I needed (Dad left the house and his retirement savings to me, and given that I existed like a junk food monk, I could have lived on at the corner of Farnum and Fairgrove until the Orchard heart finally claimed me, too). It certainly wasn't a desire for attention. I think it was because dying was all I had, the only information I could offer the world. The only way I might provide comfort to another, even if it could be for no one other than a stranger.

After some calls and letters, there were a number of New York agents willing to submit the manuscript. I went with the one with the lowest expectations.

At the time, as one editor who rejected the book put it, "Heaven's not really big right now." It was true that there weren't the number of afterlife memoirs on the shelves then that there are now. But a couple publishers liked the "hook" of my mother's Omega, and the one I decided on eventually persuaded me to add *Evidence of Heaven* as a subtitle.

I ended up doing it for a living. The talks, the fly-in-fly-out book signings. Enough to make the payments on my narrow, two-story town house outside Porter Square in Cambridge, Massachusetts, where I more or less randomly moved after the book came out. Other than this, through the rest of my twenties and thirties I lived in self-imposed solitude. No wife, no kids. A handful of publishing-related acquaintances but no friends.

That was before I met Willa and Eddie. Before something happened to me far stranger than dying and coming back again.

I fell in love.

9

Love at first sight.

This was the exhausted phrase I used when asked how Willa and I got together. It's a question put to us more than most, given my shambling height next to her squat self, her tomboyish freckles and raunchy laugh.

"How did you two meet?" the world reasonably asked.

"It was love at first sight," I said. "My sight, anyway. Not sure she even saw me at first."

"You? I saw *you*," Willa would jump in. "How could I *not* see you?"

It's a little give-and-go we did that prevented us from having to say we met at an Afterlifers meeting at the Sheraton in Syracuse, New York, where I was the keynote speaker. Following my talk, I took a chair behind a table bearing stacked copies of *The After* and readied my pen for the signing. Willa last in line.

"Who can I dedicate it to?" I asked, too shy to meet her eyes longer than my standard nod and half smile.

"Willa. Me, who's wondering if you have time for a coffee when you're done."

"I try not to drink coffee after noon."

"I mean a drink. 'Coffee' always means a drink."

"It does? I don't get invited for coffees—or drinks—much, I guess."

"Neither do I."

"Then how do you know?"

"I watch TV. How does anybody know anything?"

The thing I was thinking on the short walk down the corridor from the meeting room to the bar was how, if this woman wanted something more from me—as sometimes women at my events seem they might—I couldn't let it go any further than this. It would be dangerous. Even as we sat at a table in the corner and ordered scotches I kept an eye out for Ash to show herself in the mirror behind the bar, or turn on a stool to glare my way.

"You like single malts?" I managed to ask.

"I like having a babysitter until midnight," she said.

There was some banter about what it was like to have my job, talking about heaven to roomfuls of what she called "nervous ninnies looking for a sneak peek of the Great Beyond." I told her that whatever comes next, cosmologically speaking, is up to you. And in any case, I did less and less public speaking these days, in part because everyone who might be interested in hearing my story had already heard it.

"I've already heard it—or read it, anyway—a few times. And I'm here," she said.

"Why's that?"

"Because I was curious about what you were like outside of that photo on the back of the book that makes you look like somebody made you smile at the end of a switchblade. And I wanted to see if you were someone I could trust. Who I might be able to tell—"

"—That you know what it's like to be dead, too."

"Okay," she said. "*Okay.* Guess I was right."

45

WILLA TOLD ME THE STORY OF HER AFTER THE FIRST NIGHT WE
spent together, a couple days following our drinks at the Sheraton.
I'd driven up to her place, a yellow brick bungalow in an upstate town
called Marcellus, the morning of the day she invited me, saying she'd
arranged for her son Eddie to stay the weekend at her sister's and
wouldn't it be a shame to put a good evening to waste? We'd eaten
Chinese takeout and were finishing our glasses of wine when Willa
got up onto her knees from where she'd been sitting on the floor
and, her eyes steady on mine, pulled off her sweatshirt. For a time she
knelt there, allowing me to clear my head of whatever I'd been talking
about the moment before. Then she wriggled out of her jeans as well.

"Your turn," she said.

The next morning, when I asked why she'd chosen me over all the
other second-time-rounders out there, the unafflicted Marcellus men
who could be hers, she laughed.

"Who says it's a choice? Decisions like this aren't made, Danny.
You're just in one place one moment, and the next you're in a new
place. Hopefully it feels right."

"So does this feel right?" I asked.

She stroked her hand down the long journey from my lips to arrive
between my legs.

"Does *this*?" she said.

LATER, SITTING UP IN BED, WILLA TOLD ME ABOUT THE DAY SHE
died.

"They came in the middle of the night," was how she started, without introduction, as though in reply to something I'd asked, which in
a way I had, the question of how she came to be an Afterlifer hanging
between us since the book table at the Syracuse Sheraton.

"I didn't hear them break the window in the basement, which is
weird, because I hear *everything*, y'know? Always been a light sleeper.
Now? It's way worse. Now I barely sleep at all."

Willa's husband was a policeman, a sergeant. Judging from the one photograph of him in the front hall, the broad face that earned its moustache, the square shoulders and well-carried ring of weight around his middle, he was born to be a cop. Not one of the power-hungry types but the kind who want to help, to rescue dogs who've fallen through pond ice or deliver drunk teenagers home to their parents. She called him "a good man" and I felt I knew exactly what she meant.

They met in college in Rochester, both raised in small, outlying towns, both wanting to return to such a place. Once they married and Greg made it onto the Marcellus force, Willa found a job teaching history at the high school. After Eddie was born she planned to re-turn to work when he was old enough for day care, but "old enough" was a more slippery matter than she expected, and Greg wasn't push-ing her to go back, and the truth was she didn't have a burning desire to be back in the classroom, and so she never did. She was a wife and a mom, and untroubled in these roles. "I wasn't itchy about it the way some other women my age are," she said, shaking her head as though mildly surprised. "I was busy, I was raising a child, I was happy. Just couldn't see the shame in any of it."

Willa stopped there. It was a pause I'd seen dozens of times from others who'd told me their story. Everything up to this moment had been life, good or bad. People and events and decisions, all summon-ing their own regret, their own pride. And then the story gives way to something unrelated to all that's come before. Not the end of life, but the beginning of death.

"They came in the middle of the night," she said again.

Two men. "Known to authorities," as the local paper put it af-terward. Meth dealers, cookers. Their product, an especially potent compound, was called Superman by its users because of the strength it bestowed, the belief you could fly, the certainty that you were un-killable.

They'd chosen Willa's house because they knew that's where Greg lived. Greg, the cop who'd busted them three years earlier and pro-vided the most damning evidence at their trial and met their eyes when they were led from the courtroom after the verdict was read. Fourteen months. Once they were out they started up the business again, not knowing what else to do or where else they might do it. And Superman soon gave them an idea. They'd kill the cop who put them away and make it look like a break-and-enter gone wrong. And nothing *would* go wrong, nothing *would* touch them, because the meth made them feel so alive.

"Even though they were already dead, know what I mean?" Willa said.

They came in through the basement window and up through the dark house. The house we'd made love in the night before. As Willa described it, I could almost feel the weight of their steps on the stairs. The excited whistle of their breaths. Sounds she heard first.

"I don't know why I didn't wake Greg," she said. "He had to get up early and I think I wanted to let him sleep. Isn't that crazy? There's strangers in the house, in the hallway outside our room—our *son's room*—and the most important thing is not disturbing the cop lying next to me. What was I *thinking*? I wasn't thinking. I was sleepwalking."

They kept a handgun—a small Browning semiautomatic—in a combination lockbox on an upper shelf in the closet. Greg had taken her to the range a couple times, taught her how to hold it, release the safety, how to aim and fire. They called it the Just In Case. She never thought that she'd ever actually pull the firearm box down on tiptoes, enter the numbers that came effortlessly to mind, pull it out. Never thought she'd move as quickly as she did, thinking of Eddie—Eddie asleep, strangers in Eddie's room, Eddie being carried away—and open her bedroom door, gun raised, bright with panic and fear.

Three figures in the hallway. The only illumination the nightlight in Eddie's room, a yellowy cloud like smoke.

Two men. One boy. Hers.

One of the men had his arm casually draped across Eddie's back like they were friends, like he was a Big Brother congratulating him on throwing a strike. The other man stood closer to Willa. The leader. Both men had guns, too. One held to Eddie's head, the other rising as Willa watched until it was pointed at her.

There might have been words then, a negotiation of some kind. It's what the two men, at once wild-eyed and dopey, seemed to expect.

Instead, Willa adjusted her aim and, the barrel still moving, fired.

Big Brother's head jolted back and hung there for what seemed like a while before the spray of blood and "skull junk" appeared against the wallpaper. His face registered no pain, only incredulity. The meth afforded him a moment of false life and he tried to pull the trigger. He was standing, aim dead on her face. But he was missing the part of his brain that makes fingers move and the gun twitched in his hand like a fish.

Eddie pulled away from the man. Without the boy to hold him up, he first knelt, then slumped onto his back, emptying the contents of his head over the floorboards.

Only then did Willa hear Greg rising from the bed behind her. A sound that made things move very fast.

Willa swung around to aim her gun at the other man but he leapt to one side of the hallway, then the other, the awkward jumps and landings of hopscotch. As he went, he fired. She thought he'd missed her. But when she heard a series of half hiccups, half coughs behind her she looked to see he'd hit Greg. Her husband's hands clutched around his throat.

When she turned back to the man in the hall he smiled at her. Not jumping anymore.

Willa did a couple things at the same time.

She tried to copy what the still standing man had done and leapt away from the shot she could see him squeezing off.

She said something to Eddie, an attempt at a shout that didn't come out but that he read on her lips all the same.

Go!

WHAT SHE REMEMBERED NEXT WAS A DAY LIKE ANY OTHER OF THE preceding few years. In fact, it was a day precisely the same as one she had already lived.

Willa toweling the frying pan dry in the kitchen after making

French toast for Greg and Eddie. Greg had just left a moment ago—the smell of his shaving cream going up the stovetop vent along with the bacon—and Eddie playing with his Batmobile on the living room carpet. It was the beginning of a day. The first of the hours that march toward dinner, the reward of a glass of wine and the three of them at the table together again. Nothing special about it, no party or acceptance of an award or packing to go on vacation. A day with her son before he was schoolgoing age, just the two of them, the sun making promises through every window.

This was Willa's After.

When Eddie asked if he could turn on the TV she suggested going for a walk instead.

"Where?" he asked.

"I don't know. Maybe we just follow our noses."

Eddie stood. Jutted his chin up so that his nose pointed to the front door and he marched toward it, cross-eyed. "Like this?"

"Exactly. *Exactly* like that."

Eddie was four, turning five in a couple months. What Willa thought of as the Age of Edibility. Her love so ravenous she wanted to chew on her son's smooth legs, blow farts on his belly until it was blazing, kiss his face off. He was delicious. And she was hungry for him all the time, the same as he was for her. She thought of these days together, mother and son with hours laid out before them, as a perfect circle. Each was the unspoken answer to the other's wants.

Though she sometimes felt guilty for not putting Eddie into more programs as some of the town's skinnier, import SUV–driving mothers did—Willa could spend whole evenings hemming and hawing over her stack of science camp and beginner's piano and Go-Go Yoga! and Tennis for Toddlers pamphlets—the truth is she didn't want to yield any of this time with her son.

Not that they did anything special together. Willa was just another mom pushing her kid around town in a stroller, strapping him into the car's booster seat in the Nojaim Bros. grocery parking lot, giving him shriek-inducing "underdogs" on a swing.

And this day, her After, about the same. The happiest day of her life.

After breakfast they went to the Marcellus Town Park, where the Fall Fair had been set up: some agricultural display tables, a small midway of games and kiddie rides. Eddie chose a dragon to sit on for the carousel, Willa next to him on a winged unicorn.

"They don't make these things with horses anymore?" Willa asked Eddie, but he wasn't listening, making fire-breathing sounds so effectively his mother had to keep wiping the spit off his chin.

She'd brought lunch along but, drunk on early October sunshine, they had hot dogs instead. They both agreed they were the best they'd ever tasted, and it was true for Willa as well as Eddie. Something about the white bun, sweet as a donut, the single lines of glowing mustard she'd drawn. Or maybe it was the pleasure of feeling Eddie lean against her where they sat on a small rise behind the midway, his hand linking with hers, the sense she had of the two of them being on a "date," a romance so purely distilled that only innocence remained.

He napped in his stroller on the walk home. She took a roundabout way, admiring the well-kept homes of her town, the mature trees and quiet streets, and felt almost overwhelmed by luckiness. As she pulled Eddie up, still asleep, and carried him into the house, she wished only for things to stay like this, stay the same.

She lingered in his room standing over Eddie's bed. The weight of his body the same as her heart inside her. She didn't want to let him go yet, she didn't want to part. An impossible thought occurred to her. If she remained there, remained still, might time forget they were here and pass them by? Could she hide in the quiet of her home at midday and hold her son in her arms forever?

"In a way, the answer was yes," Willa said, using the round of my shoulder to wipe the tears from her face. "Because that's where I left part of myself. That's when the doctors brought me back. And you know what? Even though I was alive—lucky as hell to *be* alive—I couldn't have been more pissed off."

They saved Willa. Went in to stem the bleeding in the places where the bullet had gone straight through her middle, racing to re-place the blood that she'd spilled over the second-floor hallway, the ambulance, the surgery table. Near the end of the procedure she went into cardiac arrest. By the time they clamped the last artery and got the paddles on she'd been dead for almost three minutes.

When they brought her back, the first thing she remembered was the taste of hot dog in her mouth.

She asked about Eddie. The nurse watching her started to leave to get the supervising doctor but Willa wouldn't let her go. So the nurse—a mother, too, a wife—told her. Eddie was fine. Untouched. But Greg was gone. The man who Willa hadn't shot—the one who'd put a bullet through her gut and her husband's throat—had turned to Eddie after both his parents had fallen, waved his gun at the boy, steadied his aim between his eyes. But he didn't shoot. Instead, he shuffled over to Eddie and ruffled the boy's hair, the gesture of a coach comforting a Little Leaguer after striking out, and took his time going down the stairs and leaving the house by the front door. The police caught him within an hour. Blood-soaked, still high, try-ing to break into a car on Main Street. When told he was under ar-rest for murder he laughed.

"Even as I heard all that the thing that hurt most wasn't losing Greg, but having to do the grieving," Willa said, sitting straight up. "I mean, I was dead, right? I was gone, game over, buh-bye. And it was *good* over there. Then I'm here in the shit. The aftermath, what-ever they call it. And you have no choice. You've *got* to feel, you've *got* to handle it, you've *got* to *go through the stages*. I honestly don't think I would have even bothered trying if it wasn't for Eddie. You need a reason to live, a good one, I know that now. Otherwise the living can just be too goddamned hard."

I knew what she meant. I understood just as she hoped I'd under-stand, why she read *The After* three times, why she came to my talk hoping I'd be someone—maybe the only person she might ever find in the world—she could connect with. Hell is a place on the other side. But it can also be here. The experience of living without a reason to.

And with this woman, I knew that for all the risk I was about to invite into our worlds, I'd found mine.

10

When I asked Willa if she and Eddie (who could be named nothing other than Eddie, with his reddish curls and ears that stuck out like tea cup handles) would like to move into my house in Cambridge, we'd been seeing each other for less than a month. It was crazy. But it didn't feel crazy. It felt like the most sane thing I'd ever done.

Still, I didn't really expect Willa to accept. She'd buried her husband in Marcellus a year earlier. That part of upstate had been her home since birth. I figured it was too fast, that it would be too hard for her to tear herself away.

"Let's do it," she said instead.

"Really? I thought—this is your place—"

"I loved my husband, Danny. But I'm attached to people, not places. And I want you to be one of my people now."

"What about Eddie?"

"You can ask him yourself if you want, but I know he'll say yes."

"Why?"

She punched me, hard, in the arm. "He *likes* you. Probably for the same reason I do."

"Yeah? And what's that?"

She turned thoughtful. For a time, it wasn't clear if she'd answer at all.

"You understand how it can all be taken away," she said finally. "You've had that happen. But you're still here. Just like we are."

Just like Ash.

SOMETIMES THERE IS A SCENT THAT PRECEDES HER APPEARANCES, less borne on the air than held tight against my face, an invisible, smothering cloth. And soaked in this cloth an odor that carries a *feeling* with it, particular as the past. It's the same sugary, teenaged-girl perfume that clouded the rec room parties and school gym dances of our youth, combined with something foul, something gone wrong. A neglected wound spritzed with Love's Baby Soft.

In the last couple weeks since Willa and Eddie entered my life Ash has not only returned, but doubled her power. She feels heavier than before, more particular, a thing of metal or stone.

As she appeared two Sundays ago.

Standing in the kitchen, six feet from where Willa and Eddie sat eating scrambled eggs. I pushed the fridge door closed and she was there. So detailed I could see that the wrinkles around her falsely smiling lips were actually scabs, broken and healed, broken and healed.

I turned to block their view of her, to stand between them if Ash decided today was the day she would once and for all leap from the spectral into the material. And then do whatever she'd worked so hard to come here to do. Something terrible. The sort of thing she'd be curious to see.

That was her most frequent explanation, when the things she did could still be understood as the boundary testings of a smart, inquisitive child. *Curious.* That's the magic word she'd call upon when asked why she locked her best friend from first grade in the basement bathroom with the lights off until she clawed three of her fingernails into the door, after hearing the girl confess to being terrified of the dark, or why, as an eight-year-old, she picked up our neighbor's toddler from the front lawn where he was playing with his Thomas the Tank Engine and placed him in the middle of the street.

"I was only *curious*," she'd say, and widen her eyes, as though you merely had to stop and look into them to be convinced of her harmlessness. And most of the time, that *was* all you had to do. Just look into her and see how nothing bad could possibly live in those pretty blue pools.

As I looked into them that Sunday morning two weeks ago. At her.

My long-dead twin sister, parting her too-full lips to speak in a voice only I could hear.

Time's up, Danny.

11

had to get them out of the house. A roll through the car wash, a window-shop along Newbury Street, I didn't care. Any excuse to escape the room where Ash had stood, leaving a vague motion of shivering air before it was stilled again, like clamping a lid over a pot of steaming water.

A picnic. That's what I ended up suggesting. I grabbed Eddie's soccer ball, told Willa we'd get something to eat along the way, and led the two of them out the door.

We took the T a single stop and rose up into Harvard Square, picking up supplies on the walk to Cambridge Common. Just past the Civil War Memorial, beyond the cover of trees, the light had dried the dew from the lawn, and we chose our spot. It was maybe a degree or two cooler than the ideal, but as the three of us laid out our blanket and gazed across the Common, surveying the spires and chimneys of the old college, the clarity of the air was more than sufficient compensation for the chill.

Before I knew it Eddie had pulled the soccer ball out of my duffel bag and was dribbling it in a circle around us. I watched Willa as she laid out the food and poured juice into plastic cups. I thought about tickling her into submission, launching a kiss attack. But before I could Eddie called to me, sent me out with a pass, and I was running after it.

I tried something more difficult than I had any right to attempt—a kick straight up and then juggling the ball on the tops of my thighs, finishing with a jumping header—and it pretty much worked. It surprised me. Eddie, too.

"Daddy!" he shouted in celebration.

That's what I'm almost sure I heard. Not Danny. *Daddy*.

When I looked at him to see if I was right he just looked back, his face betraying no special graduation, no big deal. Maybe it was the mistake of wish fulfillment on my part. Maybe I would always be Danny, hoping for more.

The smell knocked me back a step.

A wave of rank sugar. Perfume that failed to hide the odor of moldering flesh. So thick it surrounded me like a blanket, heavy and wet. Soaked through with the foul sweetness of the dead.

I spun around, trying to find her. But the Common was peopled just as it had been: a dog walker on her phone, Willa sitting on the blanket, biting into a cookie.

And Eddie. Kicking the ball just before his attention snared on something. Something he stared at over my shoulder.

The ball rolled past me. The hush of bent grass as it carried on before coming to rest fifteen feet away.

My head swiveled. The ball there, just to the side of a wide-trunked maple.

I started over to retrieve the ball—to keep the game going, to hold off the smothering presence by pretending it wasn't there—and fought against the weight in my legs, shifting and unwieldy. It took what felt like the better part of a minute, but I got there. Almost got there.

A pair of arms reached out from behind the tree. Grabbed the ball. Pulled it back.

Bare arms. The hairs white, the fingers long, bone-thin. Limbs you might call elegant. Except they were *too* white, *too* long, so that they bordered on the off-putting, the grotesque.

I couldn't see the ball or who held it now, both hidden behind the tree. It required me to take a half dozen steps forward.

. . . three . . . four . . . five . . .

Counting them off like a child playing hide-and-seek.

Danny! Look!

She was there. Holding the ball.

I would have told her to go, insisted she couldn't be here, but no breath was permitted past my closed throat.

Ash smiled.

I looked back at Eddie. He'd taken a few steps away from the picnic blanket to improve his angle on my position so that he could see Ash behind the maple just as I could. And now he stopped. Knowing exactly what it was standing there. How the pretty girl holding the ball wasn't a girl. Wasn't alive.

I made a move to go to him, but I was stopped by a seizure of pain. A burning that started at the soles of my feet and shot up to my chest, swelling and hard.

It was Ash. Her fingers squeezing the soccer ball so tight it was an oval. Knuckles bulging against her skin.

That was my heart she held. Squeezing the life out of it. The last of its blood.

I was on the ground before I knew I was falling.

One side of my face buried in the grass, one eye looking up at her. The ball bulging, ready to burst in her hands. Her face showing the cold curiosity of watching her brother's terror, his spasming fight for air.

There was what at first I took to be a scream from my own throat. Followed by a calmly logical thought: *That's not you. You can't even breathe. So how could it be you?*

As it became clearer, I recognized the voice that shaped it. Eddie's. A shriek that shattered across the Common, sent clouds of sparrows from the trees.

Ash dropped the ball and it bounced toward me, rolling over the grass, growing in my line of sight until it was all I could see. I tried to put my hands up to stop it, but my hands didn't move. Nothing did.

You're dead.

This came to me plainly, inarguably. It didn't trigger any assessment, a life flashed before my eyes. A flat, deadened voice I recognized as my sister's.

The ball kept rolling, longer than it should've, as though nudged invisibly forward.

"Danny!" I heard Eddie calling from very far away. Not *Daddy*. Though he was running to me, desperate to help, to make the dead girl go away.

The ball touched my nose. A leathery kiss.

You're dead.

And then I was.

Again.

12

It's not a drive along Woodward Avenue this time. Not heaven. It's the smell that told me, even with my eyes closed.

Not Ash's smell, nothing outright *bad,* but unwelcome all the same. The faint odor of feet that clung to the bedsheets, of gym clothes kicked to the back of closet corners, of air unfreshened by an open window for the entire length of childhood, of boy. The room I grew up in.

My opened eyes told me I was right.

There was the *Dune* poster taped to the back of the door, its corners torn from multiple embarrassed teardowns followed by regretful remountings. There were the Dondero High Chess Club medals— one silver, one gold—with chains looped over a corner of the dresser mirror. There was the one and only family portrait we'd had done by a professional photographer who'd managed to coax halfway convincing smiles out of each of us but could not make us rest hand on shoulder or put leg next to leg on the sofa, so that we were spaced apart like strangers.

I'm home.

I'm dead.

And then another realization, more chilling than these.

Even when I was alive, it felt the same as now.

I sat up on my elbows and took a full breath. It tasted like burnt toast (Dad) and, through the crack under the door, the carpet deodorizer periodically sprinkled around the house but never vacuumed up (Mom). No Ash. Not detectable in here, anyway. Come to think of it, this room was a place she rarely entered. She called it *gross,* "too sad for words," a Nerd Hole. And while I could see that she was right on all counts it struck me that maybe, through some small kindness, she let it be mine. A sanctuary for the licking of wounds.

The curtains were pulled tight over the window but the dull light that fingered out from its edges suggested it was day outside. Early morning or dusk. The Royal Oak light of Sunday afternoons.

It was only when I swung my legs off the bed that I heard the squeak of the bedsprings and registered it as the first sound I'd heard. It held me where I stood next to the bed, trying to listen to whatever else may have been beyond the door, breathing along with me. Waiting.

Nothing I could hear. But there was *something.*

The thing you imagine when you get up in the middle of the night, wakened by what might have been a footfall downstairs. What you don't rise to search for because you'd rather talk yourself into believing it's not there. Except it *is* there. You can feel it in the stillness. The too-quiet of a creature that can hold its breath longer than you.

I shuffled over to the window and peeped through the curtains.

At first, it looked just the way the view from my room always looked. The corner of Farnum and Fairgrove through the branches of our side yard oak, the pavement recently slicked by rain that looked more like a glaze of oil. The cracks in the sidewalk beneath my window patterned like lightning bolts. A few blocks away, the top floor of the commercial buildings of Main Street just visible over the Quinlans' roof.

All of it smudged by fog. Unusual for the living Detroit. As though a cloud had descended to ground level and absorbed all the color from the world, leaving only a palette of grays and browns, stone and sand. A mist that thickened and thinned even as I watched it. Breathing.

When the fog lifted again, I saw what wasn't there.

No cars moving on the streets.

No movement behind the neighbors' windows.

But the gate to our yard was open. Swinging in a nonexistent breeze. Banging against the latch but not catching, opening wide again, over and over.

I let the curtains close. Instantly enveloped by the house's quiet. Listening for the thing that waited for me to open the door and leave the protection of my room.

If this was eternity then I had no choice.

I opened the door.

The second-floor hallway was only dimly lit, as all the other doors along its length—the bathroom, my parents' bedroom, Ash's room— were shut. Yet something moved out there. I felt it before I saw it. Down the stairs, the brass chandelier swayed an inch or two before it was stilled.

Go on.

Not a command from within. Not a voice from outside me, either.

That's the way it is with twins.

Take a look around. Old times' sake.

I started with my parents' room.

The curtains closed there, too. In the airless twilight, I could make out all the things left as they were. The bed made. The glass menagerie of perfume bottles on the dresser, the Chanel No. 5s and Diors and Oscar de la Rentas still almost full, my father's standard birthday gifts preserved like museum pieces. The full-length mirror that fattened whoever stood before it, reflecting a bowling pin–shaped me. Trembling and greasy-haired and looking even more frightened than I felt.

I was about to close the door when I noticed the outline on the bed. A body-shaped depression left atop the sheets on the near side.

As though someone had lain there not for sleep but only to recall how it felt. Followed by a clumsy attempt to smooth the bedspread.

The sort of clumsiness I'm known for myself. Like father, like son.

The body shape on the side of the bed my dad slept on. His size. The width of his head. And with this came a brief scent of him left in the air: bleached undershirt and Brut soap-on-a-rope.

He'd been here.

Which meant maybe he still was.

The bathroom next. A part of me dreading the sight of my dad on the john, or in the midst of some private act, the unwanted spectacle of him without clothes on. But there was nobody there.

The shower curtain had been pulled closed. And there was the *wink-wink-wink* of watery drips meeting the enamel tub.

"The shower game?" I heard myself whisper aloud as I slid closer to the curtain. "Really?"

Really.

After we watched a Hitchcock marathon on PBS when we were eleven or twelve, Ash made me play the game for weeks afterward. The rules were straightforward: Every time I came into the bathroom and she had left the shower curtain closed, I had to pull it open. If I didn't, I'd lose. If I didn't, there'd be "penalties."

Sometimes she'd be there, fully clothed, startling me with a "BOO!" Sometimes the hot water would be left on, steam filling the empty stall. Sometimes she'd be in the shower herself, rinsing shampoo from her hair, and when I pulled the curtain open she'd scream and rear back against the tiles as though I were bringing a knife down on her.

I pulled the curtain back slowly at first. Thought I heard the squeak of wet feet and yanked it back all the way.

No skin, no body, no scream. Just my dad's soap-on-a-rope. Spinning one way, then the other.

I was scared. I wanted to go home.

You are home. And you were always scared.

I saved Ash's room for last. The door I least wanted to open. And for the same reason then as before: I'm not permitted.

Whenever I looked in on the rare occasions when the door was left open I always saw the same thing. Ash sitting at her impeccably ordered desk or on the edge of her bed, the stuffed animals of childhood arranged as an attentive audience to watch as she wrote in her diary. Her most treasured object. Leather-bound and with a strap that could be locked to prevent anyone but the holder of its key from reading it. A gift. Personalized with a gold inscription on the back (TO MY DAUGHTER, ASHLEIGH—DAD) and therefore prized. Not "Love, Dad," only "Dad," an acknowledgment of who she was but also his distance from her. Ash saw this, too; she must have. Yet she guarded the few offerings given to her by her father all the more ferociously because of it, as though these coldly neutral presents, bought under obligation the day before her birthday or late on Christmas Eve, were sacred relics.

Other than this, I had a hard time remembering any details of what she kept in there. Were there posters of bands or movie stars? Were there bookshelves? What did Ash read or watch? What did she *like*? Nothing occurred to me in answer to any of this. It may have been because there was nothing there in the first place. No "personal items" because there was no person.

My hand gripped the cut-glass doorknob before I told it to. It felt warm.

"Ash?"

This came out as less than a whisper. The parting of sleep-dried lips.

I turned the handle but it didn't go all the way. Locked.

Except the doors didn't have locks up there.

Tried it again, driving my shoulder against the wood. There was no give. Barricaded from the inside, maybe. Or held in place by something other than bolt or bureau because I wasn't meant to open it. Not yet. I was meant to carry on and see whatever else she wanted me to see.

Down the stairs, the carpet shushing each barefoot step. The chandelier over the hall (Was it always that lopsided? That tarnished? That ugly?) swaying again. Then I felt it: a lick of outdoor air, cool

65

and smelling of wet mulch. Yet the front door and windows in the living room and family room were all closed. Which left only the kitchen. Down the length of the main-floor hall.

Nothing on the countertops or in the sink, the surfaces cleaned as though in preparation for a Realtor's open house. I paused in front of the fridge. Was I hungry? Is there food on the other side, or drink, or need for either? Whatever the answer, the idea of chewing or swallowing caused my stomach to flip.

I pulled the fridge door open. The only thing on its shelves a jug of Five Alive. What I more or less lived on as a kid, chugging liquid glucose for breakfast and keeping a plastic Darth Vader collectible cup on hand to wash down my mother's burnt dinners. Put there as a joke. But there was something about the glowing orange liquid, the only color in the white fridge, that prevented it from being funny. A treat I couldn't taste, not anymore.

Closing the fridge door let me hear it.

. . . *Croc-EEL* . . . *Croc-EEL* . . . *Croc-EEL* . . .

Outside. A rhythmic repetition I thought might have been the gate smacking shut but it was too regular to be something pushed by the wind.

I turned to see the sliding glass back door was open. Not open a moment earlier.

. . . *Croc-EEL* . . . *Croc-EEL* . . .

I squeezed out to the side yard. Tried to be quiet even though whatever opened the door knew I was there. Knew I was following the bread crumbs it had dropped for me.

The sound was coming from the back of the house. Just a few steps and I'd be able to look around the corner and see what was there. And though it didn't feel like a dream, there was that same unstoppability, the not wanting to do something but doing it nevertheless.

. . . *Croc-EEL* . . .

She sat in the tire swing I'd never seen her touch in life, let alone slip her legs through and go for a ride. Pumping it higher than it was meant to go, so that the branch the ropes were tied to bent each time the tire went back to nearly touch the toolshed, her skirt blown high around her hips.

"Want a turn?"

The search for words must've shown on my face because Ash laughed before I could summon an answer. It struck me that maybe I couldn't speak there. Maybe there I would be a mute.

But this was only the sickness of being near her again. Of hearing her voice not in my head but out in the air.

She kept swinging. Eyes on me. She seemed glad. Not one of her masks but genuinely pleased, her smile the reflex that came with the wash of relief. She swung and smiled, swung and smiled, and before I could feel it coming I was smiling, too.

"Do you know what it is to be lonely, Danny?" she said.

I was about to attempt an answer but she cut me off.

"I'm sorry! Of *course* you do."

Because of you, I wanted to say, but couldn't.

"But we won't be lonely now. I'll show you. Brother and sister. That sounds right, doesn't it?"

It did. It sounded as right as *family* or *safe* or *love.* A sound I'd fallen for a thousand times only to end up learning the difference, over and over, between the idea of a thing and the thing itself.

Ash dragged her feet over the lawn, slowing the tire. Pulled herself out and walked to the open gate where two bikes—the ones she and I rode as teenagers, a driveway-sale Raleigh for me and the fancy Schwinn she rode on the last birthday of her life—leaned against the low wooden fence. She pulled hers up and walked it a few feet away, ready to jump on.

"C'mon, D-Boy," she said, glancing back at me with her old smile now. The mask smile. "Let's go for a ride."

WE HEADED SOUTH DOWN MAIN STREET. PAST THE SAME BUSI-nesses that were there when we were in high school, though none appeared to be open despite some of the lights on inside and the sandwich boards advertising lunch specials or cheap flights to Florida standing on the sidewalks. The traffic lights all flashing red as they do sometimes after a blackout, though there was no traffic to stop. Nobody walked on the streets, nobody waited for a bus, nobody could be seen inside the apartments over the Zúmba Mexican Grille or Mr. B's Pub, readying themselves to head off to work or make dinner or do whatever they did at whatever time it was.

This was the day we died.

The movie that was playing at the Main Art Theatre—*Dead Poets Society*—told me. The front page of the *Detroit News* in a box on the corner mourning the latest indignity in baseball's terrible summer (TIGERS FALL TO BLUE JAYS IN 8–3 LOSS: NO END TO SLIDE IN SIGHT). But it was the meticulous arrangement of these details, a mirroring of a day already lived, already gone, that made me certain that this was July 9, 1989. Our birthday.

Ash rode ahead and I followed. I was even taller than I had been at sixteen so that my knees brushed against my chest with each rotation, my back hunched over the handlebars. Once or twice I caught a reflection of myself in a storefront window, tottering and comic as a circus bear. It would've been funny if I could recall what laughter was.

Was it a quality of the air, the strange, color-eating fog? A detectable element some part of me registers but my mind cannot name that told me this is the afterlife? Had I noticed a glitch in the software that made that place only *look* like Royal Oak, Michigan; something that exposed it as "Royal Oak, Michigan"? Not a fake, exactly, but a secondary creation, a shade? It was Royal Oak drained of life, its texture, its inner illumination. It appeared to be a place for the living but only in that it was a mirror world for the dead.

She didn't turn to check if I was still there behind her, knowing I would be. Rising off my saddle for a sprint of speed over the rail lines that cross Main before it joined Woodward Avenue and we left Royal Oak behind.

I looked to the right, beyond the interchange to the entrance of the Detroit Zoo. For the first time that morning—late afternoon? near-dusk?—I noticed something explicitly *wrong*. Behind its perimeter fence, a pillar of gray smoke rose over the zoo's grounds, its purple water tower tilted to one side.

And then the water tower fell.

Like it was waiting for my eyes to witness it. My ears to hear the screech of the folding steel buttresses.

"Ash!"

My voice worked.

Though I could hear myself clearly, she didn't turn. Continued pedaling down the curving on-ramp and joined Woodward, pointed her bike south.

That's when I saw the man sitting on the curb.

A felt cloak over his shoulders held in place with a knotted ribbon around his neck. Once-white gloves, now darkened and cracked. A black top hat, tall as a steamship chimney. A HAPPY BIRTHDAY! balloon held by a string between his legs. He let it go and it dropped straight to the pavement like a bag of sand.

I recognized him. The magician who entertained kids at Royal Oak birthday parties, pulling silver dollars out of ears in backyards and rented halls and, as at mine, the zoo.

He rose without looking at me. Flapped out the ends of his cloak in stagy self-introduction.

He lifted his chin to reveal his face. Makeup thick as candle wax ending at his jawline, so that by comparison the skin of his throat appeared the color of uncooked sausage. A smile of yellow teeth that showed the sinew of torn flesh caught between them.

I should have turned away from him, or pedaled harder to better my chances of avoiding his grasp. Instead, I stopped pedaling altogether. Rolled closer on a bent rear rim that moaned against the frame with each turn.

His arms lifted out from his sides. Reaching.

He smacked his gloved hands together at the same instant I passed. A trick that produced a dead bird—a dove—that he held by a wing. Waved it at me like a handkerchief in farewell, close enough that the tiny beak scratched the side of my face.

Then he was behind me.

The magician could have been charging in pursuit but I didn't look back. I heard him, though. His awful laugh, a girlish titter, that came from ahead as much as behind.

A block on I caught up to Ash, who grinned back, amused, like she'd witnessed nothing more remarkable than me spitting out a yellowjacket that had flown into my open mouth.

We rolled on without talk, without need for water or food or rest. The gray clouds darkening as we went, threatening a rain that I somehow knew would never fall.

I thought of Willa and Eddie. Or tried to. But no matter how hard I focused on them they remained at the corners of my thoughts. Their faces, even their names slipping away, becoming harder to grasp again each time they did. I wanted them with me—for the life they held, the proof of what I'd briefly managed to be—but after a time their presence caused more distress than comfort and in order to carry on I let them go altogether.

Soon we were working through the half-mile stretch of Woodlawn Cemetery on the right side and the State Fairgrounds on the left, both weed-wild and empty. Yet even with the entering of this word to my mind—*empty*—there was motion to the right.

Figures standing up and taking steps around the burial stones. Human shadows cast against the crematorium wall. Maybe a dozen people looking up at the sky, at their own feet, at us, in the reorienting way of those rising from a dream-riddled sleep.

Only seconds later there were more of them.

Two dozen. Three. And among those in burial clothes—dark suits and blouses and christening dresses—there were a handful of men in green overalls, working at the earth with shovels, building piles and slamming boots down on spade heads to make the first cut. Gravediggers. Working at plots with existing headstones. Not digging graves for bodies, but providing exit for those long dead.

Our mother was buried there. Our father.

My sister.

I returned my eyes to the road ahead. Made myself hold them there.

Don't look, don't look, don't look . . .

As we moved deeper into the city, aside from the absence of traffic, everything was the same as it was when we were sixteen and would have driven past the abandoned factories and schools with a kind of awe. Though it wasn't awe I felt then, not the giddiness of a kid imagining faces in dark windows. This was stranger and, at the same time, more real than that. It wasn't a ride we were on. It was a decision we were making. The closer we came to the black towers of the Ren Center the colder the air became, hardening and tasting of copper as it passed my tongue.

And then I *did* see faces in the windows.

Looking out at us with the dawning rage of property owners spotting trespassers on their land. One woman in a second-floor room of the Lafayette Motel cackled at me. A laugh I couldn't hear, only see, despite the absence of glass in her window frame. Her waving hands lined with cracks of dried blood.

The towers of downtown loomed on the far side of the entrenched Fisher Freeway. Most of them stood dark, though the red flight-warning lights over the Ren Center and the star atop the Fox Theatre's tower were on, lone signals that communicated the opposite of welcome. We were close enough to see the pointed teeth of the enormous concrete tigers prowling the walls of Comerica Park.

I shouted ahead for the first time in what felt like hours.

"Where are you taking me?"

Ash stopped. Rested her foot on the curb and waited for me to pull up next to her.

"I want to *show* you something."

Even as she said it I felt I knew where we were. This place—this Detroit—was a passage. From Royal Oak to the river. My After to Ash's.

The Woodward Avenue we bumped along was a bridge that led to both the good place and the bad depending on which way you went and the reasons that brought you there. I was dead. This was death embodied as a version of my hometown. But there were different paths we could take from there.

71

When I died at sixteen and drove down Woodward with my father it was a place of contentment and light. The best day I'd known to that point. But while this was the same place, the same street, it was different this time. And I knew where it would end if Ash was leading the way.

"Where am I?"

Something crossed her face. The briefest flinch that made it clear she had decided against a lie—"You're in Detroit" or "This is only a dream"—and also against the hardest form of the truth—"You're *dead*, Danny. This is *death*."

"You're with me," she said.

She cycled on, and the words she'd spoken turned sour in my head. What might have been kindness, the assurance that I was here with someone I knew and loved, echoed instead as a statement of my entrapment, the impossibility of escape.

You're with me.

I thought of Willa and Eddie again. *Home.* The loved ones held at an impossible distance, always partial, always fleeting, the same way the dead are for even the most devoted survivors.

With the return of her name I saw Willa. A reassembly of her body and face as though a puzzle I'd told myself to memorize the solution to. There was a gut punch of longing that came with the recollection of her touch, a hurt I tried to hold on to, but after a moment it diffused the same as her image and was gone.

Eddie stayed longer. All the ways he missed his dad and couldn't say how or name the ways the broken parts of him might be fixed—all of it somehow made him more full in my mind there. As though his spirit belonged to the dead in equal measure to the living.

Then Ash turned off Woodward and the change of direction wiped him away, too.

Though I saw no fire anywhere, I choked on an intake of smoke. The air acrid with burning wood and paint. Hair and skin.

I followed Ash onto Alfred Street as though compelled by a spell that overrode my own desperation to turn back, to leap from the bike and run blind into the grassy lots that separated the ruins that still stood in the fields where mansions were once lined, stone shoulder to stone shoulder. The street riddled with rocks so that the tires fought beneath me, the Raleigh leaping like a spooked horse.

Ash got off her bike and let it fall in the street. For a moment she looked up at the façade of the great house she'd stopped in front of, as though silently conferring with something that waited inside.

I watched as she walked up the steps to the front door. She only looked back at me after she'd turned the handle and pushed the door open a couple feet. Her hair pushed back by the sour air exhaled from within.

She waited for me to come up and join her, seemed about to take a step into the house, but didn't. Remained on the threshold with the cocked head and jutting hip of an impatient teenaged girl.

But there was something else in the way she stood wholly outside of the house's interior shadows. Like she not only wanted me to go in first, but couldn't go in herself at all.

Whatever was to be seen inside wasn't for her. It was for me.

I got off the bike. My feet took me to the bottom step.

I was about to start up when I met my sister's eyes. Saw, as though for the first time, what being twins meant for her. Suffering and wanting me to suffer, too.

"Danny!"

It was the fury of her voice that told me I was running.

Away from the house, from her. A defiance I hadn't expected of myself, didn't think I was capable of. Because I wasn't. Not on my own, anyway.

A boy's voice. Eddie's.

Run.

Into the fields behind the house where the grass grew high as corn around the mounds of glass and brick. My eyes on the lights around the ballpark as they came on, one tower at a time. It let me see that the tigers on the stadium walls weren't statues anymore but moving. Alive. Their tails the length of cars, flicking and snaking.

The lights also let me see that one of the tigers, the biggest one positioned over the main gate, was missing.

"DANNY!"

Somewhere behind me Ash ran, too. Getting closer.

The stadium lights a halo hovering in midair. It blinded me to what cut and slashed underfoot, what felt like bedsprings and rolled wire that almost brought me down.

"DANNY! STOP!"

I stopped.

Not because Ash told me to. Because something stood in my way.

Backlit by the stadium lights so I couldn't see what it was, though it gave the impression of being an animal. A naturally occurring creature in the living world that, there, was deformed and enlarged. An obscenity. One with triangular ears and thrashing tail. So big there was no way around it.

It stalked closer until its shadowed outline was all I could see. That, and its eyes. Red as brake lights.

Run, Eddie whispered.

I might have tried except Ash put her hands on my shoulders. Letting me know she was there, that there was nowhere I could go without her. Her cherry ChapStick breath blown cold against the back of my neck.

I watched the tongue slip out from the monster's mouth. The great legs lowering into a crouch.

And then, with a soundless intake of breath—whether mine or Ash's or the beast's—it leapt.

PART 2

The Acts of This Life

13

The first time I remember returning from the other side, after the fire, I wasn't sure I wanted to be back. If the place Ash tried to pull me to wasn't so terrible, if it was something closer to my drive down Woodward Avenue with my dad, I would have preferred to stay in the After hands down. I had little to call my own in life, little to look forward to. People are what hold you in heaven or hell or wherever you're destined to go. People are the anchors. And it's true of the living world, too. People are the reason for wanting to stay or not really caring if this is your time to go.

Back then, I didn't have anybody other than my dad, who was half gone anyway.

But this time it was different.

WILLA AND EDDIE BARELY LEFT MY SIDE AS I BLACKED IN AND blacked out over the—what? Days? Weeks? Time is unreadably stretched out on the serious postsurgical wards. It's hard to say what's a day or what's a night when the course of things is measured in dressing changes and morphine hits. But though I told them to go home, that I'd be okay, the truth was it was good to see them for the lengthening stretches I was awake. Eddie especially. Eddie, whose voice was with me in the After, telling me to run.

I took to sitting up in bed and reading to him. *The Lion, the Witch and the Wardrobe*. A gift from me only two days before the picnic. He told me he's seen the movie but liked the book better.

It was a pleasure to watch him enjoy the story. But when I glanced up from the page I searched his face for something other than his interest in Narnia. I wanted to see if he recognized he was there with me in the After that Ash tried to drag me to. Part of him, reaching across.

Did he really see the girl holding the soccer ball, squeezing the life out of it, out of me? Did he know? Or did I imagine it just as I imagined his presence in the field behind the house on Alfred Street, a link between worlds of my own making?

I wasn't sure.

But sometimes I thought I saw a hint of knowledge in Eddie's eyes, a slightly baffled recognition. Something had changed for him since what his mother called my "heart trouble," something more than a good kid trying to be nice to a guy who doesn't have much time left. If I had to guess I'd say he didn't understand it, even if he was there.

And if he *was* there, he needed to be protected. Not from the glimpse he might have had of the afterlife, but from her.

ONCE I FELT UP TO IT, IN A MOMENT WHEN THERE WAS JUST THE two of us in the room, I asked Willa what happened on Cambridge Common.

She didn't see much. One second I was kicking the ball around with Eddie and the next I'm on the ground. She called 911 and they were there almost instantly. Not that it made any difference. The way the one paramedic straddled me on the gurney, "trying to do a handstand" on my chest as a pair of firemen wheeled me to the ambulance, the radio calls to Mount Auburn Hospital with their Code-this and

Emergency Cardio—that—none of it looked good. In fact, soon after my arrival, a trauma doctor scuffed into the waiting room to tell Willa she was sorry, they tried everything, but Mr. Orchard was gone.

"Eddie took it hard. Took it *weird*," Willa said. "Kind of spaced out, right? Staring out the window at the parking lot like he's expecting someone he knows to show up. Not saying a word. So I left him where he was."

With me, I almost said.

Maybe fifteen minutes passed. Willa, in a daze herself—we were having a picnic less than an hour ago! a Sunday in the park!—and beginning to think about what she might have to do next, what forms would need signing or statements she'd be expected to provide, didn't understand at first what the trauma doctor meant when she came back to say there'd been "some unexpectedly positive developments." It turns out that while she'd been out here telling Willa that her "husband" was dead, a cardiac team had taken over and opened the patient up. Put a stent into a severely blocked valve. Paddled the heart from inside the chest cavity.

"He's back now," Eddie said before the doctor could.

"Yes," she said, with something like regret, as though admitting the loss of a bet. "That would appear to be the case."

WHEN I WAS ABLE TO TALK TO THE CARDIAC SURGEON MYSELF A couple days later he couldn't help congratulating the both of us.

"Well, we did it, Danny," he said, shaking my hand. "We goddamned *did* it."

I liked him not only for saving my life but for being a doctor of the kind they don't seem to make many of anymore, the ones who've seen pretty much everything, but who are still frequently amazed by how things can turn out.

"The human heart. An incredible machine, no doubt about it," he said, shaking his head. "But the human mind? That's what makes outcomes like yours happen. Your heart? It was finished. It was a crushed soda can in there. But here you are."

"Here I am," I said, which, for the first time, opened the gates to grateful tears. The surgeon's seen those before, too. He shook his head again.

"It's pretty unusual. Your turnaround. I'd say it's a Top Ten for me. Just glad I decided to go in there and see what I could do."

"Thank you, Doctor."

"Hey, you did the really hard work, Danny," he said. "Dead for—what?—eight, nine minutes. You want to see your chart? 'THE END.' But then we get a heartbeat. I've seen sleepers in the morgue with better prospects than you and then—*ba-bump, ba-bump!* I'm telling you, something must have scared you silly over there. Because you sure came running back awful fast."

Not that it was all good news. The surgeon told me I have a Class IV heart defect. They don't go to Class V.

"It's kind of a mess, I'm sorry to say," he said, and I was surprised once again by how his bluntness was a consolation.

"What's the problem? In a nutshell?"

"I'm a medical specialist. We don't really do nutshells, but I'll try. The left side of your heart has compromised aortic flow—the left side affecting your body and brain, as opposed to the right that affects your respiratory, so there's that to be thankful for. Low cardiac output with high systemic vascular resistance resulting in severe systolic dysfunction. You want me to unpack any of that gobbledygook?"

"Maybe later. Can you can fix it?"

"You're on all sorts of meds already. And once you get out of here, you'll be taking more pills than Judy Garland."

"What about surgery?"

"Been there, done that. Opened things up a bit on a blocked valve when you came in. Like blowing a spitball out of a straw. But there's nothing more we can do. In a case like yours, there's other spitballs floating around, and the straws around your heart are narrow. So, as far as conventional approaches go, no, there's not much we can do. Wait, *not* true. There's one more thing."

"What?"

"A transplant."

"Okay. So how——?"

"You're already on the list."

"That's good. Right?"

"It's not a short list."

"Oh."

"But if an appropriate donor appears, sure. If the procedure goes well. If your body accepts the new heart."

"That's a lot of ifs."

"It's an iffy business."

"So I guess I've got to say my line now. What're my chances, Doc?"

"If it were me? I'd put my affairs in order," he said. "Say my 'I love you's. Because transplants are damn hard to come by. And if this happens again? You're a lucky man to be here right now, Mr. Orchard. But you're not coming back next time."

ASIDE FROM THE PAIN THAT CAME FROM WHAT FELT LIKE HAVING had a grenade go off in my chest, I felt pretty good. I didn't have what I'm told a good many other cardiac patients suffer from after an "event" like mine: the vertigo, the struggle for breath, the paralyzing exhaustion. Soon I was even going for little walks, the humiliating post-op parade of those pushing their IV poles down the hall, goose-pimpled legs on display. They would only let me out if I showed them I could shuffle around on my own, reliably make the journey between mattress and bathroom and back again. That was the ticket to freedom: to convince the nurses I was ready to live bedpan-free.

So I worked at being the best patient I could be. Because I had a reason to want out of there. Two reasons. Willa and Eddie being the difference between just wanting *out,* and wanting to *go home.*

But there was a question I needed to have answered first.

"I'm going to say this once," I said to Willa one of the afternoons when she was on her own in my room. "I have to say it, and you have to really hear it. And when you answer—whenever you decide you can answer—I want it to be honest. Even if it hurts. Even if it feels like the worst thing you've ever said to another person, okay?"

"Jesus, Danny. That's one hell of a windup. Why don't we talk about whatever you want to talk about when—?"

"It can't be later. I've got to say it now."

She sat in one of the two uncomfortable chairs they had for visitors in my room. It gave a little shriek at the acceptance of her weight.

"I'm all ears," she said. Stuck her fingers behind her ears and flipped them out. It made her look a lot like her son.

"You don't have to do this. Once I get out of here. The whole *recovery* thing. The whole *waiting it out until the end*. You and Eddie have changed my life in a very short time and I can't tell you how grateful I am. But it has been just that—a short time. So short there would be no blame—no blame from me, I promise you—if you decided it would be best to go back to Marcellus or wherever and not have to deal with me. Because we have to face it—I'm just a problem now."

"Danny. Listen—"

"What I'm saying is you're free. Any promise you've made—any suggestion of commitment—it's clear. We're good."

Willa pursed her lips. Raised her eyebrows. Made an are-you-finished? face.

"Are you finished?" she said.

"I think so."

"Okay. I understand what you're saying. But what you don't understand is me."

Willa got up from her chair. Lay on her side next to me on the bed so that she could whisper what she said next into my ear.

"I don't run from things, Danny. And I don't say things because they sound good at the time. I say them because I believe them."

"I love you."

"Like that, for example."

"No. I really love you."

"Ditto. So that's all you need to know from me on this offer of yours. You had to say it, you've got your answer. And you can never open that door again—not unless you're the one who walks out of it. Got it?"

She kissed me. And though I must have smelled considerably less than sexy, though I couldn't get my lips to work right, it was a real kiss, not just a gentle deal-sealer. And when it was over and she started to roll away I pulled her back for another.

OTHER THAN LYLE KIRK, PRESIDENT OF THE BOSTON AFTERLIFERS, who came by with a six-pack of Rolling Rock ("Not sure they let you have this in here, but you only go round once—or twice, or maybe three times—right?"), my only visitors were Willa and Eddie. If it wasn't for them, I would've been alone in there with the nurses and doctors who came and went, taking blood and asking how I was doing in a way that made it clear the answer wouldn't make a difference one way or another.

The cardiac surgeon was the only other visitor I actually looked forward to seeing. I got the sense that he didn't have to check on me as often as he did. He seemed to take a special interest in those near the edge, like me. Life and death. The inarguable line in the sand. It's probably what brought him to the job in the first place.

"Danny Orchard," he announced as he came into my room once. "Why didn't you tell me you're famous?"

"I'm not. Not really. D-list at best."

"Modesty! Some of the nurses have told me you've been on TV, and they take TV very seriously. They've even brought your book to work but they're too shy to ask you to sign them. So I volunteered on their behalf."

He produced three copies of *The After* from his satchel. Placed them on the bed beside me and slapped a ballpoint pen on top.

"Would you mind?" he said.

I asked for the nurses' names and set to inscribing the title pages. Out of the corner of my eye I could see the doctor watching me with an amused stare. It's an expression I'd grown used to over the years.

The curiosity that came with being next to someone who may have a handle on Life's Big Mystery.

When I finished he continued standing there, nodding down at the books I'd returned to him.

"I'm a man of science. Never seen a spirit in my life, holy or otherwise," he said. "But I went to Catholic school growing up. I'm no stranger to what I'm *supposed* to believe happens to us after we go. And in my line of work, I'm often the last one to see them before they do. But I've got to say you're a first time for me. You've come back *twice.*"

"Three times now, actually."

"See! I'd think you were a nutcase if I saw you on TV saying that."

"I probably would, too."

"What I mean is that I know you, and take you as more or less sane. Which makes me want to ask: On this most recent occasion, do you have any memory of what you saw over there?"

"Yes."

"And how was it? Heaven, I mean. Have they done any renovations to the place since you were there last?"

That's not where I went this time. This time it was someone trying to pull me the other way.

"It looks a lot like Detroit," I said.

ONE AFTERNOON, AFTER WAKING FROM A NARCOTIC SNOOZE, I opened my eyes to find someone in my room. One of the candy striper volunteers I'd noticed walking the halls, pushing carts stacked with newspapers and magazines and stuffed animals. Did they make them hang out there as a condition of some suspended sentence, counting the hours they had to put in handing out three-month-old *Peoples* and *Times* instead of a stretch in juvie detention? Or were they just good kids trying to help?

This is what I wanted to ask the teenaged girl who stood with her back to me, flipping through the newspapers on her cart. I was trying to think of a polite way to put the question to her when she spoke first.

Special delivery for Mr. Orchard.

Everything stopped. Her back, the sway of long hair over her pink smock, the comings-and-goings in the hallway outside the door, all of it stilled.

Wasn't easy to find this, I can tell you. But we aim to please.

The girl turned. Mimicked the look of horror on my own face with widened eyes, her mouth stretched into a black oval.

No.

This wasn't a word, wasn't a failed scream. It was the hopeless denial I've felt every time she's come to me. The wish for her to go away that's never once been granted.

She frisbeed the newspaper onto my lap.

I recognized it instantly, though I hadn't laid eyes on it in years. The *Detroit Free Press* of July 10, 1989. The paper that was tossed onto the front porch of our house in Royal Oak the morning after the fire that took Ash's life and mine. The headline on the bottom corner of the front page pored over by my father, the paper laid on the kitchen table but never opened. TRAGIC FIRE CLAIMS ONE LIFE, ALMOST TWO: TWIN BROTHER AND SISTER IN BLAZE, QUESTIONS REMAIN.

I looked up and she was standing there. Looming over me at the edge of the bed.

Ash reached up and put her hand around my IV bag. Weighed it, swung it back and forth on its hook. Then her fingers tightened. The bag collapsing, forcing the fluid down the tube and into my arm. I felt it swell, followed by a shooting pain up my arm. My shoulder blades, my neck, my chest on fire.

She let go.

The bag expanded, sucking up the contents of the tube. This time, it brought blood along with the saline. Curdling the clear liquid, from pink to crimson to something darker still.

She squeezed it again.

And with it, the pain found a home inside me. My heart. Crushed as though held between the teeth of a vise.

My eyes squeezed shut. A red road map against the backs of my lids, the capillaries enlarged and throbbing.

From somewhere very close, Ash's smell. Her lips—the skin flaked with dryness, the touch cold—brushed my ear.

I miss you, Danny Boy.

I threw a blind fist out at where she stood but it met nothing but the IV pole, knocking it back. Opened my eyes.

The saline clear. The pain in my chest gone as though it was never there at all.

No Ash.

No *Detroit Free Press* on the bed.

But the smell still there. The lingering trace of perfume that sent me stumbling to the bathroom to vomit onto the floor after missing the sink.

I miss you.

14

After almost three weeks, and given there was little more they could do for me until a heart came through the doors in an ice bucket, they finally let me go home. The surgeon I liked was the last one to sign off. He brought his own fresh copy of *The After*. I signed it "For Helping My Achy Breaky."

"Cute," he said, snapping the covers closed. A finality to it that made it clear he would never open them again.

"I wish I could do more to thank you," I said. "You play golf? Red Sox tickets?"

"Gave up my membership at Brae Burn when I realized all the drivers I kept throwing into the creek were going to bankrupt me. And I've already got first-base-line season tickets at Fenway. But trust me. Your insurance has covered me just fine."

"Well, then. Until we meet again."

"Hmm?"

"The transplant?"

"Right."

"If something becomes available—"

"Absolutely. We've got fingers crossed, I can tell you that."

He gave me a look that said he believed in miracles as much as the next guy.

"I know everybody's been all over you about not exerting yourself," he went on after he asked if he could drink the untouched cup of orange juice on my breakfast tray. "But you really have to take it easy. Hang in there so we can keep spinning the wheel at our end. Not too much excitement, okay?"

"So you're saying I should go easy on the hot-tub sex and half marathons?"

"I'd definitely drop the half marathon. That doesn't even *sound* fun. But I'm sure as hell not going to be the one to advise a fellow against the other activity if he's given the invitation."

WITHIN THE HOUR WILLA AND EDDIE WERE WALKING WITH ME out the doors to the car, the sun hurting my eyes. Eddie was next to me the whole way, holding my elbow. I would have told him I was okay, it wasn't my legs that were in lousy shape but my heart, but his need to help was greater than my desire to make a show of a hopeful exit, and I leaned on him a little.

It's a short drive between the hospital and our place off Porter Square. Willa took a roundabout route that afforded a glimpse of the Charles, Harvard's spires, the rush hour traffic along Mass Ave. The faces of other passengers hinting of other stories-in-progress: the pissed-off, the anxious, the fulfilled, the bored. On the sidewalks everyone holding either a giant coffee or a cell phone, as though a law had been declared against public displays of empty-handedness. Everyday sights that struck me as original, heartbreaking, and funny at the same time. Too much life to digest all at once.

"What's wrong, honey?" Willa asked when she glanced over to see me drying my cheeks with a shirt sleeve.

"Nothing's wrong. I just remembered how good it could be."

"How good what could be?"

I gestured out through the windshield. Kept my hand moving to point a thumb at Eddie in the backseat, then brought it up to graze Willa's neck.

"This," I said.

15

It was Willa's idea to get married.

She asked me. I asked if she thought it was a good idea. She told me to shut up and give her an answer. I said yes.

This was on a Monday, less than a week after I was released from the hospital.

On Tuesday, we booked a church for the coming Friday. After that there wasn't much to arrange for outside of a quick-turnaround dry clean on my tux and a reservation at our favorite restaurant in the Square for dinner after the service. You keep the numbers small and slip in a "Truth is, I've only got a couple months to live" here and there, and you can put a wedding together in a couple days, no problem.

Which isn't to say I didn't have doubts about the whole thing. Just because my ticker didn't have many miles left on it didn't mean I deserved a woman like Willa, a woman who had already lost one husband and was now looking at her second leaving the stage, all well before she turned forty. She told me, in her forceful way, that she wasn't doing this because of the shape I was in but because she wanted to. Because she loved me. She told me the same thing she said when she slid on top of me in our bed and I asked if she thought Eddie was asleep, if he might hear us.

"Just do what feels good," she said. "Can you do that?"

As it turns out, I could. Even after a lifetime of training myself otherwise, a lifetime of Ash showing up to remind me that anything of the kind—a woman's love, the yielding to pleasure, the making of promises—was against the rules, I could feel good with the best of them.

And I was feeling pretty damn good standing at the altar of Marsh Chapel on the BU campus with Eddie, my best man, next to me, and the two of us turned at the organist's playing of "All Things Bright and Beautiful" to see Willa start up the aisle. She was breathtaking. Literally. So lovely in her silk suit and hair tied up in a ribbon of flowers that I forgot to inhale for the first half of her journey toward me, and I eventually gasped, my heart tom-tomming, the bow tie tightened around my neck.

Don't die here. Not now. Let me put the ring on, let me raise a toast to the bride, and then I'm yours. But not now.

It sounded like a prayer, but even as I thought the words I realized I didn't address them to God. I was begging Ash for mercy I'd never known her to show.

There were maybe a dozen guests sitting in the church, including the minister and ourselves. The remaining attendees were friends and family of Willa's. Other than Lyle Kirk nobody on my side because I didn't have a friend to invite. My public speaking agent? My publicist? The guy who does my taxes? Though it probably shouldn't have, it stunned me to realize I hadn't talked to anyone in years who I didn't pay to talk to me.

Except Ash. Not that she'd require an invitation anyway.

Which is why I was relieved that, when I scanned the pews, I didn't see her sitting at the back, or balancing atop the organ pipes, or peeking through a crack in the chapel doors as I half expected her to be.

Willa made her way up the altar steps, blowing all my worry away.

She wasn't a tall woman, my wife-to-be. Yet she was so much stronger than me. You could see it as she took my catcher's mitt of a hand in hers and leaned her head against my side, a lending of power that made me stand straight.

Then Eddie handed me the ring. The same one my father gave my mother. A couple decades spent in the dark of a bank deposit box, then glittering on Willa's finger.

It was a long way down to her lips for the kiss. And once I was there, I took my time.

Not now. Please.

Eventually, the spell was broken by a sparse round of applause. The minister had pronounced us husband and wife but I hadn't really heard him. I pulled Eddie in, made a circle. I was a married man and this was my family. I could happily say this out loud every couple of minutes for the rest of my waking life.

We were walking down the aisle toward the doors when I heard her.

Up here, Danny.

I didn't want to look. I never want to. But I always do.

She stood at the altar where we had stood a moment ago. Dressed in bridal white, a veil over her face.

"Danny?" Willa followed my line of sight. When she saw nothing there, she looked up at me. "You okay, baby?"

"I'm great. It's just—I thought I forgot something back there."

"Forgot what? You got all you need right here," she said, slipping my hand around her waist.

We carried on to the doors. Some of the guests threw confetti even though there were signs asking them not to. I could feel some of the papery bits get stuck in my eyelashes and slip down the back of my neck. Tickling and cold as snow.

Before I was out, before I was blinded by the afternoon's clear sunshine, I looked back again.

Ash wasn't standing at the altar anymore and at first I thought she was gone, was never there at all. But then I spotted her. Walking closer behind the rest of the guests. Lifting her veil.

Her face burned, clawed by fire. The skin peeled back, white bone beneath. The flesh hanging off her forehead and cheeks on strings of tendon.

You may kiss the bride . . .

I told myself not to run. To keep moving out of the church, just try to smile at the cameras, make it to the limo waiting by the curb and everything will be okay. Just pretend she wasn't there. The same game I've played my whole life.

Not that I've ever won.

16

The morning after the wedding, as a honeymoon gift, I took Eddie into Porter Square for breakfast and let Willa sleep in. We hit the bookstore first. I expected him to want out of there as soon as I grabbed the *Globe* I came in for, but I was happy to see him wander into the YA section and start pulling books off the shelves. I assumed kids didn't read anymore outside of the passing Harry Potter and Twilight spasms, and even those mostly limited to girls. I'd been reading C. S. Lewis to him before the heart attack, but I figured he was only indulging me. Yet there was Eddie, a kid of few words, scowling at the spines and riffling through the pages of the titles he selected, the favored covers writhing with dragons and bosomy elves.

"I just remembered we have to get back to *The Lion, the Witch and the Wardrobe*," I said, sitting next to him on the floor.

"I finished it."

"Really?"

"In the hospital."

"Wow. That's amazing. I didn't know you liked to read."

"Me neither."

I checked out some of the books he'd stacked up.

"So you're thinking of some more fantasy?"

He looked at me through a veil of real fear. "But no witches. I don't like witches." Then he brightened. "Battles and dragons and all that are cool, though."

We looked together for a while before I handed him a special boxed set edition of *The Lord of the Rings*.

"I loved this as a kid. I mean *loved*," I said. "And not a witch in the whole thing. But I bet you've seen the movies, right?"

"Mom won't let me yet."

"Really? Well, we could get around that by reading it."

He held the books in his hands as though judging their merit based on weight.

"Is there magic in it?" he asked.

"Lots."

"Do you like magic?"

"I don't think I'd be here without it."

I searched his eyes for anything that might show he saw that I might have been talking about him. That it was his presence, his magic, that delivered me all the way from the night field behind the house on Alfred Street to this café, this untroubled Saturday morning.

"Okay," he finally announced. Handed the box back to me. "Let's read this one."

"Take turns with it, you mean?"

"No, like the Narnia book. You reading to me. Except we'll finish this one."

"It's a big book. *Three* big books."

"We've got time, right?"

After a faked trip to the Reference section so I could blink away the threat of grateful tears, we bought our paper and books and walked down a couple stores to Cafe Zing for cheese croissants and drinks, a mango smoothie for Eddie and black coffee for me. We found a table near the back with plans of sneaking in a page or two of

The Fellowship of the Ring when Eddie said he needed to visit the bathroom first.

"I'll be here."

He gave me a don't-be-a-dummy look. "I know," he said.

Once I saw the men's room door shut I pulled out my cell phone and sent a text to Willa.

I miss you, Mrs. Orchard.

She wrote back almost immediately.

You've been gone 45 mins!! (Sweet tho—I luv being yr Mrs!)

I was thinking of my reply, grinning the idiotic grin of a man unused to composing love notes but enjoying himself in a way he can't contain, when I became aware of someone stepping close to the table. Not passing by on their way to the rear hallway but pausing, as though reading over my shoulder. Someone who now sat in the chair across the small table from mine. Eddie's chair.

"That didn't take long—"

I looked up.

It wasn't Eddie.

Writing to your girlfriend?

Did the people around me hear her? Did they see the uglybeautiful girl leaning closer to me, pushing me against the back of my chair? A glance around the room confirmed that none looked our way. None heard Ash speak in the voice that seemed to come from within my own head.

She scanned the room just as I did. It seemed to remind her how little time she could stay, because something changed in her face. The triumphant cruelty slipped away and left her anxious.

I need your help, Danny.

"Help?"

It's time.

"Leave me alone."

You have no idea what it is to be left alone.

"You can't hurt me anymore."

But that . . .

Her face changed again. A blank. Her true self.

. . . that's not true.

Ash lifted her hand and let it hover over the table. At first I thought she was preparing to count down the seconds with her fingers, or maybe lift Eddie's croissant to the chapped skin of her mouth. But then the hand drifted forward, toward me. Slow as a spider, which it now resembled, the long fingers extending, the knuckles staring at me like empty eyes. She didn't reach for me, though. The hand stopped before my full, still steaming coffee cup. Picked it up, making sure she had my full attention. Poured it over my hand.

Even as the scalding coffee burned my skin there was a clear thought running through my mind, more troubling than the idea of what she might do next or the strain on my suddenly racing heart.

She picked it up.

This is what shouted through my head so loud I was sure everyone sitting around me could hear. So sure that when I met their faces I was astonished to see only the curiosity of those witnessing a nasty accident-in-progress.

She picked up my cup but she's supposed to be dead.

I stood, almost knocked the table over with my knees. It fell against Ash, tipped her back in her chair, the metal frame toppling to the floor. But when I returned the table to its place, she wasn't there. Only the chair, rolling on its back before settling in a puddle of coffee.

A moment later Eddie found me by the condiments table, telling the barista there was no need to call an ambulance as I daubed my hand with napkins. Trying to hide the already blistering skin from his view.

"What happened?"

"Nothing. I spilled coffee on myself, that's all."

"Does it hurt?"

"A little."

He didn't believe me. Not just the part about it only hurting a little, but the part about me spilling the coffee on myself. I could tell by the way his nostrils flared, detecting something familiar in the air. The way he scanned the room looking to catch a glimpse of something that was there a moment ago.

"Danny? Do you——?"

"Let's go home so I can bandage this thing up. All right?"

Eddie nodded. Let me lead the way out the café's door as he brought up the rear, keeping an eye on the room as though in readiness against attack.

ONCE I GOT HOME, MY HAND IN A BOWL OF ICE WATER, I THOUGHT about how Ash's latest visits had been different from any that came before.

She'd never done anything so *physical* as pouring boiling liquid over a bare hand. Not to me ever, and not to anyone else since she died. But that morning she made something move in real time, an alteration of the world as she occupied it. Not a ghost, not a poltergeist or projection or whatever you'd call the shadow that had followed me for twenty-four years. She was *there*. For the moment that she reached out and made something happen, she was real.

What she'd done at the chapel was new, too. The burned face she revealed when she lifted the bridal veil was a different mask, a new trick. She could put on costumes now. She could show herself not only as she appeared in life, but how she looked as the flames licked her skin.

And another thing.

We'd never had a conversation like the one we had in the café before. She's spoken to me, delivered messages directly into my head, left behind notes of a kind. But then she was speaking across the table and when I replied, she heard me. Whatever barrier that made our communications a game of broken telephone had been removed, and she was present, her voice clear and sickeningly sweet as it had been in life.

So what had changed?

I'd died.

Ash killed me and brought me to Detroit, the one she'd been assigned to, the one she tried to show me inside the house on Alfred Street. Had I gone all the way up those steps and through that door I would never have come out again. Because I would have been hers.

The good news is that didn't happen, because I came back.

The bad news is I brought her with me.

17

That night, after reading the opening pages of Eddie's new book to him, Willa and I stayed up late drinking the champagne one of her friends had left with us as a wedding gift. It helped push aside the image of Ash sitting across from me in Cafe Zing and the even worse image of her walking down the aisle. The sweet bubbles of the wine, looking only at Willa, feeling the promise of her hand on my thigh. It almost kept her away.

"Cheers," Willa said, raising her glass.

"We've already clinked."

"You can't clink twice?"

"I could clink with you all night."

"I like it when you talk dirty."

Love is silliness. I didn't know that before. It's serious, too, and rearranges what's inside you in ways that are not always the most comfortable. But at that moment, half drunk with my beloved, it brought out the kid in me, the goof. The goofy kid I never had the chance to be.

Why not?

And this is how it goes.

Happiness with Willa and Eddie reminded me of how little happiness I'd had in my life. Which is followed by asking why.

Then the answer.

Her hand tipping the cup over mine. Lifting the white veil.

"Willa?"

"Yo."

"I love you," I said, changing my mind.

There is only a very small number of people who might believe me if I were to tell them that my long-dead sister is an afterlife stowaway. And I imagined Willa stood as good a chance of being among them as anyone. But I wasn't going to tell her.

I wanted to protect her. Eddie, too. From knowing what I see, the injuries I'm ready to privately bear. That was the reason that topped the list. I would do what I'd always done: I would contain Ash within my own world, hold on to the secret of her radiant evil so that it might shine only on myself.

That was the plan.

It didn't work then, my younger, unsilly self pointed out from somewhere below the champagne fizz. *Why would it now?*

"I love you, too," Willa said, and clinked my glass a third time.

SINCE THE HEART ATTACK, WILLA HAD INSISTED ON DOING THE cleaning up around the house, telling me to leave it to someone who knew what she's doing. She said it as a joke, the bossy wife claiming her domestic domain, but I knew it covered a real worry about me doing too much. Specifically, me going up and down between floors. The house is narrow and tall, as are the stairs, a common feature of the colonial-era town houses in old Cambridge. Climbing them required a leg raised higher than usual, a miniworkout to go from main-floor kitchen or living room to second-floor bathroom or bed. You had to watch yourself on the midway landing in particular, a tiny platform that turned sharply to the right, which could be a bit tricky if carrying a bucket or a vacuum.

It's where I met Willa. Me halfway up, she halfway down with a hamper of dirty laundry in her arms.

"Where do you think you're going?" she said.

"Eddie in his room?"

"Reading. Why?"

"I wanted to talk to you."

"Sounds serious. And we haven't been married a week yet."

"We can't do it this way."

"Do what *what* way?"

"Me the patient, you the nurse, making sure I stay consigned to bed. I feel useless."

"Useful's overrated."

"But this isn't how people *are*. Not the people I want us to be, anyway."

I expected another quip from her, but she softened. Did this thing with her nose, a *Bewitched* wiggle at the tip, that was her tell that whatever came next would be the real deal.

"Who do you want us to be?"

"A couple. A family," I said. "Not looking over our shoulders, just looking ahead like everybody else. But for now, I'd be happy just to do the damn laundry."

She didn't like it, but she could see this was something she had to let go of. She handed the hamper over to me.

"Go nuts," she said.

A couple minutes later, making a show of taking my time, I was two flights down in the cool of the unfinished basement. The laundry room is at the back of the house, farthest from the stairs. Just a roughed-in drywall square, plywood door, a single 100-watt bulb hanging from one of the ceiling crossbeams. I'd always liked it down there. Even when I was living alone I'd close the door and take my time feeding the washing machine, measuring the detergent, starting the cycle and lingering to hear the water pour in, the slushing of the tub.

The dryer has its charms, too. The front-entry door with its glass porthole allowing me to watch the crashing underwear and T-shirts with the same comforting repetition of the tide. If you looked long enough, you could notice subtle shifts each time around, each tumble unique. Pant legs tossed upward like a swimmer kicking his way under. A sock leaping against the glass as though begging for escape.

Or this.

A windbreaker I hadn't noticed in the wash. White with green stripes down the arm. A pattern that caught in my memory though I couldn't place from where. A flash of the nylon back, the cotton collar. The sort of retro thing you saw people wear these days, but not me. Did Willa shop at vintage stores?

I almost started upstairs but something about the dryer held my attention. A thudding from inside, like a roll of quarters I meant to cash at the bank, or one of Eddie's toy cars.

Except the thudding started in the middle of the cycle. The moment I raised my hand to switch off the light and go.

Instead of turning off the light, I turned off the dryer. It sighed to a stop, the clothes collapsing into a pile.

For the first time I noticed how warm it was. The heat of the dryer contributed to it, the indicator light next to HOT still blinking red. But something more than that, too. Air escaped through the cracks of the machine as though it were a living thing.

I bent down and pulled on the door. It yielded a quarter inch before sucking back into place.

I curled the fingers of both hands around the handle. Heaved it back.

The air came out so scorching and baby powdery it stung my eyes, an oven that had been baking sheets of Downy at 500 degrees.

And then I saw the windbreaker move.

It could've been just the last thing to settle, a belated resting of its slippery material amongst the firmer cottons. Except it did it *on its own*. Lying there on top of the other clothes and then, with a clear reach and pull of one of its sleeves, it made its way two inches closer to the open door.

An everyday illusion. The sort of thing you start trying to write off the moment after it's happened.

Then it moved again.

The other sleeve pulling itself up from the back of the piled clothes and slapping down next to the other. Two sets of green and white stripes, side by side.

My colors.

This came out of nowhere, like the name of a lost acquaintance you'd long stopped trying to recollect.

My high school colors.

I reached in and grasped one of the sleeves around the wrist. Felt it crumple in my grasp. Yet as I pulled, the jacket rising up from the dryer's other contents, the arm expanded, solidified. Something forming inside the sleeve, the shoulder, filling out the windbreaker's chest. The other sleeve rising and jerking on its own, too. Learning to move again.

"Fuck!"

I released the sleeve and leapt back hard this time, my full weight slamming against the furnace. The bent-metal roar of it echoed up the vents and into the house above.

The windbreaker writhed and shivered.

The sleeve I'd been holding reached all the way out of the drum. A hiss of nylon as it extended its full length, then suspended itself a foot over the floor. Nothing for a time. Like it was thinking. A snake waiting for its prey to walk by.

Then it moved. A round bulge made its way down the sleeve on the inside like a reverse swallow.

Something appeared from the hole of the wristband at the end. Hard-knobbed, gray-nailed, but most of it black, shining wet in spots. It paused as though making sure it had my complete attention. Then it came out all the way. A burnt human hand emerging to crack its fingers wide.

I squeezed my back against the furnace and it moaned in complaint. But I didn't run. Hypnotized by the hand. Its swaying, cobra-head dance.

Now the other sleeve joined its twin. Both out of the dryer and bending at the elbows to place charred hands on the floor. Clawing all the way out. The rest of the jacket filled out, embodied.

Including the head.

Slid out from the collar like a turtle from its shell. A partly exposed skull of bloodstained bone and matted hair. Once blond, now speckled black with charcoal.

She stood.

Wearing the green and white windbreaker zipped all the way up. Over her heart, the Dondero High coat of arms.

Go! Oaks! Go!

Our high school cheer. Chanted from the bleachers on game days, now shouted inside my head by Ash with mock cheerleader enthusiasm. Ash, who was never a cheerleader, would never have been a part of something so lame, so peppy. Though now she rotated her arms as though her hands held pom-poms. So close her nails almost brushed my face.

Go-ooo . . . OAKS!

She stopped. Made a disappointed, I-thought-you'd-be-happy-to-see-me face. A face of skin so loosened by burns it hung off nose and cheek and chin like dripping wax.

Go, I tried to say.

"How are you here?" I said instead.

Ash shrugged. The shoulders of the windbreaker rising to touch the hanging commas of her earlobes.

The same way I always was. But now—I've graduated.

These words so close they can be felt more than heard. The crunch of sand as you laid the side of your head upon a beach.

Before, you were my doorway. If you thought of me, dreamed of me, I could come through, she said, and slid one of her feet a quarter step toward me. *But now a part of me is here—I've got my foot in the door—and I can come and go. Talk and walk and push and pull and bite. The old me!*

Both feet took a full step closer. Her bare, rot-slicked soles making moist slaps on the concrete floor.

"You didn't look like that before," I said.

Like what?

"Burned."

That's what happens when you get left behind in a fire.

"I didn't leave you behind."

Yes you did. You left me in the basement of that house to die.

"That's why you tried to bring me back? Because you think I did something wrong?"

It's a mistake that needs to be corrected.

She raised one of her hands and I stiffened in anticipation of her touch.

You being alive is a fucking mistake, Danny.

Her hand drifted away from me to the light switch on the wall.

But you can start to make it right. You can help me . . .

She flicked off the light.

In the dark, I could hear her breathe.

Another thing I didn't remember from any of the times before. She didn't need to breathe then. But now she was practicing a forgotten skill, the rattling in and out. The warm stench of her insides.

"Why?"

It's the same question, asked in the same cracking voice, that I put to her over and over when we were kids. One word standing for the implied others.

Why are you doing this to me?

And she answered in the voice of the dead. Clear and unhalting, but also hollow. A recording of words already said at some other place, some other time, and now overenhanced to compensate for the absence.

We're still twins, Danny. We'll always be twins. And twins look out for one another.

She pressed against me in the dark.

Twins never let go.

The windbreaker crinkled, bunched up as it was pressed to my chest. Through the material her ribs and collarbone slipped out of place and back again, unhinged. She rose up on tiptoe to place her hand on my face. The flesh rough as a horse brush.

"Don't. *Please* . . ."

The forefinger found my lips and slipped between them, the taste liverish and sour.

The middle finger next. The pinkie. Pushed past my tongue like she might slide her entire fist, her arm, all of her into me just as she'd slipped through the sleeve of a jacket.

Then I went blind.

A rush of lemon-light. Too much all at once to discern what was there.

"Danny?" Eddie said.

I focused on him. Let his eyes tell me that Ash wasn't there anymore.

"Let's go upstairs," I said.

"Should we call a doctor or something?"

"No. But I think we should go. Now."

"Okay."

He stayed with me as we made our way to the base of the basement stairs, where I did something I shouldn't have. I asked him not to tell his mother about this. To pretend he came downstairs to check on me and I happened to be coming up at the same time and all was well. No problem, no freaked-out Danny discovered spitting onto the laundry room floor with the lights out.

"It'll just worry her, you know?" I said, standing aside to let Eddie go first up the stairs.

"Sure."

"We're good, then?"

"Great."

I was about to follow after Eddie when he turned on the second step. His face twisted with worry. And sweat. A silvery line just under the curls atop his forehead.

"Who was that?" he said.

"Sorry?"

He glanced up the stairs to make sure nobody was standing there.

"I can tell you don't want to talk about it. Like every time I've been about to open my mouth your face is all *Don't do it*. But I don't think I can do that anymore."

"Okay. *Okay*. So what are we talking about here?"

"The witch," Eddie said.

107

18

Why hadn't I thought of her as that before? It came to me only then that, for decades, whenever I saw a cutout figure of a woman flying on a broomstick taped to a school window at Halloween, whenever I got up and left the room if someone was watching *The Wizard of Oz* at the scene when Dorothy's house is spinning around in a tornado and the mean lady who wanted to destroy Toto flies by, I saw Ash, green-faced and cackling.

"The one who picked up my ball in the park when you . . . when you fell," Eddie went on, still two steps above me on the basement stairs. "The one who was in the laundry room just now."

I was nearly sick moments earlier when Ash stood so close to me, but it took an even greater effort not to be sick now. The worst part was the expression he wore. The eruption of panic that shaved years off him, returned him to darkest childhood, confused and exposed. The revelation that he'd pushed deep all this time for my sake, for his mother's, and that he couldn't carry any more.

He looked like me at that age.

"She was my sister," I said.

Eddie took a sharp breath and it seemed he might weep with gratitude. With those four words, he wasn't alone in his fear anymore. It occurred to me, with gratitude of my own, that I wasn't, either.

"She was my twin," I said. "But she's something else now."

"She's dead, isn't she?"

"Yes. But there are some people, for one reason or another, who don't entirely stay that way."

Eddie nodded, like this was all he needed to hear, and he would now start back up the stairs. But he was only gathering himself for what he said next.

"She's going to kill you."

"Eddie. Hold on. Listen—"

"That's what she *told* me!"

I sent my arm out for something to hold me up. It was sheer luck that my hand found the railing.

"She's spoken to you?"

"A couple times."

"In person? I mean, has she *touched* you?"

"No. In my dreams," he said, searching for the right words. "At least they seem like dreams, but they're not. That's how they might have started out but now they're getting, I don't know, *solid* or something."

"What did she say?"

"It's hard to think of things she said. If she's not in front of you, she gets blurry. Like she's covering the trail she leaves in your head."

"Just tell me what you remember."

It was his turn to reach out and hold on to the railing. His skin drained pale and papery as a napkin.

"How she won't stop until—"

"It's okay. We don't—"

"—until she pulls you down under the ice."

For a moment neither of us spoke. And in this pause I realized we were still underground, the washing machine commencing its spin cycle, rattling and pounding. Part of me wanted to turn and keep an eye on the laundry room door but I didn't want Eddie to see how frightened I was.

As I glanced up the stairs again, thinking I might have heard footsteps on the kitchen floor above, it hit me all at once. This was precisely the position where Ash stood in the house on Alfred Street when the fire wrapped itself around her. Down in the hole of the cellar, looking up. Her fear of being alone greater than her fear of burning alive.

Don't leave me here! DANNY!

With the memory of her scream came a whiff of smoke.

"Do you smell that?" I said.

Eddie sniffed the air. "It's stew in the slow cooker," he said. "And *her*. Like girl deodorant or something?"

This was the longest conversation the two of us had ever had. And it was about Ash. The closest I'd felt to this boy and it was her we had in common.

"She's already tried to kill you, hasn't she?" he said. "She *did* kill you."

"Yes."

Something shifted inside Eddie. He stood straight, lifted his chin.

"What can we do to make her go away?"

"I don't know. There was never really anything you could do about Ash. Nothing I could ever figure out. And I'm talking about when she was a living girl. Now? I don't know. I really don't."

Eddie mulled this over. I assumed he was trying to work up a solution, getting his head around the impossible. But his mind had been hooked on a detail.

"Ash," he said, as though the word belonged to a foreign language. "That's her name?"

"Ashleigh. She hated it, though."

"Ashleigh Orchard," he said to himself, testing its shape in his mouth. *"Ash-leigh Or-chard."*

Then he did something that startled me. Eddie looked over my shoulder toward the laundry room and shouted into the basement's darkness.

"Fuck *you*, Ashleigh Orchard!"

The thought passed through my mind that I should tell him that's not a suitable word for a ten-year-old. But I agreed with him. It was the very thing I'd wanted to shout into the dark many times myself.

"We have to tell Mom," he said.

"I know."

"Do you want to do it?"

"We're family now, right? We do it together."

Eddie started up the stairs and I followed. Though not before one last glance back at the laundry room, now still and dark with the end of the washing machine's spin. There could have been anything in there and you would never know.

19

In the living room, we told Willa about what Eddie and I spoke of in the basement.

Later, in our bedroom, I told her everything else.

How Ash and I were stillborn and something about the experience stole a part of her. How she died in the fire and I died, too, trying to help her, how I never knew why she went to the house on Alfred Street but it may be that it was against her will. How she piggybacked onto me when I came back after my collapse on Cambridge Common. How she's stronger this time. Not a bedeviling spirit anymore but a material being, acquiring new skills, learning all the things she can do.

Willa looked at me, unblinking, for the time it takes to breathe in a chestful of air.

"Okay," she said. "We're getting out of here."

I TRIED TELLING HER IT WOULDN'T MAKE ANY DIFFERENCE, THAT IT wasn't the building or rooms in it that were haunted but me, that

Ash was able to follow us wherever we went, but Willa insisted we get a hotel room somewhere and, even if I was right, "she can mess up the damned Holiday Inn instead of my house for a change." She meant to be funny. But I could see how scared she was.

We picked Eddie up from school in the afternoon and, telling him we were going on "an adventure," we got a suite at the Commander, the sitting room windows overlooking the Common, so that we could see the very spot where I collapsed, the tree Ash hid behind.

I pulled the curtains closed. Let Eddie watch back-to-back movies on the TV. Ordered up burgers and chicken wings and beer for dinner.

It was almost fun enough, distracting enough, to think that maybe I was wrong. Maybe we'd shaken her. I even did the mental math of calculating how long, if I sold the house in Porter Square and liquidated my savings, we could afford to stay there, living in fluffy bathrobes and eating room service every night. A couple years at least.

Eventually, none of us could fight sleep any longer. Within minutes of Willa turning out the bedside light over the table between our bed and Eddie's, it started.

Small things at first. The tap in the sink turned on (maybe Eddie forgot to turn it off after brushing his teeth?), the TV flicked back on with the volume cranked (maybe Willa rolled over onto the remote?). I got up and silenced them both. Returned to bed with a shrug, an unconvincing show to Willa that maybe that would be it.

The door to the room opened.

The hush of the rubber runner along the bottom grazed over the carpet. The column of light from the hallway widening over the curtains, our clothes piled on a chair. It remained held open for a moment before it was released. Closed with the solid *ka-thunk* of the weighted latch.

Everything still. The faint noise of traffic coming out of Harvard Square, audible a moment ago, was silenced. I could feel Willa awake next to me, head raised from the pillow, scanning the darkness. Eddie holding his breath five feet away.

Maybe I was the only one to hear it.

Only a whisper, at once too close to my ear and too far away to assume anyone not used to the sound might detect it. But it was clear to me all the same. Her bright, lifeless voice, announcing her readiness to play a new game.

Wakey-wakey!

The bathroom taps, the shower, the TV, the ventilation fan, every light in the room. All of it went on at once. A second later Willa's scream was added to the cacophony.

I ran around the room turning everything off. As I went, Ash followed me. So close I could almost feel her chin on my shoulder.

In a moment the room was returned to quiet. The only thing to hear was the door open and close across the hall, the hissed "Shit!" of the guy who got out of bed to see what the hell was going on in Room 614.

I stepped out of the bathroom and found Willa holding Eddie against her, the two of them standing at the end of his bed.

"We heard it, Danny," she said. "We both did."

"Of course you did. It was loud as—"

"Not the TV and stuff. The voice."

Eddie stepped away from his mother's arms to stand between us.

"Wakey-wakey," he said.

20

When we made it back home Willa took Eddie up to our room and assured him they'd sleep next to each other for the rest of the night. I told them I'd be fine on the sofa.

Besides, I had some calls to make.

I'd thought of her before that night. Violet Grieg. The old woman who went to hell and brought her father back with her.

A good man.

She was the only Afterlifer I'd encountered whose experiences were similar to ours. The NDE that resulted not in consolation or wisdom but a curse.

Wherever I go, he follows.

It was four in the morning but I called Lyle Kirk's home number anyway.

"The fuck is this?"

"It's Danny Orchard, Lyle."

"Danny? *Jesus*, man."

"Sorry for calling at this hour, but I'm in a bit of a situation."

There was a moment as I heard Lyle straightening from whatever futon or floor he'd been lying on.

"Sure thing," he said. "That's what we do."

"Remember the last meeting I came to? That lady who collapsed after talking about her father?"

"Debbie Downer. Absolutely, yeah. I remember."

"Her name was—"

"Violet Grieg."

"That's right. You have any contact info for her?"

"No, I don't. And even if I did, she can't talk to you, Danny."

"Why not?"

"She's dead."

I was standing. But now I sat.

"How do you know?"

"I set up Google alerts on everyone who comes to the meetings," Lyle said. "You know, staying informed on news among the membership and all that. Her name popped up a couple days ago."

"How'd she die?"

"Suicide. Got it right the second time around."

I looked over my shoulder. The sensation of being watched. A sensation I've had, in greater or lesser degrees, my entire life.

"What the hell's this about, Danny?"

"Thanks, Lyle. I'll let you get back to sleep," I said, and hung up.

VIOLET GRIEG MAY HAVE BEEN GONE, BUT ACCORDING TO THE IN-ternet white pages her sister Sylvie was still with us. I didn't warn her I was coming to Gloucester to see her, which it occurred to me, as I pulled off the 128 and made my way past the fishermen's outfitting shops and FRIED CLAMS! stands near the harbor, may not have been the best idea. It's a long way to have gone just to get a door slammed in my face.

The door in question belonged to a whitewashed two-story at the corner of Prospect and Main, across from Flannagan Gas Station, the air a rank competition between gas and sea. I parked directly on the street in front and got out, the chain-link gate at the sidewalk's edge screeching when I swung it open. I was trying not to think about what I'd say, what I came there to learn. There wasn't time for thinking. Every time I paused, every time I started to wonder if it was over, if Ash was gone—that was when she liked to come. I had to move. Up the cement steps and knocking a fist against the locked screen door.

When a woman appeared to squint out at me from the other side it took a moment to recall that it was my obligation to speak first.

"Sylvie Grieg? My name is Danny Orchard."

She didn't say anything to this. She may not have even heard it. When I spoke again I leaned in so close my nose pushed against the screen.

"I'm not selling anything. I'm just—"

"First thing, I can *hear* you. Pretty sure the neighbors a block over don't need to."

"Sorry. It's—"

"And second thing, I know who you are."

"You do?"

"Taller than I would've guessed. Got a few more gray hairs than the picture in the magazine, but I suppose I do, too, since the last time I read your book."

I figured she'd open the door then but she didn't. Continued to stand there, looking at me like a street accident she'd come to gawk at before heading back to her coffee.

"May I come in?" I said.

"Not sure why you would."

"I need some help, to be honest with you."

"Help? That could mean pretty much anything."

"In my case, it's—"

She opened the door.

"You're still *shouting*," she said.

I TOLD HER ABOUT ASH.

All the parts that aren't included in *The After*. I told her about how my falling in love and having a chance to help raise a boy seemed to have given her a new strength, one sufficient to take hold of the heart in my chest. I told her about Ash trying to lead me to hell but instead I came back and brought her with me. A series of sentences that sounded like the mumblings of a sanatorium patient even to my own ears. But Sylvie didn't react to any of it one way or another. She seemed as likely to call 911 as wrap her arms around me.

"Somebody told you about Violet," she said once I finished. We were in her dark kitchen at the back of her dark house, sitting across from each other. Every once in a while there was the crunch of floor-boards from upstairs but nobody came down. "Somebody told you a story."

"She reached out to the Afterlifers group in Boston."

"Afterlifers group! Sounds like an insurance company. Fat heap of help those tunnel-of-light piss parties are to anyone."

She slammed her palm on the table, a single smack, then returned her hand to her lap like it never happened.

"They didn't know what to make of your sister's case," I said. "And I can't pretend I do, either. But I believe it. What I heard of it, anyway."

"What good is believing it going to do you?"

She was somewhere in her early eighties but seemed even older, though this could have been an augmentation of the house and its shut-in scents, its smoky curtains and Vick's VapoRub. A sinewy, ball-knuckled woman who would've been good in a fight, all wound-up muscle ready to deliver swift, unpredictable blows.

"Maybe hearing what you know of what happened might help me," I said. "That's why I'm here. To see if there's a way I can stop my sister from taking my life so that I might have the chance to live a little of it first."

She searched the table's surface for a drink that wasn't there. Upstairs, someone marched down the hallway and stopped. It was hard to see this woman living with a husband, with anyone, though some-one was here with her.

"He started with me when I made the turn into my teens. But I was a different sort of girl from Violet—not just two years older but *different*—and he knew it," she said. "I'd tell. I'd fight. But in the end I ran away the first chance I had and left my sister there with him. You couldn't imagine the ways I've told myself how this was the only thing I could do, how I had no choice. All lies. Because she needed me to protect her. She was *alone*. And for the years I pretended I was being strong I was only the worst sort of coward, because my life was paid for through hers."

Her tears were brief and came with a shake of her head that spilled two lines down her cheeks. But that was it. The next second she was as steady as someone who'd recovered from a sneeze.

"She tried to kill herself," she said. "This was years after he died, after she was free of his hands but not what they left on her. Did her best to keep it to herself but I knew the pain she was in. Violet couldn't recover from it, couldn't shake him."

She wiped her sleeve under her nose and inspected her shirt as if it revealed the long-awaited results of a medical test. When she continued she was still inspecting it, saddened by the news it brought.

"She tried the easiest way to do it. Took a glass of wine and a straight razor into the bath and made a right mess. But she started too early. Before she had a chance to turn the taps off she was already slipping under and the water was spilling onto the floor and going right through to the couple who lived under her, dripping on their heads as they watched TV. They thought they saved her life, because she was dead for a time in that tub before the paramedics came. And that's where she met up with dear old Dad. Doctor Good. That's what they called him in our town. Doctor Goddamned Good."

"Who came back with her."

"He never let go! That's what she always said. 'Sylvie, Daddy will never let me go.'"

Another shuffle of footsteps upstairs, coming through the ceiling directly above us. I involuntarily glanced upward but Sylvie didn't follow my eyes.

"Things got worse for her after that. 'Dad walks with me,' she'd say. 'Holds my hand like he's taking me to school but when he whispers something in my ear it's the worst of the secrets he made me keep.' Things you couldn't live with if you were her. If you were anybody."

"So she tried to kill herself again."

"Made damned sure of it this time. Put our father's hunting rifle down her throat and pulled the trigger with her toe. Same way Dad did it. Using the same gun."

"My God. I'm sorry."

"You know where she got the rifle? He gave it to her in his will! Like it was a joke."

"Or a command," I said before I could stop myself.

She looked at me like I'd just blown a bubble gum bubble and it popped. "How's that?"

"He went out that way, so he was saying she had to follow him. It'd be something my sister would do."

"Oh yeah? People think she was a good girl?"

"They thought she was an angel."

The old woman nodded. It seemed to help her come to some internal decision.

"So what you came here for," she said. "You want to know if there's any way to make your sister stop."

"You know of any?"

"The only one who might is Violet, and she's not here anymore. But I know she tried. Her parish priest, those Afterlifer friends of yours, a New Age minister or whatever you call voodoo in Massachusetts. Knocked on every door she could think of. Didn't do any good. Just like I expect none of them could do any good for you."

"Why are you so sure of that?"

"Because your sister is *dead*. One foot on the far side of the river and the other on your throat. You can't *push* her back to where she's supposed to be, not from here. She can only be *pulled*."

Sylvie reddened. A bloom of heat that came upon her so suddenly she leaned against the back of her chair, puffing for air. I got a glass out of the cupboard and poured her some water. She took a sip and shivered as though she'd swallowed much stronger stuff.

"I wish you luck, Mr. Orchard," she managed. "But right now, I think I need to lie down."

Sylvie rose on unsteady feet and let me take her arm. Started shuffling toward the front door with me squeezed next to her in the narrow hallway, my shoulder nudging against the framed photos on the wall as we went. One I knocked hard enough that its wire slipped off the hook and I had to catch it with my free hand before it hit the floor. When I put it back I saw it was an image of Sylvie, eleven or twelve years old, standing in a bathing suit at the end of a dock next to a younger girl I took to be Violet. The two of them have just gotten out of the lake, their long hair glued to their necks. A standard setup for a holiday snapshot.

Yet something about it held me. Something wrong.

If you looked closer you could see that the girls' grins betrayed an effort, their closeness to each other an instinct of mutual protection as much as a sharing of warmth after a cold swim. It let me see who held the camera. How the lens and the man who trained it on them captured not only their images but their fragile, shivering selves.

We carried on to the door and Sylvie removed her arm from mine. Found her balance.

"Thank you," I said, and she murmured something I couldn't make out in reply, though the intent was clear.

Just go.

Before I opened the screen door I turned to look up the stairs to the second floor.

A man stood at the top looking down at me.

He wore his hair combed, shiny with Brylcreem, his shirt and pants dated but neatly pressed. His smile was the smile of a caregiver, a bedside hand-holder, gentle and knowing and inviting trust. He looked like a country doctor from the sixties. A good man.

I looked to Sylvie, who glanced up at where I'd been looking but didn't seem to register anyone there.

"If you don't mind my asking, do you live here on your own?"

"Since my husband passed. Sixteen years now," she said. "You looking for somewhere to stay?"

"No, no. Just a question."

I stepped out. The day unthinkably bright. My car by the curb, ready to take me away from the salt air and gas station fumes and the house behind me, all of them things I knew I would try to forget but won't.

But before I let the screen door slap shut I gave Sylvie a last wave of farewell and in doing so saw that her father still stood at the top of the stairs. His kindly expression hadn't changed, yet something passed between us. It's in his eyes. A darkening that left only a red laser point at their center, burning down at me. Eyes that pulled me in, letting me in on something. The sort of awful secret Ash liked to share with me.

And what his eyes said was that he *knows*.

Knows I have the gift of seeing others who are here but shouldn't be, that I know who he is and all he's done and that's just fine with him. It's all good.

BY THE TIME I WAS BACK ON THE 128 HEADING SOUTH TOWARD Boston the afternoon had grown muggy and windless, though I drove with the windows down instead of hitting the AC just to feel the real air swirl around me. Trying to blow all the voices out of my head.

It helped. But it didn't stop Sylvie Grieg's words from repeating themselves. Words that seemed to either open a door or close it forever.

You can't push her back. She can only be pulled.

Violet's father wanted to claim her in death just as he had in life. And now he waited for Sylvie to join them, to force her to go with him even if she was meant for another place just as Ash tried to force me into the house on Alfred Street.

What does Ash want?

The old question again. Maybe there's a different answer now than over the years she merely watched over me as a stalking cloud.

Maybe she wanted from me what she wanted from Lisa Goodale and Michelle Wynn and Winona Quinlan, the girls she tried to lead on a bike ride downtown.

She wanted them to *see*.

I closed the windows. Pumped the AC up to max. But before the fan drowned it out, I heard my phone vibrating on the passenger seat next to me. Expecting it to be a **When will you be home?** text from Willa, I tapped the screen to life only to see it wasn't a text at all but a phone message. A number I didn't recognize.

Odds are it was only a telemarketer, or my speaking agent asking if a date looks good for me to fly in to Denver or Biloxi, or Lyle Kirk wanting to know if all went well in my search for Violet Grieg's sister. But something told me it wasn't.

I was going to pull over at the next exit but, seconds later, realized I wouldn't make it.

A stab in my chest so sudden my left arm fell off the wheel and I drifted onto the soft shoulder too fast, fishtailing over the gravel, pumping the brakes until I eventually coaxed the car into a diagonal stop.

There was an excruciating swelling around the base of my neck that sitting forward or sideways didn't ease. I couldn't tell if it was a warning flare from the stress of the morning or simply the inevitable reblocking of a valve and this was it, this was where I go, sitting in a Ford Focus somewhere between Manchester-by-the-Sea and Beverly.

After a time the stabbing reduced to a throb and I was able to lift the cell again. Listen to the voice message on speakerphone.

"Mr. Daniel Orchard? This is Marion Cross of the Cambridge Police Department," a voice said. The low register of a bad-news professional. "Could you please call me back as soon as possible? My number—"

I thumbed the call off. Pressed CALL BACK.

With every ring the pain returned. It left me to whistle my breath through clenched teeth. Both fists slapping the wheel.

"Marion Cross," the voice said when it answered. She seemed to know it was me just as I seemed to know what she was about to say.

"This is Danny Orchard."

"Thank you for returning my call, Mr. Orchard. I wonder if there's any way you could make your way—"

"What's going on?"

"It might be better—"

"What *happened*?"

There was a quarter second of silence before she spoke. A quarter second of sympathy that proved she was a human being.

"There's been an accident."

21

The rest of the drive back was a blur of speed and rain. A downpour that hit as soon as I entered the Boston city limits and only came down harder by the time I parked at Mass General and ran, soaked, through the emergency room doors.

This was where Marion Cross, the voice on the phone, told me I'd find Willa and Eddie.

She said more than this but I heard only half of it, maybe less. I just tossed the cell into the passenger-side footwell and drove, weaving through everything in front of me. I heard *vehicle* and *they're doing everything they can* and *divers*. But there was nothing more I needed to know after *There's been an accident* and the name of the hospital.

I was shouting at the sleepy guy sitting behind the glass at the triage desk, asking where they were, when I felt a hand on my shoulder.

"Mr. Orchard?"

I swung around to find a middle-aged woman in a Cambridge Police uniform. CROSS on her shirt.

"Are they alive?"

It's not the question I meant to ask first, but it was the first one that came out.

"They've been through a lot today, but yes. Both hanging on pretty good, I'd say."

"You said divers. On the phone."

"Let's sit over here, Daniel."

"*Danny*. Why divers?"

"Just come over here with me, Danny. Okay?"

The guy behind the glass smirked as he watched the officer lead me to an unoccupied corner of the waiting room. I was wrong about him. He wasn't sleepy. He was just a dick who found amusement at the sight of people suffering the worst moments of their lives.

"We're still investigating the cause," Marion Cross was saying, adjusting the gun at her belt so she can sit without it jabbing her in the side. "But there was no other vehicle involved."

"What did they hit?"

She squinted, and it aged her a decade. "Didn't you hear me on the phone?"

"Not everything."

"Water," she said. "Your wife drove her car into the Charles River with your son in the passenger seat late this morning."

Two things hit me at once, both of equal weight.

Drove her car into the Charles River was one.

Your son was the other.

"But they got out?"

"Our marine unit was out on patrol, which was fortunate. They were able to reach the scene right away and send a couple divers down to get them out of there."

"Are they hurt?"

"The doctors are still assessing them. But it looks like your wife's injuries are minor."

"And Eddie's?"

"He took quite a bump to the head on impact. Regained consciousness by the time he got here, though, which is the good news.

But I think he'll be staying for a while to make sure there's no long-term damage, that kind of thing."

What felt a moment ago like a thousand questions vaporized all at once. Left me with only one.

"Can I see them?"

WILLA WAS SITTING UP AND LOOKING REASONABLY COMPOSED when I entered her room. Then she saw it was me. And lost it.

I held her as best I could and let her scream into my shirt.

"It was my fault," Willa said once she was able to. "It was *me*, Danny. But I don't know how it happened."

"We don't have to figure all that out right now."

"The hell we don't."

"The main thing is to fix the two of you up. You're both alive. Everything else—it doesn't matter."

Willa nodded, and kept nodding. Not at the truth of what I'd just said but the horror of what she was about to say.

"It was so dark down there," she began, and with the words, her eyes darkened, too. "I don't know how deep it was, but it could've been miles. I don't think we ever touched bottom. So goddamned *dark*. Black water coming in every crack, around the windows, the air vents. Slow at first, so I thought we had some time. If the glass held we could stay down there until the air ran out and how long could that be? Couple hours? Then it started to fill up. Fast. I got Eddie out of his seat belt—he wasn't awake, and there was a lot of blood coming from I don't know where—I pulled him onto me and made sure his head was as high as I could hold him. So he might have time."

She stopped to take in an enormous, shaking breath. Like she was back in the car under the surface of the Charles and this was the last air she'd ever taste.

"You saved him, Willa."

"I drove into the river for no reason," she said, and exhaled. "It didn't feel like it was me doing it, but it was. I didn't *save* him. I nearly *killed* him."

EDDIE WAS BLUE.

His hands laid atop the bedsheet, closed eyelids, his lips, all of him different shades of hurt. But it was the black line across the top of his forehead, a barbed wire of stitches, that was the hardest to look at.

I held one of his hands and warmed it in mine.

I'd died three times in my life but that was nothing compared to this. I would have done it three more times and stayed that way if it would've made his suffering go away. Made it mine instead.

Even though I was watching his face I didn't see the eyes open. One second he was asleep and then he was looking up at me, making the mental calculations of who I was, where he was, what brought him here.

He put both of his hands around my arm and I expected him to use it to lift himself up against his pillows but instead he pulled me down close.

"I saw her," he said.

"Where?"

"In the car. Just before we went into the water. I looked into the backseat and she was there. Smiling at me."

"Eddie—"

"*She did it.* Reached between the seats and grabbed the wheel," he said, squeezing my arm so hard I thought he'd never let go. "She tried to *kill* us, Danny."

22

They released Willa from the hospital the next day but kept Eddie in for what one of the doctors, choosing a philosophical phrasing, called "the indefinite future." His skull had been fractured, which was serious enough in itself. But they were worried about damage that might have resulted from the concussion, which meant tests and scans and people asking him if he remembered his birthday (got it right the first time, mixed it up with Christmas the second) and the name of his first pet (Charlie, a goldfish, nailed both times).

Over those first couple days, the cops came by wanting to know how a Buick Regal up to date on its maintenance would come to plow off Memorial Drive and into the Charles River in broad daylight when there was no alcohol in the driver's blood and no indication she was speeding. Willa told them she must have dozed off for a second. Eddie said he didn't remember. They asked the same questions a second time, got the same answers. In the end, they had no choice but to accept their stories, even if they didn't believe them.

Willa didn't feel good about it, but she had to lie.

I'd told her what Eddie whispered to me. She reacted as though a growing suspicion in her mind had been confirmed. While she didn't see Ash in the car, she *did* feel the wheel jerk away from her hands, a motion she felt sure wasn't a mechanical failure but "something intentional, something really fucking *strong*." She didn't tell me about it at first because she didn't think it was possible, that she might be subconsciously letting herself off the hook with a crazy idea.

"But then I remembered all the things you told me about your sister," she said. "How she's nothing *but* crazy ideas."

It was hard to coax Willa away from Eddie's bedside even to get something to eat or walk the hallway to stretch her legs. It left me to smuggle in decent food and dash back and forth to Porter Square for toiletries and clean clothes, along with the copy of *The Fellowship of the Ring* Eddie and I bought together and that he asked me to keep reading even if it looked like he was sleeping because "it's good just to hear you say the words."

So I kept saying the words. In fact I read aloud through the whole of the second night, hoping to shield both Willa's and Eddie's dreams with magic. Kept awake by the fantasy that I was actually helping.

I tried it on the third night, too, but, somewhere around when the hobbits are running from the Ringwraiths in a dark forest, sleep pulled me down.

What felt like less than a minute later, I awakened in the same chair I'd fallen asleep in. Eddie in his bed, eyes closed. Willa on the far side in the other chair, also out. The same room in every detail except for the quiet. No nurses bustling along the hallway through the open door, no squeak of shoes on polished floor, no PA calls for Dr. This or Dr. That. The entire hospital cottonballed.

I got out of the chair and looked around the corner.

The hallway was dark. The ceiling's fluorescent lights all extinguished, so that only the couple of desk lamps at the nurses' station thirty feet to the left were still on. To the right, a yellow haze that dimmed to nothing before reaching the next door.

I was starting back into the room. Maybe I hadn't been noticed. Maybe the doorjamb could be quietly lifted and the three of us could hide until morning, when the light would return the flapping lab coats and squeaking carts and burbling phones.

But something saw me.

A single intake of breath. Like a gasp, but of a lower register. The suck of air that pulled other matter deeper with it. Wet hair or half-chewed food or sand.

Coming from the right. From the darkness that yielded its details the longer I stared into it.

A patient.

Gowned and barefoot and tilted like a skiff in a gale. The tentative quarter steps of the unwell. A woman who should be told to get back into bed.

She slid her blue feet closer and I could see that it wasn't a bed she'd risen from.

Hoo . . .

The gasp-that-isn't again. Whistled up and out of her mouth. Or from where her mouth used to be.

The hospital gown not a hospital gown but skin. Hanging and burned.

My sister did two things at the same time.

She came closer, showing herself in the outer reaches of the nurses' station's lamplight.

She raised her arms out in front of her as if in invitation to join her in a dance.

Hoo . . . HOO . . .

I didn't go to her. I didn't pull away, either. Neither was possible unless she willed it.

The hands came up and found her face. What was left of it. The fingernails hooking in. Pulling away.

Who?

Ash peeled the skin off her face to reveal the soft tissue below it, the hard cords of ligament and muscle. Kept ripping until there was only bone. Until her body was no longer visible and she was nothing more than a white skull floating in the hallway's darkness.

Who, Danny? WHO?

23

Morning.

Noisy and smelling of less-than-great coffee and oatmeal. Eddie sitting up in bed, looking at me struggling to escape the chair I'd slept in.

"Bad dream?" he said, then shook his head. "Don't answer that."

I needed to talk to Willa. The opportunity came within the hour when one of the nurses arrived to shoo us out so she could change Eddie's dressing. I was about to try and convince Willa to step outside for five minutes of fresh air when she asked me first.

We crossed the pedestrian bridge over Storrow Drive and found shade in a cluster of trees at the edge of Lederman Park, a Little League game in progress on one of the diamonds. Every once in a while there was the crack of bat meeting ball, the hooting cheers as a runner rounded the bases. What would otherwise be reassuring sounds that instead punctuated our hushed conversation like gunshots.

"I'm scared, Danny."

She said it like an accusation. A declaration of lost patience.

"Me, too."

"But it's something else now. I mean, I thought we had something to deal with before this. A presence or whatever. One nasty little bitch of a ghost following us around. I figured that was something I could handle, because I can get nasty myself if I need to. But this. This is *fucked up*."

Willa walked slightly ahead, so that her words flew back into me, lightweight but sharp, like paper released out the window of one of the speeding cars roaring behind us.

"You're right," I said. "I should go. Leave the two of you on your own. Let Ash come after me alone."

"I don't want that. Neither of us do."

"I want you to be safe."

"You running away won't do that."

Willa stopped to let me catch up with her. We stood close enough to touch, but didn't.

"We're a part of this now because we're a part of you," she said.

That this was essentially the same thing I thought myself after Eddie told me of seeing Ash take the wheel of the car shouldn't have surprised me. Willa's answer to the question *Why us?* simply led her to the same place it led me.

"She's taken an interest in us, Danny," Willa went on, and paused to allow the cheers at what sounded like a home run to die down. "Whether you're here or a thousand miles away, she's going to stay interested."

I put a hand on her shoulder. Instead of drawing her closer, it started her shaking.

"It's going to be—"

"Don't say it's going to be okay, Danny! *Don't!*"

I pulled my hand away but she kept trembling. Her lips pale even as the breeze I'd detected before was shut off like the closing of an oven door.

"We're still alive," I said. "And I don't think that's just blind luck, either. I think we're *meant* to be."

"What are you saying?"

"Her attacks on me, driving your car into the river—attempts on our lives, but ones that didn't go all the way. If that was all Ash wanted, aren't there ways to do it and be sure?"

"She came pretty goddamned close the day before yesterday."

"But you're still here."

"Why?"

"Because she wants me to do something for her. Something she can't do herself."

Who, Danny? WHO?

The umpire hollered a strike call and a handful of boos filtered through the trees, settling in the branches like birds.

"When I was with her the last time, on the other side, *her* side, she told me she wanted me to see something," I said. "I figured it was something she already knew and was just leading me to, a windup. But I think I was wrong. I think it's something she *doesn't* know."

Willa unfolded her crossed arms and they dropped to her sides.

"You think she was murdered," she said.

"Yes, I do. She was murdered and not even she knows who did it."

For a moment it appeared that Willa hadn't heard me. She had the lowered eyelids and top-heavy sway of someone about to drop in a faint, so that I reached out to catch her if she fell. But she ended up supporting herself with an outstretched foot. Not falling. Walking away from me.

"Eddie should be ready by now," she said, her voice cast over her shoulder again as I followed behind her.

"Ash wants me to go."

It made her turn.

"You think you should do what *she* wants? As far as I can tell, that's seeing the three of us dead."

"You may be right. But she wants something else first."

"How do you mean?"

It was then that I voiced aloud for the first time the thought I'd been inching toward since that afternoon in the laundry room. A thought that gained the certainty of truth as soon as it was spoken.

"I think she wants me to find out who started the fire," I said.

Willa slid closer and I looped an arm around her. Pulled her closer still.

"I wish I was somebody who could honestly say, 'I don't believe any of this,' but I'm not," she said. "So what are we going to do?"

"Not you. Me. I'm going to Detroit."

"Today?"

"We can't wait," I said. "Ash isn't going to."

"What are you going to do once you get there? What can you do that twenty years and a bunch of homicide detectives couldn't?"

"I don't know, to be honest. But if there's something out there that might make her go away, I've got to try and find it, don't I?"

"Why *you*?" she said, pivoting to show new black pouches under her eyes. "Couldn't we hire a private investigator or something? You're *not well*, Danny. The doctors said to—"

"Nobody else can do it. All the clues are here," I said, tapping the side of my head with a pair of fingers.

"Name one."

"They're not those kinds of clues."

Willa walked up to me, lowered her head, and punched me in the stomach. A shot hard enough that it was all I could do not to double over.

"Sorry," she said. "Better you than a wall."

"You want to punch something? I'll always be here for you."

She looked up. "Will you?"

Willa made the motion with her hand that is her signal for me to bend for a kiss—a three-fingered *Down here* pull—and grazed a quick one, dry and cool, on my cheek.

"I'll explain it to him," she said. "Because if we're doing this, we're doing it now."

Then she walked back over the pedestrian bridge toward the hospital, the passing traffic howling beneath her.

I watched for as long as I could. Memorizing her shape, holding her voice in my head, breathing in what was left of her scent in the air. Hoping all of it might be brought back one more time before it was gone for good.

24

The clerk eating Taco Bell behind the counter at the airport's Budget Rent a Car who handed me the keys to my Chevy Impala asked if I'd ever visited Detroit before.

"I used to live here," I said. "A million years ago."

"Yeah?"

"Bet it's changed a lot since then."

He looked at me with genuine disbelief. "Bet it hasn't," he said.

Outside, pulling my carry-on bag toward my car, the night was high and starless, as though space itself had retreated from the earth.

Is there a lonelier place than a car rental lot after the last domestic flights of the evening have landed and no one but yourself slips behind the wheel?

Yes, there is. That lot could be in Detroit.

I'd gone from Mass General to Porter Square, thrown a couple shirts and jeans into a bag and headed straight to Logan, looked up at the Departures board and found the next flight out. The roar of the engines had lullabyed me into a deep sleep even before takeoff, so that the flight attendant had to shake me awake after the door had been opened at the terminal and I was the only passenger left.

The drive into the city produced nothing familiar, nothing to say this was a place of importance to who I am. The down-market billboards for personal injury lawyers and bail bondsmen. The land that's neither farmer's field nor residential neighborhood but the in-between of scrap metal lots and self-storage compounds and light-industry factories, all shut down, all with truck trailers backed up to the loading bay doors as though meant not to deliver a shipment but to barricade something inside.

Then I was curving onto a ramp that traded the interstate for the expressway that ran the southern border of downtown. And there they were.

The pillars pushed up from out of the horizon, their dark glass reflected blue against the night. The electric GM atop the highest tower floating so far apart from everything else it was a monogram stitched onto the night.

I knew I should find a room somewhere but kept driving instead. Through the near-empty streets of downtown to where Woodward Avenue began its long, dead-straight course away from the river. Detroit's spine.

The view outside felt just as otherworldly—an environment experienced as an animal might experience it, hyperconscious to escape routes and threats—as it did on the other side. What's doubly strange is that doing it while alive made me feel like I was dead. Which may have only been what the return home after a long time away is for anyone.

As I reached the far side of the overpass that left downtown behind I realized that Alfred Street was only a couple blocks ahead. I could hang a right and, within two minutes, park in front of the house (or the empty lot, or whatever had been built on its ashes).

I didn't.

Stopped the Impala in the middle of the lane. Pulled a U-turn. Stomped the gas.

A second later there was a warning tingle running the length of my left arm.

With one hand over my heart as if I were about to take the Pledge of Allegiance, I drifted into the garage at the back of the Greektown Casino-Hotel and shuffled to the front desk for a room. I couldn't have looked good. But they were used to people like me, traveling alone and not looking good.

Up on the eighteenth floor my window framed the city's core. Broad-shouldered stone buildings of the kind they haven't built in fifty years. The raised concrete tracks of the People Mover monorail curving through downtown, a failed solution notable among the city's history of failed solutions. Figures on the street here and there. Shadows standing on the corners, none walking when the lights changed.

My underworld.

25

Dawn arrived on crimson clouds. From the bed, I watched it color the city in Martian hues before it lightened to orange, then pink, as if the day were deciding between a palette of alien options before it landed on the yellow sun of home.

I should be sleeping. But every time I closed my eyes they demanded to be opened again to confirm I'm actually here.

Detroit.

Canadians crossing the border to buy stuff cheap always pronounced it in three syllables (De-*troy*-it), those of us in the suburbs made the *e* short (D-*troyt*), while the people who lived in the city itself stretched the vowel long (*Dee*-troyt). There wasn't a single right way to say it, though everyone made fun of how others got it wrong.

I tried each of these versions aloud as I watched the night pull off the skyline like a sheet. The police cars that lined certain streets and ignored others, the past-their-prime office buildings, the river blackly glinting through the gaps—there was no way to pretend I was anywhere else. Though that's exactly what I'd spent the last restless hour trying to do. Wishing I were home, or in one of the other Any-cities where I gave a talk and had to remind myself where I was.

Even for an Afterlifers gig, I never said yes to Detroit.

The bedside phone rang.

Did I request a wake-up call when I checked in? Being in the middle of a minicoronary at the time, my memory of the exchange was less than crystal clear.

I was going to let it ring until it stopped, then thought it had to be Willa. Willa, who wanted to be the first to wish me good morning and tell me Eddie's doing fine—maybe he would even get on the line himself—and they'd tell me they miss me already and be careful, please be careful.

The receiver was against my ear before I remembered Willa didn't know where I was staying.

Wakey-wakey . . .

I slammed the phone down. Headed straight into the shower. Cranked the hot water as if I might wash Ash's voice off my skin.

BREAKFAST AT THE HOTEL BUFFET IS ALL-YOU-CAN-EAT, AN OFFER taken seriously by the other diners who returned several times for more waffles and nests of bacon, a consolation for what, by the swollen-eyed look of them, was another losing night at the casino.

I laid my phone on the table and checked to see if the app I downloaded before I left was working. A link to the security system I had installed in the house in Porter Square a couple years ago after a rash of break-ins in the neighborhood. By clicking on the app, I could see what the tiny cameras affixed to the ceiling at the entry points to the house could see: the back door, the main-floor windows, the front door. The idea is that if there's an intruder or someone who comes in without deactivating the alarm, the phone automatically shows me what's going on by connecting to the camera where the break-in is happening.

With a couple clicks, I confirmed it was working. Checked all the cameras, hoping for a glimpse of Willa coming or going to the hospital, but nothing moved.

When I exited the security app, there was a new message from her waiting for me.

there ok?

For five minutes I tried to think of something sweet or flirty or encouraging—some of the talk we found so easy just days earlier—but it all looked false when typed onto a screen. In the end, I decided not to even try.

Here just fine. Let you know how it goes.

I waited for an **xoxo** or **luv u**, the equivalent of a pecked cheek, but nothing came.

I GOT INTO THE CAR BECAUSE I DIDN'T KNOW WHAT ELSE TO DO.

Onto Woodward again, headed away from downtown and this time passing Alfred Street and carrying on by the Medical Center buildings, the Detroit Public Library and Institute of Arts, then into the long, blasted miles of now largely unoccupied residential blocks, the thousands of condemned properties that billboards offered for those looking to START OVER FOR $10,000 . . . OR *LESS*!!

Once I was across 8 Mile Road, things started to change. With the Detroit city limits behind me, the stores were no fancier, but at least half of them were open. A couple of car lots offering new models along with the used. Here the churches had unbroken windows and signs advertising the topic for Sunday's sermon (JESUS OPENS THE DOOR . . . BUT ONLY IF YOU KNOCK).

When the avenue divided at the base of Main Street I veered right and headed over the train tracks into Royal Oak.

It hadn't changed much. Which must be considered a triumph, given that the city has seen nothing but change the past couple decades, almost none of it good. But the Royal appeared to be hanging on, guarding itself against the realities swirling around it. Here's the

Starbucks, there's the Barnes & Noble. A cookery store with copper pots and wineglasses in the window. People on the street moving with purpose from one place to another, skateboarding students and strollering moms and tie wearers. Contrasted with Woodward south of 8 Mile, it all looked set-decorated, a middle-class checklist.

Driving alone up Main Street. Not knowing where to go, who to call on, how to get out.

I felt like a kid again.

And like the teenager who drifted through town after Ash was gone and, later, the college dropout doing nothing but tweaking a book about being dead, I found myself heading into the Caribou Coffee, ordering a mug of dark roast, and hiding in the corner. Trying to sort things out. Then as now, not even sure what the question was that needed sorting.

If Ash had been murdered, the one thing that's known is that it happened on our birthday. And as far as the public record goes, the last people to see her alive were the three girls who biked behind her part of the way down Woodward Avenue before turning back.

Lisa Goodale.

Michelle Wynn.

Winona Quinlan.

Lisa, cleavaged and sleepy-eyed, came to mind first. She could have any guy at school she wanted, and she *did*—unless Ash wanted him, too. At one basement party I remember Lisa sitting next to Nathan Pohl. Nathan was two years older, his dad let him drive his BMW coupe, he did some modeling for local ad flyers—as close to a movie star as we had in Royal Oak. And he was taking Lisa by the hand, telling her that maybe they should "go for a drive," when Ash came down the stairs.

In less than a second she saw what was happening, how Lisa was brimming with triumph, and met Nathan's eyes.

"Can I talk to you?" she said.

That was it. Nathan let go of Lisa and followed Ash upstairs. It was my sister he ended up taking for a drive, my sister who didn't care one way or another about Nathan Pohl the moment before she saw how much *Lisa* wanted him, how happy *Lisa* was.

As for Michelle Wynn, it's a mystery why she was permitted in Ash's circle at all. Michelle was what you'd call obese today but what we then called fat, given to acne and noisy breathing, undistinguished in intelligence or charm. Invisible when viewed through teenaged glasses. And yet she was with Ash more than most. It may have been because Michelle went to every play Ash was in, taped every issue of the school paper with an Ashleigh Orchard byline to the inside of her locker, snapped hundreds of photos of Ash for a collage she was doing for her Fine Arts project. Even for my sister, such devotion was irresistible.

Where were they now? Who the hell knows.

But Ash wanted me to come here. She wanted me to *see*.

The Quinlans lived across the street from us. So I set off toward Farnum and Fairgrove. A place I knew how to find.

Winona Quinlan had thin lips she tried to fatten by drawing outside the lines with lipstick and red hair she cut to look like Molly Ringwald's. Academically, she was Ash's equal. Ash pretended not to care on the rare occasions the gold medal for top grade in English or Chemistry went to Winona instead of her, but she did. She knew Winona wouldn't get the scholarship she needed for college if she fell short of being top of her entire class, and this was enough to inspire Ash to edge her out into second place, denying Winona's dream of escape.

She had somewhere specific in mind, too.

A cousin of Winona's had graduated from Princeton and given her a sweatshirt with the school's crest on it when she was in sixth grade. That was all it took. She read the annual Princeton syllabus the way other girls read *Tiger Beat*. Her American History presentation in ninth grade was about all the presidents who'd gone to Princeton, her Geography project the next year about the unique landscape features of the campus at Princeton, her public speaking speech (for which she went all the way to the state finals) was titled, rhetorically, "Why Princeton?"

Winona could tell you why. Princeton meant getting *out*. To run away from the house she shared with her dope-dealing older brother and her parents, who we could hear screaming promises of divorce from across the street at night but who, by day, returned to their jobs and waved at us as they pulled groceries from their car or mowed the lawn. Winona didn't have boyfriends. She counted Ash as her best friend, which is to say she didn't have anyone.

It was a short walk to the old neighborhood. The streets the same as I remembered them though the trees were taller, a canopy that darkened the faces on the houses. Our house shrouded more than most. The side yard oak towering over half the block, some of the branches pushing against what used to be my bedroom window. In the backyard, over the fence, I could hear a couple of toddlers playing. At the end of the yard the tire swing was still there. The rope spiky and frayed, the branch it was tied to raw from the years of holding up its weight.

I turned away to take in the Quinlan place. In need of a paint job, car parts and tools littering the floor of the open garage. Still, whoever lived there now might know who the owners of this place were twenty years ago. Where their Ivy League–bound daughter is today.

It was this long shot that had me walking up to the outer glass door and ringing the bell. From inside, what sounded like two televisions and a radio tuned to a shock jock station, all on loud. I was about to hit the bell again when a woman appeared from the gloom, took me in as her thin, unlipsticked lips disappeared completely into her mouth.

"Danny?"

It was Winona. And something about her—*everything* about her—told me she never made it to Princeton.

"It's good to see you, Winona. It must be—I don't want to even count—"

"What're you doing here?"

She said this with real sharpness, like I'd already done something to anger her. Or like she didn't want to even be seen standing here talking to me.

"Can I come in?"

She looked over my shoulder at her driveway. "I don't think so."

"Just for a minute."

"You oughtta go."

"She's come back."

"Who?"

"My sister."

Her face blinked. Not just her eyes, but her entire face squeezed together and released.

"Come around to the back," she said.

Winona slammed the inside door closed and left me to slink around the side of the garage and reach over the fence to let myself into the yard.

Random piles of junk. Tools in open boxes on picnic tables, old power saws left on the lawn, the grass so high you had to watch not to step on them. The backyard of the world's most careless handyman.

"Who're you?"

I turned around to find a teenaged boy standing on the small deck by the door. Surrounded on all sides by stacked boxes of Miller Genuine Draft empties.

"My name's Danny. I'm an old friend of your—of Winona's."

He did the same face blink thing that his mother did. "You're her *friend*?"

"From way back."

"Go inside, Henry," Winona said when she appeared in the doorway behind him. But the boy didn't move. "I'm *serious*. Go the fuck *in*."

Eventually he did. Which left just me, Winona, and my idiotic grin.

"Henry. Classic."

"Henry Ford," she said, her chin sweeping across all the rusted junk in the yard. "This is still Detroit, you know."

I waited for her to step down off the deck, or offer me a seat in one of the folding chairs scattered here and there, but she remained standing where she was. The two of us weighing the effects of time on each other in the way of those who, moving into their forties, automatically make damage assessments of people who share their age.

I could only guess what she saw in me, but in her there was a whole person who'd been left behind.

The weight was only part of it, the plumped cheeks and arms that spoke of illness. But that wasn't what had fundamentally changed in her. It was the feral skittishness, the tension of someone who is alert to potential attack from any angle, at any time. A girl of words, of thoughts, who had grown into a woman of base instinct. Drugs. That's what all of it said. When she crossed her arms and her sleeves were pulled back, the track marks confirmed it.

"You've lived in the house the whole time?" I asked. "I don't re-member seeing you here when I was across the street, taking care of my dad."

"I went away. And then my parents died," she said with the blunt-ness with which one would announce a lost pair of shoes.

"Henry's your only one?"

"Three boys."

"And their dad?"

"This a fucking two-person high school reunion we're having here?"

"No. I wanted to ask you something."

"Yeah?"

"About the day Ash died. The bike ride you guys took with her."

I was sure Winona would tell me to leave. Instead, she started down the steps. Glanced over the fence at her neighbors' places, try-ing to confirm nobody was there to overhear us. Came to stand close enough that she brought her scent of cigarette smoke and unwashed skin with her.

"I told the police all about it," she said. "We all did."

"I'm just wondering if there's anything they missed. Because I think Ash wants me to figure out what happened to her. Who started the fire."

"*She* wants that? She's dead, last I checked."

"Yeah. It's kind of nuts."

"Got that right."

"But I'm asking you anyway."

"Why?"

"Because you knew Ash. And I'm hoping if I give her the answer, she'll leave my family alone."

"How's that?"

"She tried to hurt them. She'll try it again unless I help her."

Winona looked left and right. The regret played over her features like she held her hand over an open flame.

"They said at the time that whoever killed your sister probably killed Meg, too," she said.

"You have any ideas?"

"Somebody who'd take two girls into an empty house in downtown Detroit? Fucksake, Danny, it's kind of a long list. Why don't you start with the phone book?"

She was bluffing. I'm no expert at these things, but even I could see how her eyes looked around me instead of at me.

"What if it's not just some stranger who got away with it?" I said. "What if it was somebody from here, from Royal Oak? Somebody who knew them?"

She released her lips from where they'd been clenched and they came out with a pop.

"You know what I think?" she said, reddening. "I think you should leave this shit alone. It's *done*."

"Can't do that."

"Because you've got people thinking you're a medium or something? You're Mr. Heaven, that it?"

"I'm not a medium. And heaven's not where Ash went."

She seemed to listen to the ongoing noise from inside the house as though trying to discern a particular voice amid the advertising and cartoon sound effects and studio audience laughter.

"I can't talk to you," she said finally. "I'm sorry about whatever is going on with you, but what happened back then—not that I *saw* anything—I'm not talking about it."

She looked pissed off. But this was only where all her feelings ended up, worry and sorrow and love and everything else congealed into confused outrage.

"Maybe my life isn't exactly as I was hoping it would go," she went on. "But here's the thing—I'm still alive. I need to stay that way. For my boys. And bringing your sister up again—"

She didn't finish the thought.

"What about Michelle or Lisa?" I said. "You know where they live now?"

"Michelle's dead. Don't know about Lisa."

"What happened to Michelle?"

"She tried to talk about your sister, *that's* what happened to her. Called me a few times, *remembering* her, wanting to *figure her out*, just like you. Then it's her mother calling to tell me she killed herself. You know what? I wasn't surprised."

"And Lisa?"

"Last I heard she moved out west. Seattle or Portland or someplace like that. A photographer."

Winona did something with her mouth that may have been a smile. Something unpleasant, whatever it was.

"You should look up her work sometime," she said. "Bet you'd find it interesting."

She started away. Backed up without turning around as if there were some threat of me taking a run at her.

"Why do you think she wanted to go on that bike ride?" I said. "What did she want you to see?"

"Good-bye, Danny."

"But you have an idea, don't you? There's something you know that you didn't tell the police."

"You have to *go*. Just—"

"Please!"

The door banged closed.

I made my way down the driveway to the sidewalk. Across the street, there was a commotion in the backyard of our old house.

The toddlers who were playing out there before were screaming now. Not everyday kid screaming, not the theatrics of a scraped knee or protest at a stolen toy. Screams of terror, wordless and pure.

Their mother rushed out the sliding doors, almost screaming herself.

"What's wrong? My God! What's wrong?"

I couldn't see because of the fence but one or both of the kids must have pointed at the far end of the yard, because that's where their mother's eyes went to. Where she saw the tire swinging as high as it could go, higher than a kid their size could push it, back and forth without lowering or slowing, stirring the smell of too-sweet perfume and spoiled meat around in the still air.

26

hadn't been to Woodlawn Cemetery since my father's funeral. Knowing what I know about where we go once we die, I'd never seen the point in leaving flower bouquets next to tombstones or talking to the ground. This was just where the bodies end up, and soon enough the bodies weren't even that anymore. The soul—or whatever you want to call the part that can't be buried—doesn't stick around these places for long. Why would it? There's nothing here for the dead but the dead.

Yet, even in this relatively neglected parcel, amid the tilting crypts and gravesites calling out for a weed-whacker, there were the flowers and ribbons and teddy bears and flags left behind. The living showing up for their own reasons, their own loves and duties and confessions.

Dad's stone was doing better than the other two. Funny how their monuments stood now as they themselves stood then: Dad firm and tall, Ash a mystery (ASHLEIGH ORCHARD 1973–1989), Mom chipped away, the epitaph a proverb she'd chosen from a book when they'd reserved the plots.

The acts of this life are the destiny of the next.

When *The After* came out, I was asked to come here by TV producers wanting to film me standing at her stone, providing a thoughtful scowl for the camera as the voice-over explained how it was this grave where Mrs. Orchard was buried wearing her father's watch, the watch that her son was given in the afterlife and still wears today. They would have cut to a close-up of the Omega on my wrist then, Mom's tombstone soft-focused in the background. "Haunting and moving," the producers promised me, trying to talk me into it. I refused every time. I didn't want to be moved, not as a public performance, anyway. And I was already haunted.

Now, though, alone in the flat field dotted by other stones, I brought the watch to my eyes. What did it say, other than the hour? That there was something that came after our time here. *The acts of this life.* And that my mother loved me. She loved me and wished she could have shielded me but she didn't have the strength.

That's not how I wanted it to end for me. I wasn't interested in sending a message from beyond. I wanted to help my family *here.*

And to do that, I would have to tell Ash who put her in the ground under my feet.

I HEADED BACK TO THE HOTEL AND OPENED MY LAPTOP. THE FIRST thing I found on Lisa Goodale was her professional website. On the splash page, a self-portrait of Lisa. The kittenish features of her youth had given way to harder lines, a mournful widening of her nose exaggerated by the photo's stark lighting, so that she seemed to be trying to hide from the camera even as she stared into it.

Elsewhere, the rest of the site was a slick showcase for her work arranged in various galleries: Weddings, Portrait, Corporate. It's good.

Tasteful and restrained, with a strong leaning toward black-and-white. But it was the pictures I found when I clicked on Fine Art that took my breath away.

All of the images she'd posted involved a girl as their recurring subject. Always the same model, a blonde in her midteens with blue eyes that appeared to have been enhanced somehow, so that they glowed out from otherwise monochrome exposures, alien and cold. A girl who was illuminated in a kind of aura no matter what setting she was in, though the effect was somehow the opposite of angelic, the light something that would burn if you got too close. Looking directly into the camera from the back of a bus. Sitting on the roof of a car, her legs dangling over the driver side door. Laughing into a set of bathroom mirrors arranged so that a thousand of her faces repeated themselves, bending round into the glass.

She'd titled the series *The After*.

The other results I found were from news sites.

Missing-person bulletins. Stories reporting on how prominent Portland photographer Lisa Goodale, single and with no children, hadn't been seen since August 12, 2013. Two days after my heart attack on Cambridge Common.

They'll never find her.

She won't be taking any pictures that try to bring Ash back to life again, because she *was* alive.

And Lisa, officially missing, was already gone.

WHEN I STOPPED BLINKING AT THE LAPTOP'S SCREEN IT WAS NIGHT again. I hadn't eaten since breakfast, so I walked out the front doors and found a place along Greektown's single touristy block of restaurants. After I ordered, I pulled out my phone to text Willa and saw there was already one waiting for me.

how's it going, sherlock?

It took the length of a beer to come up with an answer.

Think I'm on to something here.

Not a complete lie. Either way, I hoped she wouldn't ask for more. So I asked what I really wanted to know before she could.

How are you guys?

When the answer came I had to stifle a whimper that worked its way out of me just as the waiter returned to take my order.

Missing you. Both of us.

Once I finished eating I stepped out and felt the night around me, the air hard and cool. It promised to help me think.

I started out for a walk but kept to the perimeter of the reclaimed historical buildings that now housed the casino, assuming there was security to keep it safe, though as soon as I turned the corner away from the tourist strip there was nobody on the sidewalk. Two stories above, the People Mover tracks curved toward the office buildings a few blocks away. The trains still passing every couple minutes— almost empty during the day and totally empty now. With every coming and going I looked up to see if anyone sat in one of the fluorescent cars, playing a game with myself where I could only go back inside the hotel if I spotted a passenger.

In the meantime, I tried to pull something useful out of my conversation with Winona Quinlan.

Whatever secret she was keeping, Winona felt she was protecting herself and her boys by burying it. And maybe she was right. It couldn't be denied that she was still here and Michelle and Lisa weren't.

Who else was there to ask? I could always try to dig up an old Dondero High yearbook and search the names, firing out e-mails and calling whatever numbers I could find. Yet what would I say if anyone answered? *Hi! Danny Orchard here. Ash's twin who brought a watch back from the pearly gates? Just wanted to ask if you knew how my sister might have been murdered. Oh, and remember . . . GO OAKS!* And how could they possibly reply? *Oh yes, now that you ask, Danny, I have the name of Meg and Ash's killer right here. Must have slipped my mind to share it with the police twenty-four years ago!*

Still, I knew something that I didn't know before coming here. Winona told me, however indirectly. Her nervous face-blinks, her bit lip, her fear at the mention of Ash's name.

Even if it wasn't Winona herself, someone knew at least a piece of what went on in the house on Alfred Street.

Someone was there.

Above, like a roll of thunder, the People Mover came again. I looked up to spot a face at the window. A white girl. Alone, lost.

Chipmunk-cheeked and tiny-nosed, her hair parted in the middle, Midwestern-pretty in the era of leg warmers and roller rinks. Lisa Goodale, the way she appeared at sixteen. Except she was unsmiling now. Her eyes darting around in their sockets.

Until they found me.

The train whined into the Greektown platform overhead. It would linger there for a time, doors opened, before carrying on. Enough time to climb the stairs and make it onto Lisa's car.

Taking the steps two at a time seemed doable until the chest pain returned.

Is this where I end up falling? In the empty stairwell of a People Mover station? It was the sort of thing Ash would find funny. *Pathetic*, she'd call it. Pathetic being the way she liked to judge the world, the way all except her tried and failed, tried and failed.

And there I was. Trying.

To follow the bread crumbs left by the dead. To build a wall around Willa and Eddie. It's what started me up the stairs again, telling myself the pain was only indigestion, a souvlaki dinner gone wrong.

I made it onto the platform in time to see the doors close. The empty train moaning into motion, its interior lights casting shadows against the walls of the buildings snugged close to the tracks.

Neither Lisa nor anyone else in the cars, but there was the outline of hundreds drawn dark onto the brick. The heads of men and women and children, bearded, ball-capped, long-haired, earringed. Invisible passengers staring out at the city, stuck in an infinite commute, around and around. The empty train built for the dead alone.

27

In the morning, after a call with Willa in which I learned that Eddie was doing fine and that "there hasn't been any spooky business since you left," I hung up wondering if it would be best for all concerned if I just stayed in Detroit. And I would do it happily—well, maybe not *happily*—if it meant Ash leaving Willa and Eddie alone forever.

But here's what I didn't mention on the phone but I suspected Willa knew anyway: *she won't.*

Which meant I had to show her I was getting closer to what she was looking for. Or at least looking like I was.

There was nowhere to go but back to Winona's.

I drove into Royal Oak, crossed the Amtrak line with the familiar *a-rum-de-dump* of tires over the rails. Years ago, it was a signal of being home. Safety. That was always the fantasy of this place. Harm was something that happened elsewhere. A protective spell cast by middle-class wealth and policemen whose names you knew and sweatshirts that announced which college people went to.

Perhaps it's why I was so surprised to see the yellow line of police tape tied across Fairgrove Avenue. An ambulance, police cruisers. Real detectives, so much more convincing than me in their leather jackets and unironic moustaches, speaking with neighbors who wore housecoats and track pants. A crime scene where the Quinlan house appeared to be the center of attention.

I parked a block south and walked the rest of the way up. Made it to the small group of onlookers as the paramedics brought the gurney out through the front door.

I was certain it was Winona even though a sheet covered the whole body. It was the look on her son Henry's face. Standing on the patch of lawn, watching his mother lifted into the back of the ambulance, the boy's lips moving in a search for words. There was the beginning of anger, too. The grown-up kind that will find no lasting relief, a vine no pruning will hold back until it's covered everything in its path.

Once Winona was slid into the back one of the paramedics closed the doors and the other got behind the wheel. All of us, even the detectives who looked, now that I was closer, a little *too* like detectives—too world-weary, too vainly aware of their grim audience—waited for the ambulance to roll away before we'd let ourselves say another word, pull out cell phones, move. Then, with lights still turning and strobing atop its roof, it bumped off the curb and turned left onto Farnum, the driver looking back at us as if he were considering shouting a distasteful, if irresistible, joke.

The mom who lived in the house across from the Quinlans', our house, stood slightly apart from the others. Her toddlers weren't with her, so that she had nothing to do with her hands except rub them under her eyes. When I approached she looked at me without recognition.

"Know what happened?" I asked.

"OD. That's my bet."

"Oh?"

"A body can only take so much."

"She had a history, I'm guessing."

"Everybody's got a history." She dropped the hands from her eyes. "You a reporter or something?"

"Just a friend. Of Winona's."

"Friend," she repeated. "Didn't know she had any of those."

"Actually, I grew up in the house you live in now. Way back."

She took two long steps back from me.

"You're the brother."

"Danny Orchard," I said, assuming she'd read my book, but it didn't seem to register with her. And then I realized she didn't know me by name, but because of what she'd seen in her house. The girl her children knew.

"You don't look like her," she said.

"We were twins."

"Are you . . . *like* her?"

"No. I'm not like her at all."

She moved her head from side to side the way a pitcher shakes off a catcher's signal.

"She's dead, isn't she?" she said.

"Yes."

It was clear this gave the opposite of relief. With a swipe of the air that resembled a wave but wasn't, she turned and started back into her haunted house.

I'VE NEVER BEEN MUCH OF A MIDDAY DRINKER.

When you grew up with the kind of mother I did, one who started refreshing herself with white wine spritzers to go with ironing my dad's shirts in front of *Good Morning America*, you tend to either grow into an all-day boozer yourself or barely touch the stuff, and never before five. I'm of the latter school.

Though now, returning to Main Street at a quarter to noon, I felt the overwhelming need for a drink.

Tom's Oyster Bar was already busy with the lunchtime rush, but there were still plenty of empty stools and I took one, ordered a large scotch ("You mean a double?"), and let my eyes blur over the laminated menu the bartender left behind. It took a moment—and a full, burning swallow—before I realized someone was trying to talk to me. Two people, in fact.

"Danny!"

"Danny *Orchard*?"

"That you?"

"Over here!"

I spun around to find two men my age at a round table in the middle of the room, waving my way. They wore identical gray summer suits, the same short-cropped haircuts, both dissecting their way through the same plates of peel-your-own shrimps. The Wigg twins.

The Wiggs were identicals, the only other twins I remembered from growing up. They did the whole mirror-image thing: same sets of clothes worn on the same days, same chess club vice presidencies, same bowl cuts, same beady, superior stares. For class photos, they wore matching sailor suits from kindergarten all the way into their early teens, their faces indifferent to their ridiculousness, year after year. They would often ask to be excused from class at the same time, presumably to sit on side-by-side johns, counting down to launch their identical breakfasts at the same moment. It was said that the only way to tell them apart was by their erections: one with a slight banana hook, the other straight as a ruler. Though how this comparison was ever made—or how one might test its accuracy—I never knew.

"John? Rudy?"

The two of them grinned as though I'd successfully identified them, though I could no more tell them apart now than I could in high school.

"John," the one on the right confirmed, shaking my hand.

"Let me guess. Rudy?" I said, indicating the one on the left.

"Twins know their twins," Rudy said.

John pulled out a chair and I dropped into it.

I considered opening the conversation with the news about Winona Quinlan, but there seemed little point in me being the one to share it with them. "You guys work in town?" I asked.

"We went into practice together," John said.

"Orthodontists," Rudy said.

"The efficiencies are *phenomenal*," John said.

Rudy tapped his whitened front teeth. "No business like a family business."

"You guys stayed," I said. "You didn't want out?"

"Out of what?" they both asked at the same time.

"I keep forgetting that not everyone had as fucked-up a time growing up as I did."

"Nobody had the sister you had," Rudy said, glancing down at my scotch.

I was trying to think of a way to politely leave—being around the Wiggs again, around twins, is pretty close to the last thing I need—when John took a deep breath and, against his better judgment, decided to confess something to me.

"I asked her out once, you know," he said, waving Rudy off when he made an are-you-sure-you-want-to-go-there? face. "Probably half the guys in our year asked her out. Seriously, how could you *not* ask her out? But I thought, seeing as we were both twins, she and I—maybe I could understand her where other guys didn't."

"But she was—how can I put this?" Rudy said, thinking hard. "*Mean*. She was *mean*."

"She *laughed* at me! Right in my face!" John dotted his fingers over his nose and cheeks in a pantomime of spit hitting him. "Then she pretends to change her mind. 'Maybe a double date! Twins on twins. The four of us! Question is, who gets my brother, and who gets me?'"

"She was something else, no question. A beauty," Rudy said, closing the subject. "But Danny? Your sister? Gotta say. She had a way of making you feel like shit like nobody else."

Rudy sucked a third of his pint glass of cola up his straw, daubed his lips with an index finger, pushed his face across the table at me.

"So what are you doing here, Danny?"

"I'm investigating my sister's death," I said, like it was the sort of thing anyone might be up to in a bar at noon. "My sister's murder."

The Wiggs scrunched their noses precisely the same way.

"We've always had a theory about that," Rudy said.

"The teacher," John said.

They seemed to think I ought to know what they were talking about.

"What teacher?"

"She didn't tell you?" Rudy said.

"Ash and I didn't exactly share things—" I was about to say *the way you two do*, but stopped myself. "We weren't close that way."

John nodded in what appeared to be real sympathy, the idea of twins not knowing everything about each other an unthinkable tragedy. "We saw them once," he said.

"But we didn't tell anybody else," Rudy said. "Guess we always assumed you knew, too."

"Which means maybe we're the only ones who had an idea."

An idea about WHAT, you freaks? This is what it took everything I had to prevent myself from screaming into the corners of the room.

"I'm still in the dark here, guys," I said.

"Mr. Malvo," John said, the two of them starting a back-and-forth between themselves, finishing the other's thoughts.

"The drama teacher?" Rudy said. "The director of the play that year?"

"*South Pacific.*"

"That's it. *South Pacific.* Ash was, like, the lead or something."

"She *was* the lead. Have to say, she was actually pretty awesome. Great pipes."

"Great everything. Nice teeth, too."

"Malvo and Ash in his car in the parking lot out back of the Caribou Coffee."

"Kissing."

"*Kissing.*"

I remember Mr. Malvo. At Dondero for just a single year, replacing Mrs. Regehr who was away on maternity leave. An actor himself. This is what everyone knew about him, because it was what he constantly reminded everyone of. He'd grown up in Sterling Heights, in suburban Detroit "just like you," as he said in his little introductory speech at school assembly, the *like you* dripping with the condescension of the motivational speaker, as if he was addressing a gymful of kids confined to wheelchairs and he alone had learned how to walk. After a move to the coast (never "Hollywood," never "L.A.") he'd made it onto a couple TV shows, bit parts on a soap and a cop show, both canceled. This lent him a glamorous authority we'd had no experience of. A guy in his midthirties who didn't wear a wedding ring and looked a little like a young John Malkovich if he had more hair and hit the weight room four times a week.

The next year, he was gone. Mrs. Regehr never returned after having her baby so there was an opening in the drama department he could have filled. But Malvo left Royal Oak sometime during the summer that followed his triumphant staging of *South Pacific* with its "electrifying" (*Detroit News*) sixteen-year-old star—the summer that same star burned to death in an abandoned mansion downtown—and was never heard from again.

"Ash was making out with her drama teacher," I said. "Creepy. But not exactly evidence of foul play."

"Meg Clemens was in the play, too," Rudy said. "Think about that."

"Four-eyed Meg who ended up in the same place Ash ended up," John said.

"There were people at the time who said they saw Malvo and Meg together, just like we saw him with Ash," Rudy said.

"So why wasn't he a suspect at the time?"

"He was on the list, or so I heard," John said. "But there was no physical evidence, nothing more than circumstantial stuff."

"And let's face it. It was probably a long list," Rudy said.

"But I'm telling you, there was something wrong with that guy," John said.

"Lucky sonofabitch," Rudy said.

I asked them if they knew where Malvo might be these days, or if anyone might have more information about the director's relationship to his cast, but they admitted to having no way of knowing, not exactly being the coolest kids in school at the time.

"We were nerds," John said.

"Gifted."

"Same difference."

Without noticing, over the course of our conversation, I'd finished my scotch. This middle-of-the-day-drinking thing was easy so long as you were motivated.

I declined the Wiggs' invitation to join them for lunch, thanked them for their help. Rudy wished me luck. John told me to come back anytime I was looking for a good quote on corrective dental work.

On the way out, I picked up their tab. It was the least I could do. Us freaks got to stick together.

28

How to find Mr. Malvo? I figured my one advantage was that he was an actor. And actors leave credits behind like a mouse leaves turds.

It appeared, however, his life on the silver screen was cut short just prior to his coming to Dondero High. All the TV and movie websites tell the story of his sputtered career: there's the soap, and there's his name—Dean Malvo, the "Dean" striking me as fake—deep down the cast list of a couple second-tier action flicks I could sort of remember.

Henchman #3.
Waiter in Café (Paris).
Guy With Bomb.

It seemed that he was on his way up, the henchmen graduating to indie dramas where he earned an actual character name or two.

Then it all stopped in 1988. The year before he subbed for Mrs.

Regehr and was witnessed making out with my teenaged sister and Meg Clemens. From then to the present, there was no trace that Dean Malvo of Guy With Bomb fame existed.

He had another career, though. Drama teacher. As well as a possible side interest in seducing girls of an illegal age. The sort of activities that might also leave a trail behind.

DONDERO HIGH LOOKED MORE OR LESS THE SAME, BUT IT WASN'T Dondero High anymore. A plaque outside the main entrance doors explained that Royal Oak's two high schools were consolidated into one a few years ago, and that this building now housed a middle school. Before I went in, I walked around the property and the buried memories stuck their hands up out of their graves: there were the bleachers Todd Aimes pulled me under and smeared dog poo under my shirt because Ash told him to, there were the train tracks at the far end of the playing field where Ash made kids play chicken with oncoming diesels, there was the parking lot where she would stroll from car to car, visiting the older guys with their radios blaring, sticking her head into their Camaros and Mustangs to let them get a good look, a peek down her shirt, leave a whiff of herself behind.

Only then, standing in the place where it happened, did it occur to me to wonder if Ash *liked* having her teacher's hands on her. Or was he something she couldn't control, something that took from her and made her keep a secret? Did he hurt her?

The weight of sympathy I felt for her was so sudden I needed to sit on the lot's curb and rest my chin on my knees. She was the reason my life had been the malnourished thing it had been until Willa and Eddie came along. But she was also my sister. She may well have needed me back then without saying so just as I wished she were someone I could actually talk to, actually understand. It's why the idea of an outsider making her do something she didn't want to do made me feel like the failure was mine. I should have seen what was going on, read her brooding, lengthening stretches in her room as a sign. I should have saved her.

This, too, is how it is between twins.

When I lifted my head the lot was full of parents getting out of cars, all of them staring at me, the folded-up stranger fighting to get to his feet.

The bell rang. Kids hollered out the doors and found their moms and nannies and dads.

And me among them. The fever heat of suspicion on my back.

AT THE SCHOOL'S RECEPTION DESK, A SECRETARY WEARING A RUB- ber ducky nightshirt and sleeping cap asked if she could help me. When I didn't immediately come out with anything, she looked down at her outfit and grimaced.

"Pajama Day," she said.

I asked if the school kept records on teachers who worked here in the old Dondero days. In particular, a substitute Drama department head named Dean Malvo. The name gave her pause.

"We don't have staff files of that kind. Not here, anyway," she said. "Maybe you could try the union?"

"I'll give them a call, I guess."

It seemed that was it. I was mustering up a thank-you when she leaned against the counter so she could lower her voice.

"Why are you looking for him?"

"I think he might have hurt my sister."

"Break!" she called out to someone unseen and unreplying in a room around the corner. Then she stepped out from behind the counter and walked out, leaving me to follow her down the hall to a door at the opposite end.

Outside, she leaned against the wall and looked anywhere but at me.

"He goes by Bob now," she said.

"Can you tell me where he is?"

"I can tell you where he *was*. Did six years at Baraga. Got out maybe a couple years ago."

"What for?"

"What do you think? You're here asking about your sister. There were other sisters after yours. Other daughters."

She pulled a pack of cigarettes from a pocket but didn't take one out.

"Did you know him?"

"He was a sub teacher, he moved around," she said. "I guess that had its advantages for him. But yes, he was at a couple of schools I worked at a long time ago. A good talker, that's for sure. People took notice of it at the time. So when the news came out, they took notice of him for something else."

She knew more than this. It's why we were there, out in the sunshine that appeared with the pullback of clouds, a shattered man and a woman in a nightshirt, neither knowing the other's name and both preferring not to say.

She cared in some way. Whether it was for Malvo, or for one of the girls he decided on, or for herself. Maybe she fell for him, only to later discover he was a monster. There was no wedding ring on her finger.

But if she was going to tell me about any of that, she would be doing it now. It was obvious, by the way she pocketed the cigarettes and gripped the door handle to go back inside, that she'd already gone further than she meant to.

Yet she didn't go in just yet. Looked at me directly for the first time since we came outside.

"You okay?" she said.

She saw it before I felt it. The sense of everything coming down at once.

Malvo a predator.

Winona dead, along with the other girls who made the trip down Woodward.

Eddie in a hospital bed.

"Sweet dreams," I said before stumbling off, eyes closed against the sunshine.

29

It made sense that Malvo changed his name to Dean. The kind of name to put at the bottom of 8 x 10s, Bob not carrying quite the same hint of mystery. It also made sense to change your name back to what it was once you started to come under suspicion for sexual interference with underaged girls. Not that it helped him.

Bob Malvo was charged with two counts of third-degree criminal sexual conduct relating to girls between thirteen and fifteen years old and was convicted of both in 1993. He was subsequently sentenced to eight years in prison (though as the Pajama Day secretary correctly noted, he was out in six). His crimes took place while he was a substitute teacher at two different high schools, both located in southeast Michigan, the victims both ninth-graders and students in his drama classes.

I tried searching for something that might tell me what he'd been up to for the time since his release, but nothing matched his name and profile. He could be anywhere. The chances of a convicted statutory rapist hanging around near the same towns where he committed his crimes had to be slim. Employment in teaching would be out of the question, and the professional acting opportunities for a man who would now be in his late fifties and with a nasty record would be nonexistent. Bob Malvo may well hold the secret to how Ash died in the fire. But he'd be long gone now.

The news stories about his trial named his defense lawyer as William LaMaye, of Farmington Hills, another suburb west of Royal Oak. An online search showed he was still practicing, still there. A partner at LaMaye & Durridge, a firm whose slogan, "IT'S NEVER TOO EARLY TO HIRE THE RIGHT ATTORNEY," suggested that everyone in Detroit would need a defense lawyer at one point or another, so you might as well retain one now.

I hit an ATM and withdrew the maximum amount allowed, slipped it into an envelope, and pocketed it in my jeans.

If I was heavy on the gas and the traffic was light, I might make it before the office closed.

WILLIAM LaMAYE, OF LaMAYE & DURRIDGE, WAS A CHRONI- cally underslept black man of unguessable age in a suit that was once tailored to fit him but no longer did, the shoulders sagging and front button-stretched in the places he had shrunk and expanded. After the receptionist put in a call to him he was out to see me before I had a chance to take a seat in the waiting area. His movements deliberate but forceful, a body used to being taken seriously.

"Thank you for seeing me, Mr. LaMaye."

He shook my hand, a brief clench that let me know he was prepared to hear whatever I had to say but that it didn't mean he was interested in taking any bullshit.

"Hey, I'm *here*," he said. "Office?"

I followed him back through a narrow hallway in need of a new carpet and smelling of French fries. In his office, there were sun-faded degrees on the walls from Western Michigan and Wayne State Law, two chairs, and a desk stacked so high with binders and files shaggy with Post-it Notes he had to place a hand on the top of it to prevent it from crashing onto my lap.

"So," he said once he'd found his way into his chair. "What kind of trouble you in?"

"You don't want to know. But I'm not here about me, actually."

He didn't like the sound of this and let me know by placing both hands behind his head. "No?"

"Bob Malvo was a client of yours some years ago."

"Malvo."

"He was a teacher? Convicted for—"

"I know who *he* is. I'm waiting to hear what you want from *me*."

"I was wondering if you could tell me where he is now."

He let his hands slip away and returned them to the desk, but finding nowhere to put them, dropped them on his thighs.

"I'm not permitted to give out client information of that kind," he said.

"Trust me, I'm not a journalist or revenge seeker or anything like that. I'm just family."

"Family?"

"Bob's brother."

"He didn't mention he had a brother."

"He wouldn't. I'm of the Long Lost variety. That's why I want to find him. Say I'm sorry for what I've done, that I forgive him for what he's done. Clean slates. Know what I mean?"

"What's your name?"

"Name?"

"Yeah, you know. Those words at the top of your driver's license?"

"Danny. Danny Malvo."

"Danny and Bob."

Did he believe me? William LaMaye was a man who dealt with liars for a living, so I'm guessing not.

"Smart guy, your brother," he said after what either was a long while or what he made feel like one. "Gift of the gab."

"He was an actor."

"He *acted* like an actor. Know what I'm saying?"

"Afraid so."

If there was any polite humor in his tone before, what he said next was drained dry of it.

"Still owes part of my fee, you know."

I handed over the envelope I'd stuffed at the ATM. Six hundred dollars. An amount William LaMaye didn't blink at, just counted, once, before opening a desk drawer and shoving it inside.

It appeared that was it. I'd made a contribution toward Bob's overdue legal bill, and there was nothing coming back the other way. The two of us sitting across from each other thinking about what might be said next. It had been a long day for both of us.

All at once he opened a leather agenda on his desk. Flipped the pages and, finding what he was looking for, reached for a memo pad. Wrote something on it and ripped the sheet off. Flipped it over to me.

"That didn't just happen," he said.

I didn't read the note until I was back in my car.

An address. A street in an area I could locate in my mind, but one I'd never visited in my life even though I grew up no more than a mile away from it.

Bob Malvo lived in Detroit.

30

The east side of Detroit is even more lawless and unoccupied than the lawless and unoccupied west side, and McDougall-Hunt is a neighborhood situated at the very heart of the east side.

This is where William LaMaye directed me, whether to see me find his client or see me lose my wallet or worse, I wasn't sure. There was no reason why he should be trusted. Knowing this didn't stop me from driving right past after I turned onto the street and, after driving through a field where other houses used to be, finding the house I was looking for, standing alone in the tall grass like a farmhouse on the Dakotan prairie. Of the half dozen places still standing on this cracked stretch of pavement, it was the only one with a porch light on. A bare 40-watt bulb under siege by a dive-bombing moth the size of a bag of chips.

What did I think was going to happen here? Knock on the door, ask the man if he'd like to discuss his possibly being a murderer along with a sexual predator? It was only there, only then, that the foolishness of my journey was wiltingly brought into focus, the ridiculous sight I made in the rearview mirror, baffled and greened by the dashboard light. It was a fight to talk myself into parking a hundred feet short of the address, the only car to be seen, behind or ahead. It was another ten minutes to convince myself that this unlit street-that-is-no-longer-a-street was where I would find the thing that would save my family.

I got out and made my way to the front door. The night was windless and hot. Despite the wide space between the lopsided outlines of distant homes, I had a sense I wasn't alone, that my clean car with the Budget sticker in the back window—that I, polo-shirted and deck-shoed, stepping out of it—was a spectacle that had already been taken note of. A quiet that came not from people sleeping, but people waiting.

The doorbell didn't work. Knocking wasn't much better. My knuckles on the wood next to the square of gated window in the door swallowed the sound up inside.

Anywhere else, you'd say there was nobody home. Here a dark house didn't mean a thing.

I tried the handle. Locked by way of multiple bolts secured on the inside frame.

A walk around the outside of the property revealed ground-floor windows curtained with newspaper. A yard so dry that nothing, not even crabgrass, grew. In the distance, a broad rectangle with a smokestack rising out of it like a middle finger salute.

I looked up. A rear balcony over the back door that led into what I guessed was a second-floor bedroom.

The way in.

If the sliding glass door could be wrenched open. If I could climb up there without breaking my neck. If hands or dog's teeth or buckshot didn't pull me down.

I was hugging one of the two wooden supports that held the balcony up when I saw the hammer.

A ball-peen lying next to a rusted can of paint next to the back door. The can dented like someone realized they picked a tool without a hook to lift up its lid and figured they'd beat it open anyway. When that didn't work they quit, leaving both behind.

Now I was picking the hammer up. Throwing it into the air and getting lucky when it landed on the balcony with a metallic ring like it found a gong up there.

Then I was wriggling up the post again, splinters stabbing through my shirt. At one point I swung out with only a hand and the toes of one foot holding on, and there was time to see I was going to fall, my head leading the way.

But I didn't let go. The swing brought me around to the railing and I used the momentum to pull myself up and over. Made the same gong sound with my face as it hit a steel mixing bowl, left out there as if to catch the rain.

I was ready to use the hammer on the sliding door handle but didn't have to. It had been left open an inch.

Even though the gonging and hammer tossing and body crashing had already alerted any conscious people inside to an intruder, I pulled the sliding door open as quietly as I could.

Nothing came at me from out of the dark. Until something did. A dead-aired wall of body odor, sweetly foul as a sack of rotten oranges.

It was even hotter inside than outside. A stillness that slowed the capacity for movement as well as thought, so that I put observations of the room together in a linking of sluggish logic.

No bed or furniture
means nobody sleeps here
means there's nothing here to see
means keep going, Danny

On the second-floor landing, three other doors. One to an empty bathroom. One to another bedroom similarly bedless and unfurnished, the closet vacant except for what appeared to be a nest made of dried grass and ripped-up magazine pages and pieces of IT'S YOUR BIRTHDAY! ribbon on the floor. The last opened to the third bedroom where, by the look of it, by the smell of it, somebody came to sleep.

Though all the rooms were small, this was the biggest of the three, with a single bed (no sheets, no pillow, the mattress polka-dotted with mold) and a bureau. Inside the drawers a couple pairs of track pants with RED WINGS down the leg. A lone pair of boxer shorts patterned with the Major League Baseball logo. Three identical T-shirts: all XXL, all with THE ROAR OF '84—DETROIT TIGERS WORLD SERIES CHAMPIONS on the front. The wardrobe of someone who did a one-stop shop in a sports store bargain bin.

There may have been more in the closet but it was padlocked.

I was wondering how I might get in there when I felt the hammer in my hand. I'd been carrying it with me from room to room the whole time. If I used it on the metal brackets on the door's frame it might be enough to rip it off.

There was just enough thinking still going on to tell myself to go downstairs and check if there was anyone there first.

A front hall of curled linoleum and rat droppings. A kitchen at the back with an unplugged fridge holding nothing but rolls of toilet paper on its shelves. A dining room with a fold-out chair and oil drum for a table.

The living room was where the living happened.

A coffee table with a glass crack pipe, balls of tinfoil, and a pair of disposable lighters on its surface. A sofa with the springs pushing through. Fast-food bags and sandwich wrappings—all crushed, all Church's Chicken—tossed on the floor like a paper archipelago.

A couple thoughts arrived as I heaved in the hot fudge air of 3380 Arndt Street.

First, whether it belonged to Malvo or somebody else, I had just broken into the house of a crack-smoking stranger.

Second, crack-smoking strangers *didn't like it* when their houses were broken into.

And then the slo-mo conclusion that followed: if there was nobody here now, they'd be back soon. Because there on the table, nested in tinfoil, was a pale, unused rock. The only thing of value in the whole rank, slope-floored place.

Unless there was something in the padlocked closet upstairs.

I started up but had to take three breaks for my heart to calm. The hammer gaining weight in my hand the closer I got to passing out.

I'm close, Ash. I'm trying to help you. But I need you to help me.

In the bedroom, I lined up the hammer and the lock brackets. Testing the arc, the point to make contact. Then I brought it down.

It did nothing but make it feel like both my wrists were broken. Not that it stopped me from trying it again.

And again.

On the fourth strike, the wood split. The bracket screws pulled halfway out. Another swing and they fell to the floor. As did the hammer when I tossed it behind me so I could pull the door open.

Ash.

Clippings of newspaper reviews of her in *South Pacific*. Every picture with her in it published in the Dondero yearbook of 1989.

Along with photos I'd never seen before.

Ash sitting in the passenger seat of Dean Malvo's car wearing a strangely nervous smile. Ash's face in close-up, eyes closed and lips open in a lustful pose that betrayed a falseness, as though she'd been told to shape her face that way. Ash naked. Sitting on an earth floor, lying on a blanket and looking back over her bare shoulder, reaching her hands out to the one who held the camera, legs wide. The shock of her skin. The leering angle of the lens.

She wasn't the only one.

Meg Clemens was taped there, too, closest to the floor, as if the images had been arranged in the shape of a tree, a time line where Meg was the roots and Ash the trunk. Higher up, many other girls for the branches and leaves. All about the same age, similarly posed, though more active the closer they got to the top, the photographer's demands grown bolder over time until parts of himself were visible, too.

On the floor, a metal cashbox. But no cash inside. Notes. Folded pieces of lined paper for the most part, but also memo pad pages, index cards, the back of a Get Well Soon card. Some a back-and-forth correspondence between someone who signed off only with "D." and another who wrote in girlish script. Signed "Ash" with a little heart over the top of the *h*.

Her hand.

Her voice. Or one of them.

I can't wait to see you! Feel you too. I just want to make you happy. You know that, don't you? After last night, how couldn't you?

You are my man. My teacher. (You say you don't like it when I call you that, but I can tell you do. I'll show you tomorrow. I'll show you . . .)

Please tell me these rehearsals are almost OVER! I love the show but I am SO tired of seeing you every day and not being able to touch you and kiss you every day too. We're going to have that soon, right? We can have our Alfred any time we want . . .

This showed up a lot. A code word. A place that had been turned into an interchangeable verb/noun.

Wanna Alfred after school?

Let's meet for an Alfred.

This girl needs her Alfred!

"Turn around."

The voice was slurred at the edges, stoned but hyperalert. The way his two-word command both threatened and conceded a point, as if he'd been expecting this very moment for a long time and now must go through the actions that were required of him.

When I'd shuffled a half circle on my knees I noticed that Bob Malvo held the hammer in his right hand. It brushed against his pant leg. His grip white-knuckled.

"You one of the dads?" he said. "An uncle or something? Or one of them hire you?"

"You think I'm here to hurt you."

He looked me over, searching for a weapon. "A lot of people want that."

"I do, too."

"But you're the one on your knees."

He was bigger than I'd anticipated. Wider and man-boobed. He wore his fourth THE ROAR OF '84—DETROIT TIGERS WORLD SERIES CHAMPIONS T-shirt and green surgeon's pants, both so voluminous that when he moved they took a half second to catch up with him.

"How'd you manage to keep all your souvenirs?" I said, and started to rise but he raised the hammer waist-high and I held myself still. "I would've thought they'd taken all this stuff before you went to prison."

"Storage units. You know how *cheap* that shit is?"

"Why keep it at all?"

"My memory's not what it was."

He exhaled. Blew out his lips and a drizzle of spit fell over my face.

"Are you going to let me go?"

I tried to prevent it from sounding like a plea, but it did anyway. Not that he heard it. His mouth widening to show root-dead teeth and black gums.

"You're the brother. The twin," he said. "She always said you got the shitty end of the stick."

"You raped my sister."

"That makes it sound so *one-sided.* And like I said, my memory's a little foggy about the particulars. But I'll tell you this. She *ruined* me. Once you've tasted berries that sweet, the rest needs a little extra sugar on top. Know what I'm saying?"

Nothing changed in his face but it was clear now, in that moment, that he intended to smash my skull in with the hammer. It would happen without warning. He didn't think anymore, he only acted, a jittery collection of impulses. Just like the men who invaded Willa and Eddie's home. Just like Ash. The mistake you made was trying to find the humanness in them, the line between what they might do and would never do, and while you were looking, they brought the hammer down.

"Did you murder them?" I said, my hands drifting in front of my face in a reflex of defense.

"You might need to clarify—"

"Did you bury Meg in the bottom of that house? Did you try to do the same to Ash but something went wrong and you trapped her down there instead? Started a fire? Did you kill my sister?"

Did you kill me?

Malvo stood over me. Not hesitating. Recalling.

"She was the most amazing actress," he said. "I didn't even know what part she thought she was playing half the time. Victim. Cocksucker. Headfucker. Ingénue. Great performances, every one of them. It wasn't until later that I figured out *that wasn't real! And that wasn't, either! Or that!* None of it was."

He absently lifted the hammer level with his shoulders. The sweat-darkened rubber handle. The gouged ball of its head.

"I gave up after that girl," he said, and lowered his eyes to mine. "I never acted again once I fucked your sister. All it left me with was fucking other little sisters."

I know he said this—*other little sisters*—because I heard the words. But there was something going on at the same time he spoke them. Something I was doing. Lunging at Bob Malvo's legs and wrapping my arms around his calves. Uprooting him. Howling at the hammer as it struck the middle of my back.

Then it was fingernails and fists and teeth.

A sickening animal screech when the hammer found its way against my ear. Malvo's thumb in my eye, working to push it through to the back of my head.

I was aware of making some decisions. The biting of his unshaved chin. The pinched-off artery, or tendon, or something cordlike and tender in his neck that made him gasp. The kneeling on the wrist that sprung open the fingers around the hammer's handle.

It fell to the carpet.

Definitely blood on it now. Definitely mine.

It glued my fingers to the handle. Kept my palm in the right place long enough for me to swing it through the air like a pendulum, cracking into Malvo's jaw as it went.

Partly because of my revulsion at the sound the bone made when it broke—a bone in his *face*—and partly because of the black fish swimming around in my head, the hammer flung out of my hands so that it tumbled once before landing with a sigh on the bed.

If it were me on the floor, jaw-broken and bitten, I'd be done. But it was as if Malvo didn't feel a thing. As if he were just waking up.

Bucking me off him. Slapping me away with the back of a hand. Reaching onto the bed for the hammer with the other.

How is he moving so fast?

There was a corner of my brain that found this question genuinely interesting. There was another corner that realized staying where I was would give him the time to paint the walls with the insides of my skull.

I was on my knees in the bedroom. Then I was moving.

To the landing. Banging off a wall. Into the empty bedroom I first entered.

Heaving back the sliding glass door to the balcony.

Spilling over the side.

Stumbling away from the house. One hand over my gut, the other held out in front of me. The pose of a 1950s running back, protecting the ball as he barreled toward the goal line.

I didn't know if Malvo was behind me or not. I didn't look back.

Clawed open the driver side door and stabbed the keys into the ignition.

Put one foot over the other and kicked them both down on the gas.

31

I drove through the night along streets I'd always heard mention of but never traveled alone. Gratiot Avenue. Conant Street. Mound Road. The traffic lights flashing, all saying *go, go, go.*

But there was no going back to the hotel, no sleep, not after what I knew. Because it wasn't enough that I knew it. Ash needed to see it, too.

And what was that, exactly?

That Dean Malvo was an emptily charming monster who sought substitute teaching for the access it afforded him, and drama for the parts he found most useful to play. Caring Dean. Sexy Dean. Boyfriend Dean. Daddy Dean.

What else? He went to prison for only part of the damage he'd done. Because there were two lives he'd taken in Royal Oak. Malvo murdered Meg and Ash to prevent them from exposing him for what he was, burned down an empty house downtown with Meg's bones and a still-alive Ash in it—the same house he'd take the two of them to, where he took pictures of them, his first pieces in what, over years, went on to grow into an extensive collection of memorabilia—and got away with it.

It fit. It worked.

But it didn't answer every question that had me drifting through the dark fields of Detroit.

If it was Malvo who started the fire, wouldn't Ash have known it was him?

Maybe she didn't see who it was who locked her in the cellar.

Maybe she didn't think he could have done it.

Maybe she needed proof.

Maybe she knew it was him, but needed to see him pay.

The photos and letters and whatever else he kept in the cashbox would do it. Show how she wasn't the only one. That would convince Ash as well as the police. It would surely be enough to substantiate murder charges, the closing of a nagging file. Malvo doing time until his time ran out and then his real punishment would begin.

The problem was, I didn't have the cashbox.

Somewhere along the way, after hundreds of random turns, I got lost and didn't bother trying getting unlost. The leaning houses, the cars propped up on cinder blocks, the fenced acres of buckling cement, the inexplicable frequency of motorboats, tarped and rusting in otherwise vacant lots—a monochrome procession just outside the headlights' reach.

I only stopped after I drove into a seesaw.

An asleep-at-the-wheel detour over the curb and through what must have once been somebody's backyard but now was neither back nor front of anything. And in the middle of it, the remains of a playground. The metal bar on a pivot, the red saddle at each end. All of it toppled over at the end of my folded hood.

I backed up to the street again, made another couple turns, and parked. Made sure the doors were locked. Let my eyes close.

It felt like I was out for less than two minutes when I heard the tapping.

Hard metal on the driver side window. A pipe. A blade. The end of a gun.

Tap, tap, tap.

It was meant to wake me up. So I pretended to stay asleep.

Tap, tap . . . CRACK.

I opened my eyes and pushed away from the door at the same time. The flinching anticipation of the end of things that I knew was only the beginning of something else.

There was the spiderweb of cracks over the window, silvery and fine. What I heard had weight. Wanted in.

Not there now.

I checked all the windows. A horizon of night. Not a face to be seen, not a figure. Not a vehicle other than mine parked along the length of the street that looked more like a country road, bordered by grass so tall it could have been a farmer's crop ready for harvest.

Was there time for someone to run across the street and hide in one of those fields? No. Though maybe there was time to drop out of sight. Squeeze under the car's chassis. Wait me out.

The smart thing to do would be to start the car and drive. Keep going even if I rolled over whoever might be under me.

So I tried to be smart. It didn't help turn over a dead engine.

Four times I hit it, priming the gas, the battery waning. On the fifth try it didn't even lend the dash enough light to see what time it was.

The time of death.

It had been so long since I'd heard Ash's voice in my head I almost welcomed it. Except I knew that if she was there, if she'd come by to witness what was going to happen next, it couldn't be good for me.

I unlocked the door. Kicked it open.

When nothing immediately attacked or fired or stabbed, I stepped out of the car. Bent down to look under it. Walked around and popped the trunk to confirm that nothing had found its way in there.

Then I remembered my phone. So long as there were still bars showing on the thing, I could put in a 911 call and wait for the cavalry to arrive. Out here, it could be a while. Some guy who didn't know where he was saying he'd hunkered down in a parked car with somebody trying to smash their way in? They may not find me for a couple days. They may not come at all.

Either way, it was worth hitting the numbers. And now that I was standing out there, the inside of the Impala looked relatively cozy.

I got back in. Closed the door.

In the next breath, I took in the smell.

Perfume and soil and spoiled meat. Overwhelming and close.

Why not let me drive awhile, Danny?

Her hand on the wheel. Pulling it hard to the right just as she did to drive Willa and Eddie into the Charles. Showing me it was her. How she did it. How she'll do it again if she likes.

The hand drifted up to me. The burnt fingers landing wet and bone-nubbed on my chin. Pulled my head to look at her. The darkness so dense only the white balls of her eyes, the sheen of congealed blood shone back.

He's waiting . . .

I knocked her arm away. Then I was falling out of the car, hitting the street flat on my side. The same ear that took the hammer stroke earlier smacked the concrete and blared new trumpets of pain.

When I rolled over and looked into the car, Ash wasn't there. The passenger door open as if she'd run off into the field beyond the curb. Not that I was about to go looking for her.

So I looked the other way. A pavement-eye view straight down the length of street.

And saw that I was back where I started. Arndt Street. Malvo's house a couple hundred feet away, the porch bulb still dimly burning, still a sun for the orbiting moth.

After I'd rolled through east Detroit for half the night I parked here, passed out here, was awakened by my dead twin sister here.

Why not let me drive awhile, Danny?

This time, when I walked up to the front door, I knew I'd find it open.

I knew that nobody would be sitting on the living room sofa, that the rock of crack would still be where it was in the tinfoil, the pipe untouched. The kitchen empty, the rolls of toilet paper greenly glowing in the fridge.

But there was somebody there.

Upstairs. Where I had to go.

Where I was going now. Thinking of Willa and Eddie. Working to make them as present as I could so that I could take the next step up the stairs, and the next. There was no reason to face horror directly before, only the impulse to obey. It was why Ash had kept me where I'd been for so long, telling myself I had no choice. But there was always a choice. There was *this:* walking into the dark knowing something waited for me. So long as the idea of them stayed with me, I could raise my foot and look up into the second-floor shadows. I could do something other than hide.

Even in the dark of Malvo's bedroom I could see the flowerings of blood on the floor. The closet open, the cashbox where I'd opened it. The photos a checkerboard of flesh on the walls.

But the ball-peen was gone.

I checked the other two bedrooms. The same as they were before. The sliding door I'd barreled through still open, a tongue of outside air pulling back as though in revulsion at the taste.

Which left the bathroom.

The door was ajar. It let me slip past without touching it, squinting into the tub, around the corner at the toilet.

Nothing.

Though there was a sound. The hush of something sliding over the floor.

It spun me around to see the bathroom door drifting closed. The sound coming from Bob Malvo's bare toes leaving visible trails in the dust. The extension cord he used to tie around the hook in the door and his own neck pulled his head even with mine, so that his empurpled eyes seemed to appeal to me for help. His mouth fat-lipped. Hands black oven mitts over his crotch.

I want to show you something.

I plucked the photos off the closet wall and stuffed them into the cashbox along with all the clippings and notes. Picked the box up, cradled it with both arms against my chest like a baby I was carrying out of a fire. Down the stairs, out the door, leaving it open behind me not knowing if that was a good idea or not.

185

Both car doors were still wide open. Ash could have climbed back in since I went inside. Or somebody else entirely.

None of it stopped me from jumping in, dropping the box in the passenger footwell, and closing the doors. When I turned the keys in the ignition the engine started with an untroubled roar. Gentle on the gas. A weightless roll toward the pink line of dawn.

This time, when I made it to Alfred Street, I took the turn.

32

The house was still standing.

The brick blackened by fire, the roof a makeshift cladding of plywood sheets, the foundation buttressed by a pair of steel beams jammed against a side wall. It would have been so much easier to let it fall, but somebody had gone to a minimum effort to see that it didn't. A sign wired to the fence provided part of the explanation. DESIGNATED HISTORICAL SITE. It didn't say what history happened here worth holding on to.

This block of Alfred Street was only one among five thousand abandoned residential blocks in Detroit, and looked, at first, just like the others. The broad spaces between what was left of the existing structures, the surreal touches of a Dali painting—a stacked pile of real estate placards mutely calling FOR SALE, a naked mannequin propped against a wall, her arm raised in invitation. What was different about this street was that the houses were manors, even more haunting in their fall from grandeur. Less than a hundred years ago, the wealthiest people in the Midwest lived here, kept their shining horses in stables out back, parked the first automobiles ever made by the curb.

They're all dead now.

It's no trouble pulling open a slash in the fencing and squeezing through. A crunch through the waist-high grass brought me to the broad front steps, where it again proved easy to make my way inside. Someone before me had done some work with a crowbar on the wood barrier, returning it to a hinged door that could be pulled open and slid shut again, obscuring evidence of entry.

Which meant I could go in the same way.

Which meant there may be others in there with me.

It was dark, but not without spokes of light here and there. It let me advance in a shuffle, plowing through the rusted cans and wet newspapers and waste, animal and human alike.

There was nothing familiar about it, even though it was the place everything had changed for me. Only the smell. The acrid trace of carbon, burnt wood, and the chemicals used to start the fires that followed ours. The places that were once around here all torched on the Devil's Nights, the orgies of citywide arsons the day before Halloween. But this house was still there. A crypt. A holder of secrets.

Just as I was. The cashbox in my hand doubling in weight the deeper inside I went.

If this was what Ash wanted, how was I supposed to give it to her? If it was the police I needed to hand it over to, how did I do that without instantly stepping forward as a prime suspect in Malvo's death myself (not to mention Ash's, my name probably still high on the list)? And then there was the question that arrived with every return of Bob Malvo's swollen, plum-colored face: What difference does it make now?

What brought me there was the idea that, as with any detective who has answered his client's question, it was time to present my findings.

I stopped myself from falling through the floor at the last second. A black square that my foot wavered over before being pulled back.

On my knees, I put the cashbox next to the hole in the floor.

It didn't seem to be enough to simply leave it there. Isn't the rule with ghosts that a speech is called for? A summoning? If a spell was required to make the witch return to her grave, I needed the right words to bury her.

I meant to say *Here it is* but instead said, "I'm sorry."

Because I was. Sorry for what was done to her despite what she did to innocent others. I didn't forgive her, I never would. But I was sorry for whatever it was she saw on the other side when she was born just as I was sorry I couldn't have pulled her up, shown her I was ready to die for her because she was my sister, my blood.

"It was the teacher," I said to the empty house. "It's all here. You and all the other girls, too. And Meg. It was Malvo. It was him."

I waited for a reply that didn't come. Yet there was something now that breathed along with me. Something in the house. Or the house itself.

"Now I need to ask you something," I went on. "I need you to leave them alone."

Quiet.

Not even the breathing anymore.

There was the feeling that if I looked over the floor's edge into the cellar I'd see her there, but I didn't look.

I stopped at an electronics store on 7 Mile Road and bought a disposable cell phone. Called the Detroit Police and told the guy who answered to write something down. Bob Malvo's name. Meg Clemens. Ashleigh Orchard. The address on Arndt, the address on Alfred. Directions where to look for a cashbox in a corner of what used to be the main-floor living room, a box with evidence that showed Malvo was their murderer, as well as maybe some other missing girls in central Michigan over the last couple decades.

When I was done I pitched the phone over the guardrail onto the I-94 as I drove over it.

Then I was on my own cell. Calling Willa.

"Danny?" she said when she answered. "I've got good news."

"Me, too. You first."

"Eddie's coming home. Can you frigging believe it? The doctors say he's looking better than they expected, he can be monitored just as easily by me as by them—it's all I do at that damn hospital anyway. He's coming *home*, Danny!"

"That's wonderful," I said, but nothing but a weepy garble came out.

"What's that?"

"I said that's so fucking wonderful!"

"He can't wait to see you, you know."

"Me, too."

"So what's your news?"

"I'll tell you tonight in person," I said. "I'm coming home, too."

AT THE AIRPORT I SAT DOWN TO THE FIRST PROPER MEAL I'D HAD since the breakfast buffet two days before. Fajitas and cold beer at a Mexican place that tasted so good I ordered another plate halfway through the first just in case. Nothing on my mind but ways to shave time off the trip between the airport and Porter Square after we landed. Maybe I could ask for a seat closer to the front once I got to the gate. Or reserve a car so that one was waiting for me instead of joining the lineup for a cab.

As I ate, a couple of laughs came over me so abruptly I had to slap a napkin against my mouth. It was the Budget guy's face when he came out to take a look at the Impala, the same guy who was behind the counter when I arrived. Took one walk around the car, noting the smashed front hood, the scratched driver side window, the missing hubcaps (which I hadn't actually noticed).

"They invented insurance for a reason," he said. He leaned on the side of the car and, with perfect timing, the whole front fender fell off.

My second dinner arrived. I might have started into it, too, but it was time to head to the gate for boarding. Still, it wouldn't take more than a minute to see if I could line up a ride. I picked up the phone to start searching for car services at Logan when it vibrated in my hand.

Not an incoming call or text. The home security app I had installed before I left. Filling my screen with the live image of my front hall.

At first, it appeared to be a malfunction of some kind. There was nothing to see. No alarm to be alarmed about.

I was about to turn the thing off when the door nudged open.

A narrow band of darkness seeping in around the edge of the wood that grew wider, inch by inch.

Along with an alert running across the bottom.

. . . Unauthorized Entry . . . Unauthorized Entry . . . Unauthorized Entry . . .

Ash walked in. Wearing the same candy striper uniform she'd worn at the hospital. Looked straight up at the camera. At me.

Waved.

33

I repeatedly tried to get Willa on the phone while running down
the terminal hall to the gate. Left two messages on the landline.
Okayed a 911 call through the app to report a break-and-enter in
progress. Fired off three texts in between.

GET OUT! NOW!

She's INSIDE

i'm serious.

Then my flight was being called, the doors closing, the PA announcing the last boarding call for *Mr. Orchard, Mr. Daniel Orchard*. I
considered staying where I was, working the phone some more, trying to do something from my end before I was cut off in the air. But
I knew that the only thing I could do was try to stop Ash myself,

and I couldn't do it from Detroit, so I ran to the door and slipped through, took my seat with the curious gaze of the other passengers burning into me.

The one hour and forty-eight minutes roaring through the night between Detroit and Boston were the most wretched of my life, and that included a childhood with Ash. It included hell itself.

My heart added a new kind of pain to its repertoire, a crushing weight pressed hard against its bone cage. More than once I thought my efforts to contain a scream would fail, that I would start kicking the chair in front of me or ripping the oxygen masks out of the ceiling and we'd have to land in Buffalo or Albany so I could be pulled off in handcuffs. I needed to stay calm until I got there. And then I needed to be ready to—to what? Change the game. I was through with trying to figure out what Ash wanted. That was the only thing that kept me in my seat the whole way. Conjuring all the ways I would make *her* feel something for once.

As soon as we landed I was on the phone again. Multiple texts and voice messages popped up. I ignored them all and called Willa before we were parked at the gate.

It rang close to a dozen times before she answered. Her voice hoarse. In the background, the sound of electronic bells ringing, the muffle of institutional air.

"Oh, *Danny*. Oh my God. This—oh my *Christ*—"

"Slow down, baby. Okay?"

"—this *isn't* fucking *happening*—"

"Just tell me where you are."

"The hospital."

"Eddie?"

"He was *fine*. Everything was *fine*. They couldn't believe how well he was doing. When they said he could go home you should have *seen*—he was so happy. And then I went up to his room to bring him something to eat and . . ."

"And what?"

"He was *gone*, Danny."

A howl. It's the only way to describe the noise I made, loud and brief and unforeseen, cut off by putting my mouth against my shoulder.

"Willa," I said when I was able, the flight attendant opening the door of the plane and everyone up and wrestling for their bags in the overhead compartments. "Gone how?"

"Out. Asleep, but not asleep. I tried. I *tried*. But I couldn't wake him up!"

"A coma. Is that it?"

"They're not using that word. But yeah, it looks that way."

The passengers were shuffling down the aisle and out the door. Each of them taking a look down at me, the cause of concern in the second row they were glad to be putting behind them.

"I saw the messages you left," Willa said.

"It was too late. I'm so sorry."

"How do you know it was her?"

"The security camera. I saw her. Coming into the house."

"She did this to my son?"

"Yes."

"But you said everything was okay. That you'd figured things out—"

"I thought I had. I must have been wrong. Or maybe I was right, and it just doesn't make a difference."

"If she did this, what's stopping her from—from coming back? From *taking* him? If she could get into the house she could get into the hospital, too, right?"

The hospital candy striper uniform. Showing me where she'd go next.

"I'll be there soon as I can," I said.

"Danny? What are we going to do?"

The plane was emptied out except for me. The flight attendant looking my way, a look that said she was used to crazies who had to be pulled out of the sardine can at the very end of the day.

But I was getting up all on my own. Rushing into the terminal, passing others, a dash toward the GROUND TRANSPORTATION sign that

194

lit a new fire in my chest so that I couldn't answer Willa's question even if I had one to give.

You'd think a heart attack would hurt most where your heart is. But it can show up anywhere: down the length of your leg, the back of your head, a knuckling behind the eyes. I had three-alarm versions of them all as the cab descended into the Callahan Tunnel crossing from East Boston to downtown, the fluorescent tubes strobing as we roared through the earth.

Then we were rising into the city at night, the driver weaving through the old streets designed for horse carts, running reds in pursuit of the extra hundred promised him if we did it quick.

They were close now. The pain retreated like a rat when the lights get turned on.

"How's *that*?" the driver asked in thick Dorchester-ese as we pulled up to the hospital's doors.

I gave him everything I had.

Willa didn't touch me.

I wasn't expecting an embrace or a kiss or anything—I'm not sure what I was expecting—but the way she jolted back when she saw me, an instinctual aversion to a known carrier of disease, threw me back as well. No mirror was necessary to see how I appeared to her: unclean, glassy-eyed, the yearning reach of the terminal case. Damned.

We stood in the hallway outside Eddie's room and took a moment to recover. Not as lovers, not as husband and wife, but as Adults in a Situation. The minimum control that made human speech possible. She told me Eddie's coma had been confirmed, that the doctors were puzzled by how it came about, one saying it was like "someone reached inside him and turned out the light." I told her the facts of what I discovered in Detroit and how I must have been wrong in thinking the discovery of the truth would stop Ash, wrong that the truth was what she was after in the first place.

We stared at each other. Me concluding that there was no way to tell her how sorry I was. Willa trying not to swing her hand across my face.

"Can I see him?" I said finally. Asking permission. The fantasy that I was his dad, his *almost*-dad, over in four words.

"He loved you, you know," Willa said, then took longer than she needed to correct herself. "Loves you."

I took Willa in. My happiness in the shape of a woman, short and salty and firm. She was mine for a time I knew might be brief but now felt like it never was at all.

HE WASN'T MY SON. HE WAS A BOY I WAS STARTING TO GET TO know. One who came with the package, the two of us connected by shared circumstance and low expectations and unspoken ground rules. But that didn't stop me from being glad the door was closed and the room was otherwise unoccupied when I saw him in the bed, complicated by breathing tubes and monitoring wires, and let the grief pour out.

The same sun-dotted, jug-eared kid assembled there beneath the white sheet, but absent in the ways that matter. You can *feel* it: the vacancy of the artificially life-supported, their claim on this world the weight of a penlight's beam through the fog.

His eyes were closed but the lids were twitching. I'm sure it was only some aspect of bodily autopilot and not an indication of consciousness, but it was like he knew I was there. The spooky feeling of being watched from behind, except from someone laid out in front of you.

I held his hand. Told him I loved him. That I wasn't totally honest when I said I never wanted to be a replacement dad to him, because a part of me did, right from the start, a part that grew every day we spent together. I never told him because I didn't want to scare him away, and because I was happy just being around, learning how trust might be made between two beings shaped by suspicion and loss.

I told him all this. And then I told him something else.

"I'm going to find her, Eddie. I'm going to send her back so she'll never hurt you or your mom again. You just have to hold on. Just think about that. Concentrate on that."

He heard me. There was nothing to indicate this, no telltale squeeze or effort at speech, but I knew he did. I'd been where he was now. You can see and hear a lot from the middle ground. Some of it pulls you back, some of it pushes you all the way over.

I leaned in close enough for him to feel my voice as well as hear it.

"Wherever she has you, I'm going to make her let you go."

Then I stood up while I still could. Released Eddie's hand and stepped out into the hall.

Willa wasn't there. Probably in the lounge area, or the bathroom.

I headed the other way.

You can't push her back to where she's supposed to be, not from here.

Down the elevators to the main floor and out into the swampy night that smelled faintly of the sea. Took a lungful in. Tried to remember this, too. The simple in-and-out of air, overlooked and miraculous.

She can only be pulled.

And that couldn't be done from this side.

I ran.

A full sprint, or as close to it as my knees allowed. Plowing across busy Cambridge Street, almost knocked down by one of the cars that hit the brakes so hard they didn't have time to lay on the horn. Into the narrow streets of Beacon Hill, fighting the slopes and slippery cobblestone, unworried about which way to go because I wasn't going anywhere in particular. Only running.

From a distance, in the dark, I would've looked like another late-to-the-game health nut trying to stave off the inevitable.

In fact, I was a suicide-in-progress.

The night was still but there was a rush of blood in my ears, howling at what it was being asked to do, how it wasn't getting to the parts where it had to go. And soon the pain, too. All the new kinds, as well as the crushing pressure in the chest. Signs I ignored along with the traffic lights, clopping the length of Louisburg Square and south to Beacon Street, banging through a clutch of drunk tourists and into the Public Garden on the other side.

Even then, right at the end, there was an appreciation of beauty.

You'd think there'd be more serious considerations as the legs finally gave way just short of the duck pond and the stars extinguished, from dimmest to brightest, the heavens short-circuited. But as my head hit the ground and the willows and light-pricked buildings along Boylston Street and the sickle-shaped moon were turned sideways I was thinking, *It's so pretty here.*

The air.

That's what you end up clinging to. That old, lung-filling need. One more deep one for the road—

But that was it. The last breath of this world tasting of grass. A sip of dew.

So pretty . . .

Then, right before the darkness, someone else added a thought of her own.

Not so pretty where you're going, Danny Boy.

PART 3

Motor City

PART 3

34

Before I open my eyes I work to remember everything that brought me here. So long as I stay in the dark I can make most of it come back, shape it into a sequence of events I can almost make sense of. Memory is one of the first casualties of the After—I know this if nothing else—and while so much of my life is something I'd rather forget, some of the most recent past has been good, the best I've known, and I don't want to let it go.

Too late.

This is the present.

This is now.

Nothing else counts but *now*.

Ready, Danny? It's time to move. For them. So open your eyes on three. *One . . .*

The smell tells me where I am just as it did before. But it's different this time. I'm back in my room. Where I am now. In the present that feels stretched out forever. Except this time, forever smells *bad*.

The stale sheets and unwashed gym clothes, the burnt toast and lilac carpet deodorant, all of it sharpened to the point that when I wake it's with the gagging cough of having smelling salts held under my nose.

 . . . two . . .

There's a new odor, too. The foul leavings of animal urine and shit. Neither dog nor cat but something wild, a creature born of another continent altogether. A meat eater.

 . . . three.

I sit up and count the marks of its fury.

The room torn apart from ceiling to floor. Gouges left in the walls from the sweeps of claws the size of crowbars. The *Dune* poster, half shredded, half still hanging by a taped corner. A chaos of scat-smeared clothes and splintered wood colored by blood. Ribbons of it over what's left of the window's glass, the headboard. And on the floor, faceup, the forced smiles of the one and only Orchard family portrait. Ash looking back at me as if to say I should have known it would end like this.

Whatever was here was hunting. And when it didn't find what it was looking for it left a show of its power and size and the terrible things it can do.

You can be afraid in the After. You can feel the terror of death even in death.

I'm up and tiptoeing to the door, careful to avoid the upturned nails and wire ends. When I spot my chess club medals I nearly bend to pick them up, wonder why, and instantly answer myself: they are proof of the only game I was ever good at. My specialty was escape. Hiding the king, hoping my opponent slipped up. The same tactics I employed against Ash.

At least in chess it sometimes worked.

The hallway has been scratched and soiled and bloodied, too, but not as badly. As though the animal knew where to look.

There's confirmation of this in my parents' room which, while visited—the door ripped off, territorial sprays of piss over the wallpaper—is largely undamaged aside from a crosshatching of gore on the bedsheets where, last time, the indentation of my father's body had been left behind.

I back out to the top of the stairs. Wonder whether this moment is an opportunity to get out of here that will be missed if I linger, if what I'm here to do will be stopped in the first minutes by a rending of claws.

Which begs the question: What have I come here to do?

Do what Sylvie Grieg told me. *You can't push her back. She can only be pulled.*

Try to save the living by dying.

But dying only gets me here. It doesn't save anyone. All it means is I'll never see them again.

No. Not allowed to think about that. If I stop moving I will be held in place forever. That's how it works here. You stop to ponder the past and it will screw you to the spot.

So let's try it again, Danny: What have you come here to do?

I'm here to yank Ash out of the living world and anchor her here, in the After. Her hell. Now mine as well.

How is it done? Sylvie Grieg didn't know that part and neither do I. But I'm pretty sure of the first step: I need to find the part of Ash that's still here. Play a different chess game than what I'm used to playing. Be the hunter instead of the hider for once.

Ash's door is the only one that remains untouched.

I'm expecting it to be barricaded as it was before. But this time the doorknob turns. The door whispers open over pristine carpet with a single nudge.

"Ash?"

I find my voice on the first try. Brittle, but audible. It summons nothing but the overpowering scent of the room. The same as it smelled when we were alive but denser now, so strong I raise my hands to push it aside. Fruit candies and lavender and talc. The industrial essence of 1980s girlishness.

Everything as it was. A space so clean and organized and free of character—no posters, no photos, no books—it feels like a film set. A script that called for A Good Girl's Room and neglected to provide any details aside from the arrangement of various framed Certificates of Excellence on the wall, shelving that supported nothing but trophies. Tennis. Math-a-lympics. Swim Team. Science Fair. Best Actress.

The only thing on her desk is her diary. The leather strap holding it closed. Locked.

TO MY DAUGHTER, ASHLEIGH—DAD

Left here for me. But not the key.

I could cut the strap but that's cheating. And I'll be punished for cheating.

So I start out looking under the bed and feeling the closet floor on hands and knees. In the end, I throw everything onto the floor, smash the glass on the Certificates of Excellence, sling the trophies against the wall. Grind the little plastic tennis players and actresses under my shoes until they crack.

When I find the key it's on a second pass through her underwear drawer. Buried deep among the panties, so that I have to feel its hard copper through the soft cotton and silk. Another joke. Making me look like the horny brother, caught in the act. *Pervy,* as she approvingly described any boy who looked her way.

I unlock the strap. Start on the first page. Flip to the next. The middle, the end.

All three hundred pages of it the same.

I'm not here.
I'm not here.
I'm not here.
I'm not here.
I'm not here.

The handwriting careful, unhurried. A written self-portrait that was as close to the real Ash as she could get. Her autobiography.

All at once, the room's perfumes double in intensity. It forces me out to prevent myself from vomiting all over the carpet.

By the time I make it to the bathroom and kneel over the toilet, it passes. I'm partway to standing again when I hear it.

A drip of water from the faucet into the full tub.

It will require me to pull back the curtain to see what's there. The shower game. This time, there will be something other than a spinning soap-on-a-rope waiting for me.

There's no point waiting.

A body submerged beneath the still surface except for the head at the far end. My mother. Naked and drunk as the day I found her after school.

Her bloodshot eyes blink open and pull me into focus.

"Danny?" she says, a hand breaking through to hold on to the side but without the strength to pull herself up.

"It's me, Mom."

"You're here, too?"

"Yes."

"Why? What did you do?"

"I'm here to find Ash."

"Of course," she says, nodding so deeply her nose dips underwater and she has to sneeze it out. "Funny how it's hard to think of your children—how they run out of time the same as we do. The last thing a mother wants to think about."

"Nobody likes to think about it."

"Of course. Why would they?"

She's doing her best just as she always did. The *Of courses* and overstated gestures an attempt at an unruffled control of her own thoughts and words. As in life, she does it for me more than herself.

I kneel down on the bath mat and stroke the wet hair from her eyes. "Can I help you out of there?"

"Would you?" she says. "I don't know—I must have fallen asleep."

"It happens."

"How dreadful! A son shouldn't have to lift his mother out—"

"It's all right, really. It's fine."

She squeezes up a smile at this. There's gratitude in it, and enormous sadness. But there's relief, too. She has been alone so completely these shared words are like the warmth that comes with the first swallow of wine.

It's a little easier getting her out using a thirty-nine-year-old's arms than a ten-year-old's. Not that it still isn't a struggle.

Once she's out and sitting on the mat I go into my parents' room and find her something to wear. A billowy summer dress she reserved for "cleaning days," the afternoons of incomplete vacuuming and abandoned miniprojects. I get her to raise her arms and, together, we pull it down over her. She slaps the wet floor, inviting me to sit, and I settle my back against the wall opposite her.

"Did you see whatever happened here, mom?" I ask, casting my eyes out into the damage in the hallway.

"Look at that. Terrible. I thought it was a dream."

"What was it?"

"I only heard it. I suppose I was trying to pretend it wasn't really here so I didn't want to look. But it was *big*, whatever it was." She shakes her head. The same disbelieving shake she'd give the TV news at the announcement of a fresh round of layoffs or lousy weather forecasted for a holiday weekend. "There's odd things on this side, Danny. Some more odd than others."

"Is Dad here with you?"

"No. But I wish he was."

"What about Ash? Does she visit?"

"I wouldn't call it visiting," she says, blinking. "She comes and goes and sometimes I happen to see her when she does. But she's not here for me."

"What's she here for?"

"She doesn't say."

"Do you go with her sometimes? Out of the house, I mean?"

She cocks her head like I might be teasing her.

"This is my *place*," she says. "This house. It's where I stay. Even if I wanted to, I couldn't leave."

"But Ash can."

"She roams."

"How?"

"It must be because she wasn't properly attached to anything—to anyone. Back then."

"The thing that was here. The animal. It can roam, too?"

She crosses her arms as though against a sudden chill. "I don't know about much outside these walls, Danny. I'm here on my own. I'm *meant* to be here on my own."

"I can't stay, either, Mom."

"Oh?"

"There's something I have to do."

"You mean outside?" My mother reaches out her cold hand and hooks her fingers through mine. "Promise me you'll be careful."

"Why? What's out there?"

"Monsters. People," she shudders, as if the second of these is the more hideous.

"What can anyone do to us? We can't die. We're already *here*."

"There's always a new way to die," she says. "Just like there's always a worse version of here than here."

She slides forward over the puddled floor and pats my hand the way she did when I was a child.

"Dying is different in this place, but it still happens. And it's *awful*," she goes on. "When you come back the next time everything's the same—you still come back to your *here*—except there's even less sun, less order, less hope. Less of the good things you're able to remember from being alive."

The good things. What were they for her? Me, I feel sure. But she couldn't think of me without thinking of Ash as well, which situated me in the purgatory of the bittersweet.

She wasn't always the way she was. In the photos of our parents taken before we were born they were often laughing, wearing funny hats at a New Year's Eve masquerade, Dad dipping her low in some dance competition while she playacted a swoon, the two of them beaming and lipstick-smeared outside the church at their wedding.

The best day of her life had to be back there somewhere. Starting out together with Dad, buying this house on the edge of what was then a still prosperous city. And if I'm right about that, it means that this is the dark flip side for her. Alone in a house that her husband avoided as much as he could, blacked out from drink in a cold tub. My mother's After is the hell of denial. Her being here proves that not doing what we ought to do can condemn us just the same as doing what we know to be wrong.

That, and making the wrong kind of prayer. The wrong kind of trade.

"I'm glad you got it," she says now, nodding at the watch on my wrist.

"Why didn't you give it to me yourself?"

"You were in a place I couldn't go. But sometimes the things we carry can pass through, even if we can't."

When I stand I offer her my hand to help her to her feet but she refuses it. Splashes a hand in the water on the floor as if to say she's fine where she is.

"Can I ask you something, Danny?"

"Sure."

"You knew, didn't you, that Ash was with me when I died?"

"With you how?"

"Here. In this room. By the tub."

"Not helping you."

"Not helping me, no. Rather the opposite of helping me."

She watches me like a doctor waiting for an injected drug to take effect.

"She *drowned* you?"

"It didn't take much, God knows."

"Mom! Oh *Christ*—"

"The funny thing is I thought she was going to wash my hair. Her face was almost gentle. Almost *sweet.*"

"She *murdered* you!"

"It only took one hand on my head to slide me down and keep me there. She didn't seem angry or anything like that. She didn't say a single word. It was like she was only vaguely interested in watching me take the water in and fight as best I could, try to pull myself up by her arm. I remember looking up at her pretty face and thinking,

It's like she's watching a show on TV. And then I thought, *A show she's already seen."*

She shakes her head at the memory as if a trick had been played on her, one she had to admire for its cleverness.

"I'm going to find her," I manage, the room spinning. "I'm going to stop her from hurting anyone else."

"Stop her?"

"That's why I'm here. To put an end to it."

"But this *is* the end."

I try to think of something to say but none of the candidates is anything that would mean anything here.

I'm sorry.

There was nothing you could have done.

She lost her soul the same day she was born.

"You better get on your way," she says before I can try any of them. "The days are bad. But the nights . . . you don't want to be out there at night."

I find a brush on the counter and use it to untangle her hair. Lay a dry towel over her legs. Bend down and kiss the side of her face. She surprises me when she turns her head to kiss me, too.

"Good-bye, Mom."

"I'd rather not say the same to you, if it's all right," she says. "The thought you might come back is something I'm going to try to hold on to."

She turns away from me to look out the small rectangle of the bathroom window, where she can see only pillows of fog pushed along by a whistling wind but never clearing.

"Happy birthday, Danny," she says.

35

I have to go no farther than the sidewalk to see that my mother was right. The After has different levels.

You need only look both ways along Farnum to know this place is farther down the slide than where I was when Ash brought me here. *Less sun, less order, less hope.* The formerly well-tended gardens and lawns now high with thistles, thick vines crawling up walls to join fingers with others as though pulling the homes into their graves. The pavement cracked, huge slabs heaved upward like an ice-jammed river.

All of it seen through the fog-that's-not-a-fog. Selectively obscuring, veiling, disappearing. Making distances difficult to judge. Casting gray doubt over everything you think you see.

More disturbing are the screams. Every couple minutes a new howl of agony or protest, some sounding a half mile off, others no more than a block or two. No sirens. No reply of gunshots.

Which way to go?

To wherever she is.

The places Ash knew, the emotional landmarks, the ones with

meaning. Where the very worst thing happened to her. For most, a short list of such places would immediately come to mind. But for a girl who didn't feel as others do, it could be anywhere or nowhere.

I'm not here.

I start by looking for something that might be useful. Transportation, above all. Figuring my old Raleigh might come in handy, I hop the backyard fence where my bike and Ash's used to be kept. The shed, too. Nothing with wheels is still here. The same with the neighbors' yards and garages. The few parked cars—in the middle of the street, on what used to be front lawns—gutted long ago, sitting on corroded rims, the hoods ripped off. The Motor City has no motors.

I start west. My watch says it's noon. It has said that since I got here. Winding it, tapping it, knocking it against brick doesn't bring it back to life.

When I get to Main I cross and carry on the couple blocks to the high school. The same walk of my teenaged years, made with the same dread. Ash never let me make the trip with her. Instead, she walked ahead or accepted the ride from one of the older boys who rolled next to her in their cars though the school was less than a quarter mile away. Sometimes I'd spot her in the hallway over the course of the day and turn the other way, pretending I'd forgotten something in my locker, if only not to see how she didn't see me. Talking to her friends or laughing at the report of a practical joke by one of the basketball guys, Ash always at the center of the pack no matter its composition, and she would pass me without any sign.

Later, once we were home, she would find me.

"I *saw* you today," she'd say, as if my being visible was another instance of poor judgment on my part.

Maybe this is why I climb over the rubble where the main doors to the school once stood and enter the building's dust-choked insides. Maybe she's already here, having walked on ahead of me.

I stop at the office, noting how the counter where the secretary in the nightshirt had stood on Pajama Day has been hacked apart. Try all the light switches at the main board but nothing comes on. The result, as I start deeper into the school, is hallways bathed in near darkness, the smashed windows offering light that reaches only a few feet inside before fading to chalky grey.

The classrooms are destroyed. The desks overturned, burned. Ceiling tiles ripped away to expose the spidery wires and ducts above. A wall of presidential portraits amended to create a pornographic mural of self-pleasuring. In the library, the books have been pulled from the shelves and spread over the floor. The pages soaked and dried so many times they have puffed up soft, an orange shag carpet.

I open the door to the theater. Because there are no windows in here the only available light enters from behind me. The rows of seats, the panels depicting scenes of Detroit's industrial and cultural ascendance, the stage, all in total darkness until a moment ago. And though it's still dark, the weak glow is enough to reveal two things.

The first is that the *South Pacific* set used for the production Ash was in remains onstage. The palm trees that used hockey sticks wrapped in brown construction paper for their trunks, the painted background of a distant island. All of it just the same as when Ash stood before us to accept a standing ovation for her winning "I'm Gonna Wash That Man Right Outa My Hair."

The second is that someone sits in the audience.

Only the back of a head is visible but the hair is long. A woman staring stageward in the middle of the rows, not turning around even as the dim light is cast over her.

"Hello?"

There is no reply beyond a distracted flap of her hand, as though asking me to keep my voice down and not interrupt an ongoing performance.

I go down the aisle and slide in to sit two seats away from her. See that it's someone I know. Knew. Michelle Wynn, one of the three girls who went down Woodward Avenue with Ash on her birthday. Though this Michelle is one I have never seen before: midthirties, ample-cheeked, her girth spilled over the handrests. The state of things when she took her own life.

"Michelle? It's Danny Orchard."

She turns. Her mind catching up to my words. "Danny?"

"Remember me?"

"Sure, I remember you. I think about you all the time."

"You do?"

"I think about *everything* all the time."

"The old days."

"No, not because of that. Because you never know what will end up being part of the answer."

"The answer to what?"

She smiles a don't-be-stupid smile.

Of the three girls who pedaled along behind Ash, Michelle was the one hardest to see being there at all. There was the pedaling itself, which she would have found difficult, trailing farthest behind, the heaviest and least athletic of the girls. Then there was her neither-here-nor-there place in the Dondero universe. She was distinguished primarily by her transparent need to get along with everyone, which in high school marks you as guaranteed to be rejected by all.

And she was big.

"It's my *glands!*" Michelle would protest whenever teased for her weight. It turned out to be a misguided defense. Boys would only stuff half a hamburger in their mouths as she walked by in the cafeteria and shout through bun-blowing mouths, "*Ooh!* These *glands* are so *delicious!*"

"What are you doing here, Michelle?"

"I'm waiting for her to come on," she says, jutting her chin toward the stage.

"You've seen her here before?"

"Many times! Starting with opening night. May 14, 1989. And the six shows after that. She was *amazing.*"

"You came every night?"

"This was my seat. I'd sit here, trying to figure out how she could *do* that. Become someone else, have everyone *believe* in whatever you were doing, moment to moment."

"What about here? The theater on this side," I say. "Has Ash come back here?"

"She hasn't spoken. And it's too dark to see her. But I've sensed her standing up there, looking at me. I could feel what she was thinking."

"What was that?"

"The same thing I felt her think whenever she looked at me then: 'Why do you even *bother*?'" Her Ash voice is impeccable. An impersonation so good it makes me look around to make sure it's not actually her. "'*Look* at you! Why live when you have no *reason* to?'"

"I don't understand why you'd be here for her when she wasn't there for you."

"Because I *loved* her! When she talked to me, made me feel like a friend, let me in on some secret—I'd never felt that way before. I never felt anything like it again."

Michelle shifts in her seat, or tries to.

"It's why," she says, "when she told me to take a razor blade and—I did it. I *did it*. For once, I had all of her attention. And I never felt anything like it."

One of her hands briefly rises, fighting against the seatback in front of her, and I see she wears a wedding ring. Whoever she left behind, the children she may have had, none of them equal to a girl whose lesson was that life wasn't worth living unless you could live it like her.

"Do you remember the day Ash died, Michelle? When you followed her on your bike on her birthday?"

"I remember."

"Did she say anything about meeting someone?"

"Someone?"

"A date she had, maybe. A secret she wanted you to keep."

Her face sours.

"Like Dean Malvo?" I ask. "The teacher? Did she ever mention him?"

"Nice seeing you, Danny."

"Wait. Don't—"

But she's gone. Her gaze returned to the center of the stage as if a spotlight has been turned on. The folds of her body tensed in anticipation of the first strains of music.

I make my way back up the aisle. She doesn't look back. When I leave, I close the doors behind me, leaving Michelle in perfect darkness once more.

36

There are people out on Main Street.

Not many, maybe a dozen scattered over the three blocks of Royal Oak's downtown strip, including some I even vaguely recognize. Gus of Gus the Barber's, standing on the corner in his white barbor coat with scissors poking out of the chest pocket but wearing no pants, staring skyward as if gauging the chance of rain. One of my dad's friends from the office, chewing on an unlit cigar as he stares down through a sewer grate on hands and knees. A cashier from the Holiday Market, dragging a stroller stacked with fallen birds.

As I pass them they give me the same look of distaste, one that shifts to a hostility I can feel growing with every moment they hold their attention on me. It's my freedom of movement. The way I walk around them and keep walking, heading south. I haven't found my place yet. My ability to decide on a direction and pursue it at will—to *roam*, as my mother said of Ash—is what fills them with rage.

A couple of them start to follow me, murmuring to themselves, before giving up when I quicken my pace. None venture beyond the rail tracks. All of them loyal to the Royal.

By the time I make it to where Main meets Woodward, the light has begun to fade. The gray mist rippling like an aluminum curtain. Above it, the clouds remain a solid mass, their underside untextured as a bedsheet. Somewhere behind them, the sun has started its decline, though it does so according to a pace of its own choosing. Whether in two hours or five or fifteen—whatever shape "hours" take in this place—night is coming.

The Detroit Zoo is just ahead, on the far side of Woodward's multiple, buckled lanes. I'm climbing over the iron spokes of its fallen water tower when I spot the magician.

Running between the ticket booths at the entrance, his top hat wobbling but somehow clinging to his head. The same man who was the entertainment at my one and only childhood birthday party. The man in the cloak and gloves I cycled past when I was here with Ash and he pulled a dead dove out of thin air.

The magician climbs over the water tower's remains. Noting me but without slowing. His eyes darting in different directions.

The roar stops us both. Something like a lion, but not. Coming from inside the zoo's grounds.

Next to me, the magician releases an involuntary squeak of terror. Lurches on.

A zebra next. Squeezing through the gap where the turnstiles used to stand, whinnying. When it's out it can't decide which way to go, so ends up standing next to an overturned cotton candy cart, white froth dripping from its mouth.

Another roar.

Followed by others, coming from other sources. Some distant, some very close.

A tiger jumps onto the roof of one of the ticket booths and looks down at the three of us as if taking roll call. Zebra, magician, man. All here.

There's enough time to see that it's not really a tiger. It has the same stripes, the lashing tail, the whiskered chops. But its orange

parts are too orange, its black too black, as though painted and lac-
quered. And it's twice the size of any tiger in the living world. Its
teeth and nails bigger still.

It comes to a decision.

Locks eyes on the zebra. Leaps from the roof—an effortless air-
borne crossing of the thirty feet between them—and falls upon its
back.

The zebra emits a catlike yowl, then nothing more. Black-and-
white-striped legs falling to the ground, still kicking. Claws parting
head from neck with an audible pop.

The magician sees what's coming next before I do. Starts to run.

Which reminds me I should, too.

And I'm about to when something new comes over the ticket
booths.

A second tiger. And another. The third one bigger than the others
by half. Muscled and smooth as though its fur has been greased. This
and its eyes mark it as the creatures' leader. The irises glowing red,
dazzling even now in waning daylight. The same red I'd seen in Violet and Sylvie's father's eyes as he stood at the top of the stairs. The
red of Dr. Noland, my mother's delivery room doctor.

It ignores the other two tigers and makes the jump onto the top of
the felled water tower tank. Taking in the view to the south, over the
twelve miles of blasted flatlands to the black pillars of the Renaissance Center. Seeing it all as its own.

I run past the multilevel parking lot, pounding the sidewalk south.
My heart may be just as defective in the After—it certainly struggles
to make my legs do anything more than a thigh-burning jog after the
first couple hundred yards—but the fear of a death-in-death isn't
as sharp as the fear of the shiny tigers, and I carry on until I can't
anymore. The corner of LeRoy and Woodward where the gray slab of
the Ferndale First United Methodist Church stands. Where I see the
magician again.

We notice each other at the same time. He sits leaning against a
tree in the grass median. When he sees me, he stands. His waxy face
betrays a look of disbelief at this—*In a thousand acres of wasteland you*

had to leave a trail to where I'm sitting?—before he turns to new considerations.

He looks up his tree but it's too low, too exposed to bother climbing. To the south, Woodward continues on, wide and open. He swings his head, choosing between the streets on either side, when he stops.

I follow his line of sight and see the biggest of the three tigers coming down the middle of the southbound lanes, a half dozen blocks off. Its red eyes locked on us.

The magician runs into the church and I follow him.

The sudden dark holds me in the entranceway a moment. Even when I make my way down the aisle of the nave, there's no sign of the magician.

Red Eyes had to have seen us come in here.

The pipe organ next to the altar has been smashed, all but a few of the keys removed so that what's left looks like a boxer's gumline. But most of the pipes are still there. The gaps between showing a shadowed space behind them. Maybe big enough for a man to fit into.

Climbing onto the pile of the organ's ruins I'm able to pull myself up to the platform holding the pipes. That's the easy part. Getting to my feet without falling is harder.

The tiger enters the church just as I squeeze against the wall and slip behind the pipes. It pads along the aisle, its head lowering to sniff the floor. When it looks up again it gazes at where I stand.

There's a full moment of the two of us held like this. Measuring, listening. Then it starts forward again.

I'm sorry, Eddie.

The monster stops directly below me, where the organist would have sat. My feet a couple ladder rungs above the top of its head.

I wish I could have gone farther. But I tried. I did.

With a movement so sudden there isn't the time to gasp, the tiger leaps backward onto the altar. Its roar shaking islands of plaster off the ceiling.

Almost instantly, the magician jumps out of the darkened vestibule where he'd been concealed. He attempts to pitch himself past the creature and run for the door. As if in anticipation of this very action, the tiger raises one of its great paws and plows it into the man's side, knocking him into the pews below. The top hat tumbling to the floor.

The magician cries as the monster takes its time pulling him apart. A human wailing not for himself but for something left behind, the last of what he remembers of being alive.

And when its teeth find me, it will be my turn to do the same.

37

I stay where I am through the night. So does the tiger.

Lying next to the magician's bones and licking its glistening fur, grooming itself clean of blood. It paces the walls for a time after that, stretching, testing the air for something it detected earlier but now seems to have lost.

I have no choice but to watch it. Crushed behind the organ pipes, fighting to stay awake as the light dims, darkening the monster into a lustrous, moving body of oil. The red eyes burning.

It doesn't feel like sleep, but that must be what it is.

Outside, through the smashed stained glass windows, the dawn is stalled. I wait for it to build, to show how this day might be different from the last, but it only brightens enough to coat the world in gray sand.

The tiger is gone. Or is it? There are corners of the church I can't see, places where it may have curled up in the night. It's a hunter. It has time.

And it's after me.

I know because I've seen it before. When I was here last time and Ash took me down to the house on Alfred Street. She couldn't go inside, though she wanted me to. And when I ran I was stopped by a creature I couldn't properly see because of the baseball stadium's lights. But the eyes shone clear. Lit from within by fire.

I climb out from behind the organ pipes. Step through the door into the monochrome morning. The fog gauzy, metallic. Woodward almost empty except for a handful of distant human stragglers, pacing the sidewalk blocks.

Starting south again, I wonder if it would be smart to travel by way of the smaller, residential streets, then dismiss the idea. Woodward is the way downtown my father took, the way Ash went on her last birthday, the line that runs through the heart of Detroit. The devil you know.

The walking is slowed by the rough shape of the sidewalk, so I keep mostly to the street. The doors of the businesses along Ferndale's commercial strip are either closed or open or missing altogether, but nobody appears to go in or out. The few others out here occasionally stop to look in but eventually turn around to pace the same block they've just made their way down. For some, hell is window-shopping.

After an immeasurable time (the Omega still reading noon, or midnight) I make my way across the lanes of 8 Mile and into the city of Detroit. Just as in the living world, the downgrade is immediate. Fields on either side of Woodward. The remains of cinder-block sheds where the end-of-the-road businesses, the tow truck and demolition and self-storage lots once operated. A greater number of dead.

A number that doubles when I reach the quarter-mile stretch with Woodlawn Cemetery on the right and the concrete space of the State Fairgrounds on the left. As for the latter, parts of the midway still stand. An unmoving Ferris wheel. Rows of game stands, most with the roofs ripped off. A tilted Tilt-A-Whirl.

Some walk around the attractions, stopping to look at the rides or the Crown and Anchor wheel as if expecting them to start moving all on their own. One couple strolls hand in hand, looking lost. They never seem to notice the other. They never let go.

The trees on the cemetery side offer the promise of fresher air, as well as a place to rest that's out of the long view of Woodward. It's what has me joining the other shufflers, trying not to meet their eyes.

They try to meet mine, though.

I can feel their stares, varying in intensity, from puzzled to hateful. So far on my journey none have come close enough to touch me, which has me hoping this is a rule of the After.

There's a decorative boulder a couple hundred yards in and I sit, lean my back against the stone. It isn't comfortable. Not that it stops me from falling asleep.

Something hits my shoulder and I open my eyes. Three people stand over me who weren't there when I closed them.

A woman and two men. One curly-haired man in his twenties, the other shirtless and elaborately tattooed, maybe twenty years older. The woman, dark-skinned and with hair bleached yellow, could be anywhere between the two in age.

"The fuck," the younger man says.

"The *fuck*," the older man says in agreement. Then he kicks me in the face.

Mom was right. You can die when you're dead. You can also lose a tooth and spit it into your hand with a fire bell ringing in your head.

It's clear that if I don't get to my feet—if I don't do it *now*—they'll all start in and won't stop. The looks on their faces tell me. The light returning to their eyes, the nostrils stretched into circles. A strangely girlish, tittering laugh from the woman. That old excitement that comes with seeing that something interesting is about to happen.

I make a good decision by accident. Instead of trying to rise right away, I turn my back to them. A turtling move that allows me to use the boulder as a kind of ladder, my fingers finding ledges in the surface to lift against. At one point I grab a stone from the ground, clutch it in my fist. A weapon I forget about as soon as I pick it up. All this while their kicks find my back instead of my face.

Once I'm up I put one of my own feet to the rock and push back. Use my backpedaling weight to cut through their circle.

"You see 'at? Muthafuckin *see* 'at?" the older man says.

A quick look around. If I'm going to run—and I *am*, I'm going to run until they tackle me and boot me into jam—which way to go?

No one direction looks better than any other. It's because the activity of the last moments has attracted something of a crowd. A gathering of shufflers closing around the boulder, their expressions all doing the same thing. The turn from vacancy to seething rage.

And with it, faster steps. Their anger returning the full use of their limbs.

My legs were never sufficiently muscled for their length. The result being slow starts. But if I have the room, if the knees don't crap out, I can build to a gallop. Not unlike the zebra as it ran up to the turnstiles.

This is how I must look to those who now pursue me. Ungainly, panicked. An animal to pity for a second or two before starting after it.

The chase is quiet. No whoops, no *Get him!* or shouted orders. Just the pounding of all our feet on the hard earth. A herd on the move through the tombstones.

I'm going the wrong way.

This comes to me too late to be of any use. If the ones after me are fixed to Woodlawn Cemetery, if they aren't roamers, I should have tried to make it back to Woodward to see if the boundary held them back. Instead, I'm running deeper into the grounds.

What makes it worse is that now I'm lost. The snaking lanes that once let cars park close to visit loved ones' graves—loved ones who now flail after me—all lead back upon themselves. Every time I think one will take me to the main gate, it feeds into another circle with a named crypt in the center.

DODGE
HUDSON
COUZENS

I'm turning the corner on the last of these when I see a man standing outside a smaller crypt down a slope. Not starting after me, but raising his arm. Beckoning.

38

I go to him.

Keep my head lowered so the ones behind me might not see me on the way down. Rushing inside the smaller crypt at the bottom of the slope. Leaning against the cold stone wall as the man pulls closed the wood from a crate bottom he's fashioned as a door.

A few bands of silty light find their way through the slats, but it's almost as dark in here in the middle of the day as the church was at night. The man here with me but I can't see him. Can't hear him, either. Only the pounding steps of the dead outside. Some at a distance, guessing wrong as to which way I went. Others passing close.

And then they're gone. All but the one standing in the dark.

"Should've known I'd see you again," his voice says. "Nobody looking for her could come to a happy end, could they?"

He takes a step out of the corner. Younger than when I found him in the house on Arndt Street. The way he looked in his drama teaching days, when he was Henchman #3. When he was Dean.

"Do you know where she is?"

Malvo weighs this question in his mouth. "You're still looking for her?"

"Have you seen her?"

"Wait," he says, silencing me with a raised hand. "You came here to *find* her! See? I tried to *tell* you. *That* is the kind of thing that bitch can make a man do."

"I'm not doing this for her."

"Really? If money meant anything here I'd bet all I had that you're wrong."

He paces from one side of the darkness to the other, kicking stones against the walls.

"Why'd you help me?" I ask him, hoping he'll stop making noise. He doesn't.

"A familiar face. Plus I know what it's like. I'm new, too."

"They're after you?"

"Not as much as at first," he says. Arranges his features into a look of thoughtfulness. "Death is predictable. What happens *once* you're dead isn't."

"Why do they hate us in the first place?"

"It's like prison. The new ones get the worst treatment because they still smell like the outside. It's like you're rubbing their faces in it just by being here. Reminding them of life, when the only good part about being inside is that, once you get into the rhythm, it can help you forget."

Malvo sounds friendly. But the way he slows his pacing and faces me isn't.

"Why are you here? The cemetery," I say. "Why is this your place?"

"I'm not sure. I think it's because the Fairgrounds are across the street. That's where I'd *like* to go, but the ones here won't let me. Because they know."

"Know what?"

"That the midway is where a lot of the kids end up. The girls."

"Why do the ones here care about that?"

"Like I said, it's like prison," he says, and shrugs. His voice sharpening with the loss of patience. "Full of the worst motherfuckers in the world but there's still laws. And people like me? We're the rock bottom. Worse than the random killers or torturers or Ponzi schemers. We're *shit*."

Malvo pouts. A show of self-pity he glances up to see if I've noticed. If I'm on his side.

"You've found your place," I say. "Not the Fairgrounds. Here."

"Oh?"

"The worst of your life was the years you were sent away, and that's what this is. The penitentiary. Your identity exposed, not getting what you want most. You're meant to be here."

The pout is gone now. His hands drifting out from his sides as if to block any move I might make for the door.

"Let me ask again," I say. "Do you know where Ash is?"

"Why would I know that? You just said I'm stuck here."

"She might have visited. She's not like you or the others out there. She can move around wherever she wants."

Except the house, I think, but don't say. *She couldn't go into the place where you set the fire.*

Malvo's expression changes just like the ones who tried to hunt me down, like every other face I've seen.

"Why would I tell you?" he says. Not acting anymore, not charming Dean. He's Bob. Swallowing the taste of hatred in his mouth. "Why would I give a flying fuck?"

"To do something good after all the pain you've caused."

"Listen to you! *Pain*?" He laughs at this. "It's like I used to tell my girlfriends. *It doesn't hurt if it's a secret.*"

"It's not a secret that you killed my sister."

"I didn't kill her."

"Bullshit. You hung yourself."

"She *told* me to do that."

"You did everything she told you to?"

"Didn't you?"

Malvo is very close now. I make a move, a turn of the shoulders, and he slides the couple inches over to match it.

"Isn't that why you're here?" he says. "Because she wanted you to come?"

"Tell me who did it."

"That girl? Who knows? She was a walking billboard that said *Love me!* or *Fuck me!* or *Kill me!* depending on who looked at it."

Malvo lets his mind rest on this. Sighs like his memories of my sister were nothing but sweetness and sunshine. Acting again. It holds at bay the aggression that's seizing him. But not for long.

"Can I tell you something, Danny?" he says, a white line of spit ringing his lips. "I thought I wouldn't mind a little company over here. Someone who knew me back in the good old days. But you're kind of a *drag*, to be honest. *Who killed my sister? Tell me! Please!* Puts me in mind of a note from one of my directors. 'When you don't know what to do, do *something*.'"

He brings his hands even with his shoulders. At the same time, I back up, thinking I've left at least a foot between myself and the wall. But I'm already there.

"So what do you say?" Bob Malvo says as he locks his fingers around my throat. "How about we *do* something?"

Willa!

A thought-message that goes nowhere.

Eddie!

It's the boy's name that has me trying to punch Malvo's hands away. It doesn't work. Not even close.

But it reminds me that I still hold the rock. The one I'd grabbed when I was kicked awake. A stone the size and weight of a large marble, nothing more. Enough to give my fist ballast. Pushes the knuckles out, jagged and hard.

All I can hear is the sucking away of sound that precedes blackout, the floating orbs of light.

My fist swings up and I watch it as if from a distance. An event outside my control.

It finds the underside of Malvo's chin. I know the sound's back on when I hear the crack of teeth. His. Spat out against my face. One chip finding the corner of my eye so that I push blindly against him after his grip loosens on my throat.

Within seconds, we both discover that driving the other against the wall is a better tactic than a fistfight. For a time, there are only the bass notes of bodies meeting stone.

In one back-and-forth I give Malvo more room than I mean to. It allows him the space to drive at me, elbows up like the horns of a bull. I manage to jump aside before contact. His momentum, the missed hit, my own hands on his belt—all work together to see his head meet the granite behind me.

It barely slows him down. His frame straightening as he emits a hiss through his now missing front teeth.

All of which takes a little time. Time I use to knock the wooden door down and run over it into the gray light. Up the slope where I'm able to make a guess as to where Woodward might be and start toward it, arms pumping.

Malvo close behind. The hissing now a throaty gargle, as if he's preparing to sing.

Through the trees, one of the lanes widens where the administrative building sits, graffiti-tagged and roofless. Just beyond, the avenue's concrete river.

A dash toward it I'm not alone in making.

Other footfalls joining Malvo's now. All of them wordless. The whole earth trembling with the weight of their lengthening strides.

The idea that I'm not going to make it helps. Spurred on by hopelessness.

I jump off the curb. On my first step down, the toes of my left foot catch on a piece of upturned road and send me rolling to the median. As I go I catch sight of the crowd stopping at the edge of the cemetery's property line.

Malvo there before anyone. Hands reaching for me but legs planted to the ground.

From out of nowhere, my father's voice.

There's a border in the middle. An invisible line.

It's the same for the rest of them. Malvo, the two men and woman who ran me down, along with half a dozen others who watch me get to my feet and limp on. Across the way, at the edge of the Fairgrounds, the same hand-holding couple have come to see what the commotion's all about.

That's forever, Tiger.

For a moment, the two sides of the dead face each other across the divide. Curious only in the way of those spotted while speeding along the highway, those glimpsed pulling the mail from the box or hanging laundry on the line. Existences like your own on the face of it but different in ways you can't even guess at, and when they're gone, they're gone.

39

Thoughts are hard to hold on to in the After.

Basic facts of who I am as difficult to recall as the names of primary school teachers or second cousins or, in my case, the once memorized roster of the 1984 Detroit Tigers.

Lance . . . Parrish? He was the catcher. Chet Lemon, center field. Kirk Gibson. Or Kurt? Either way, born in Pontiac, Michigan.

I remember the team finished first that year with a .642 winning percentage, but not my mother's first name.

This must be the struggle of Alzheimer's, of old age, of time itself. The horror of feeling the details escape your grasp replaced by the greater horror that eventually you won't even miss them.

None of it as bad as forgetting the ones you love.

I keep Willa and Eddie with me as I make my way down Woodward toward the black towers. But even this comes with a cost. The more I think of them, the more difficulty I have remembering what I've come here to do. There isn't room for both.

One foot on the far side of the river and the other on your throat.

This comes back to me, though I can't remember from where. *You can't push her back. She can only be pulled.*

PAST THE FEATURELESS GOLF COURSE IN PALMER PARK, A FEW players scattered over the fairways, looking for lost balls in the quack grass around a drained pond. Then over McNichols Road, where Woodward loses its median and the north-south lanes join, the road wider but in even worse condition, some of the concrete slabs pointed straight up like an ancient wall. On either side of the avenue, dollar store after fast-food island after parking lot. The latter with more cars in them now, a littering of American product both recent and historical, so that an Escalade sits next to a Packard, an F-150 next to a Studebaker. All wrecks.

For a few blocks, in North End, things briefly improve. The Cathedral of the Most Blessed Sacrament still mostly intact, an anchor for the massive homes along Boston and Chicago boulevards. It takes a longer look to reveal the differences. A poplar tree growing up through a hole in a roof. A man in a tux and woman in a maid's uniform, dry-humping on a side yard tennis court.

Then it gets bad again.

Not just the damages to the landscape, the cinder-block bars and Check 'n Gos, but a chill in the air that has grown more solid over the past few blocks. The distance between where I started and where I am now has brought on a change of seasons, from dreary fall to dreary winter. With every mile I get closer to downtown the temperature drops another ten degrees. The fog hardening.

If I ever reach Alfred Street the ground will be frozen. So will I.

I'm crossing Grand Boulevard when I hear the roars again.

Hide.

Eddie's voice. Breaking through from wherever he is. Which means he's closer to this side than he should be.

Something's coming.

"No! Eddie? Go back!"

The sound of my voice echoed by an Amtrak overpass. The dead

233

seeking warmth under cardboard blankets raise their heads to see me shamble past.

Hide!

There's a car lot on the left. Jimmy Dale's Pre-Owned. Random stock here and there, along with piles of scrap metal. A chain-link fence, still upright, stands between the lot and the street. A vine of some sort has snaked through its honeycomb of holes, acting as additional cover. It'll have to do.

The problem is the fence. Climb over? Look for a gate? No time for either.

I'm about to run on when I spot a tear along one of the posts. Wide enough for a man to squeeze through if he doesn't mind getting grated by cut metal.

Another round of roars.

Now.

When I make it through to the other side, my chest, stomach, and legs crosshatched with cuts, I look for cover. If the beasts are as close as they sound, the sales building is too far away. There is only a sculpture of steel rods and fenders and car body parts, thirty feet to the right and against the fence.

I'm falling to my knees and scrambling around behind the pyramid of scrap when Red Eyes roars beneath the railway overpass. Its voice louder and deeper than the other two, thrumming and hypnotic.

There is no way to confirm whether it has seen me or not. Not without moving. And moving means it will hear.

Even thinking is a risk. Because if I can feel its thoughts, it must be reaching out for mine. And I *can* feel its mind. Subtle as radio signals picked up by the fillings in your teeth.

Quiet.

This is new, too. The whole of Detroit suspended in the airless silence of a vacuum.

How much time passes before I decide to crawl over and take a look out at the street? Enough for my hands and feet to go numb.

I wriggle through the dirt, staying low. Nothing there.

Maybe it thinks I've gone farther along than I have. Or it knows

I'm watching and will do some hiding of its own. It doesn't matter. I have to start walking again or freeze.

I come out from behind the piled metal. Start toward the gap in the fence. Feel something watching me.

My feet stop but my head turns.

Wolves.

Guard dogs of no discernible breed to begin with, but now, on this side, enlarged and mutated. Wolves combined with the grotesque creations of dollar store Halloween masks. Eyes sunk back in their skulls. One brown, one spotted like a cow, one black. Stepping out from what was once Jimmy Dale's office.

Even as I start to think of what I might do next, they spread apart. A widening semicircle that cuts me off from where I'd been hiding. A couple seconds later, one of them stands between me and the hole in the fence.

There is no going ahead. There is only what's behind me.

I swing around and run for whatever's there.

A Crown Vic sedan. Long and wide as a tugboat. Judging from the faded blue stripes along the sides, a decommissioned Detroit Police cruiser.

It's all simple now. I make it there, the door opens, the windows are still intact, I get in, and all of it holds. Or the wolves rip the feet off my legs.

The passenger side door is closer, but it's closed—possibly jammed, possibly locked—and I can see that the driver side door is ajar. I figure the odds of a sure thing are better than an unsure thing, even if I have to get to the other side.

The wolf-things close in behind me. Teeth chattering with excitement. The promise of meat.

I hit the front of the car instead of shearing around it, a painful meeting of fender and thigh. It doesn't stop me, though. My hip slides over the end of the hood and I find my feet again on the far side.

One of the creatures, the brown one, jumps onto the hood. Its teeth would be on my arm if its nails didn't slip on the smooth surface, a scratching dance that makes it snarl with fury.

I'm rounding the partly opened door when the black wolf comes out from behind the car. Behind me, the brown makes it off the hood. Lands on the spotted cow, who shrieks with surprise.

There's a fraction of time when all three see how easy it will be to take me down. Time enough to also see there will be a race between them as to who gets me first.

It's why, when they come at me, they jump earlier than they likely otherwise would.

I fall sideways into the driver seat. Grab the handle as I go. Most of me inside when I slam the door closed, but not all. Not the foot of my already injured leg. The foot the door closes on.

The brown is on it instantly. The teeth tearing neatly through the sides of my shoes. Sinking into skin. Pulling me out.

I'm another tug or two from being on the ground when the other two wolves fall upon the first.

It lets me pull my leg back in though it costs me a scream. Which returns the creatures' attention to how I might be removed from the car.

With a yank, the door clicks shut at the same time the monsters throw themselves against it. And again. Their heads used as battering rams against steel.

I try to move the foot that the brown chewed on. It throbs like a swarm of hornets are attacking it, but doesn't seem broken anywhere. If the pain can be tolerated, I can likely still put some weight on it.

So it can carry me where?

I'm not leaving this car with those leaping, howling things out there. And their seeing me here every time they jump up for a look only doubles their frenzy. Makes them run their heads against the door again.

After a while, it knocks some sense into them.

The spotted wolf jumps onto the trunk. The black onto the front hood. The brown takes running leaps at the rear passenger window on my side, which is open a few inches and already webbed with cracks. Pounding, scratching. The three of them in a race to find the way in.

I try to think of my family, the ones left behind. Summon a face or spoken word in their voices. But I can't remember their names. There is nothing but the wolves. Wailing with an almost pitiable need.

At the same time as the brown knocks a mug-sized chunk out of the rear window, the black smashes its snout through the front windshield. The teeth snapping two feet from my face even as the shards slice its jaws.

I don't want to think of her. But she comes anyway. Her name. The exhilaration she felt when she saw something was going to die.

"Ash?"

Curious.

She'd be interested to see which wolf finds my throat first. And while I called out for her, even as I reached out for her, she would feel nothing for me. Only disappointment if her pick didn't win.

And then, all at once, I'm not alone.

40

Someone sits in the passenger seat next to me who wasn't there a second ago. Not Ash. There isn't her smell, for one thing. And there isn't the swallowing sadness that comes before the confirmation that it's her.

A man. A uniformed cop with a moustache that suits his wide face. He's not oblivious to how bad this is—he sees the wolves-that-aren't-wolves as well as how they now see him, his eyes darting between their three positions. Yet his features remain open, the professional skill of communicating calm to others who need it.

Greg.

His name comes to me even if it doesn't return his wife's—my wife's—with it. Her first husband who took a bullet to the throat in his own home. *A good man*, she'd called him. A soul sent to a better place than this, but here all the same. Come here for me.

Things, feelings, people. Souls. Maybe they can go back and forth more than we think.

"I know who you are," I say.

He nods. A kindly, distinctly masculine gesture. A signal of peace between those who might otherwise have conflicting interests.

"I'd say we ought to get a drink somewhere," he says. "But I'm pretty sure this is a dry county. And you don't have the time."

The black wrenches its head out of the hole in the windshield and drives it back through. The whole snout in the car now, almost the ears, too. Once it gets past those it will come in to the shoulders. More than far enough for its teeth to find me.

"Here," Greg says. "You need this more than I do."

He reaches inside his Marcellus Police windbreaker and pulls out a gun. Not his service revolver, but a small Browning semiautomatic. He flips it over in his hand, smiles at the return of a memory.

Greg hands the gun over to me. The surprisingly heavy metal of a proper weapon, the density of purpose in the palm of my hand.

"We called it the Just In Case," he says.

I nearly thank him but he gives his head a slight shake to indicate it's not necessary. And then it's his turn to almost say something to me.

I know you loved them, too.

He opens the passenger side door and steps out of the car. The wolves pause to watch him walk away just as I do. A cop's untroubled saunter around the side of the sales building and he's gone.

Once he's out of view, the monsters start fighting to get in again.

Two of them do.

The brown through the rear passenger window, tumbling onto the bench seat. The black through the front.

The glass falls away from around the black's body at the same time I raise the Browning. It bites the hand that holds the gun. Its teeth cutting through skin as my finger squeezes off the shot.

The bullet explodes through its back. The creature releases its hold, looks at me like this was only a game and it can't believe I took it as far as I have. An expression it holds as its head collapses onto my lap.

I spin around and fire into the back of the car without looking.

The first shot misses the brown, but startles it. Gives me the chance to align my aim and put the next bullet into its skull.

Which leaves Spot.

Until a moment ago, it was banging away at the rear window. Now nowhere to be seen.

I open the driver side door and let it swing out a few inches. I've got the gun aimed at the gap but no teeth come snapping into it. Did the missed shot find it? It's possible that it lies on the ground at the end of the car but I don't think so. It was smarter than the other two. Using new tactics after it saw what the gun did to its brothers.

Kick the door open wide. Step out with the gun at arm's length, scanning the lot. When my left foot finds the ground it sends an initial note of pain straight up to the back of my head so intense it brings me close to passing out. Then, just as quickly, it recedes. Finds a throbbing rhythm I can just about manage.

I leave the Crown Vic behind, start backing up toward the fence where I found a way in. My eyes traveling around the edges of everything, looking for a shape to emerge from its hiding place. It's why, when the spotted wolf comes at me from behind and off to the side, I don't see it until it's too late. Running silently from the same pile of scrap I used for cover from the tigers. Plowing into me.

But it doesn't take me down.

My legs hold me against the impact and still do even as it clamps its incisors through my pant leg and pulls back. It wants to topple me over. Instead, I shoot it in the hip.

It lets go. I start backing away again, thinking I've got some time, but then it's charging at me. Its lame rear leg bouncing around like a hammer tied to a wire.

I shoot it in the chest.

It puts in another two strides before it falls.

The lot is quiet again except for the Browning, clicking and clicking as I keep pulling the trigger before dropping it next to Spot. Then I pass through the fence and start south without looking back.

41

'm expecting the gunshots and howls to have brought more people out along Woodward to see me. Instead, the blocks that follow are oddly emptied of movement. Perhaps the Detroit of the afterlife is like the living Detroit in this respect: when you hear trouble, you don't call 911 or come out to see what's going on, you mind your own goddamned business.

It's only after I've crossed the I-94 that I see people once again. Most of them standing at corners in Pistons and Lions wear, waiting for something that will never come to take them home. Others look like tourists. Out-of-towners in brightly colored golf shirts or floral skirts. One wears a money belt around his waist, another squints at a map she's holding upside down.

They're here because this section of midtown once attracted them here. A stretch of Woodward Avenue that has the Detroit Public Library on the one side and the Institute of Arts on the other. The white stone of both structures riddled with handprints and smears, loops and commas—not a word, not a name, not a picture—all of the same dark brown color. Graffitists who have used human feces for paint.

"That's all the high culture this town has left," I remember my father saying as we drove between the two buildings on the day he took me to his office. "Blink and you'll miss it."

It was a remark I didn't really understand at the time, but now see was directed not at the institutions themselves but the very character of the city. How little the place he'd poured his working life into had to show after the decades of prosperity and seemingly unstoppable growth, all of it so swiftly peeled away. The way Detroit would always be the Motor City even after the motors stopped being made.

The tourists stop to study me the same as the others do. I can feel their interest turning to something else, something I notice for the first time emits its own vaguely sulfurous odor. As before, I keep my eyes down. Don't look at them in the hope they'll let me pass.

I would guess, if this were the living world, it would be late afternoon now. Here, under the uninterrupted dome of cloud, the sun never shows itself, the shadows not lengthening so much as thickening.

The Ren Cen towers loom larger now, their curved skin visibly pocked where windows have been smashed out. Before them, the older, Art Deco office buildings look porous and brown, as though made of wet sand. In the gathering gloom, the Stars and Stripes hangs from a pole atop the First National, the flag shredded to a limp pom-pom.

I'm close enough to see the baseball stadium, too, set off to the east. The light towers surrounding the outfield wall like sentries.

The view from Alfred Street.

THE HOUSE IS STILL HERE. IF ANYTHING, IT'S IN BETTER SHAPE than it is on earth.

It doesn't need the steel posts to hold up its walls, and the distinctive turret at the corner of the building has not yet collapsed so that, in the lowering light, a degree of its former grandeur is returned to it. Because almost every other mansion along the street has been razed, it stands alone for hundreds of feet on every side. The solitude only adds to the suggestion of haughtiness, a refusal to be around others unworthy of its company.

The other difference is that the house has no boards nailed to its doors or windows. What air and light is available passes through its rooms, though from where I stand, where the sidewalk used to be, nothing can be seen inside.

When I leapt from my mother's car on our sixteenth birthday I didn't hesitate as I do now. Back then I had a feeling. An Ash feeling, therefore good as certain.

Now there's nothing. *Less* than nothing. A hollowness inside me I hadn't detected since coming here. Maybe I'm just noticing how I'm becoming like the others, losing myself as I come closer to finding my forever. Which may be here.

I enter the brown light of the house's front hall where the floor is less littered now, only low dunes of dust and tumbling bits of paper on the floor. The silence so dense I try to imagine something in it, the hum of another's blood in their veins, but the quiet only reasserts itself.

"Are you here?"

I sound sixteen again. Or younger still.

When nothing answers, I make my way to the hole in the floor. Somebody has left a wooden ladder where the stairs once went down. So lightless at the bottom I can't see where it touches ground.

I put a foot on the second rung. When it doesn't snap, I get into position and hold on to its sides. It squeaks in complaint but feels sturdy enough. With another couple descending steps I'm swallowed by increments of darkness.

It takes longer than I'd guess to touch bottom. The open rectangle above shrinking to something unreachable, the light at the end of a pier seen from a ship after it pulls away.

The moment I'm standing on the earth floor I only want to start back up. But all at once I'm shaking so hard I don't think my hands could keep their grip on the wood.

Because it's cold down here.

Because I'm terribly afraid.

When my vision adjusts to the dark I blink into the cellar's space and guess where its corners are. Eventually, different shades of black become readable and I start away from the ladder. Hands out in front me.

"I know you're here."

This isn't true. But it feels like the sort of provocation that might bring her out. A statement of superior knowledge she'll be tempted to challenge.

"I'm not scared of you anymore."

It triggers a noise. The shuffle of feet over the slats of the floor overhead. Followed by the long scrape of wood on wood.

I turn around in time to see the bottom end of the ladder disappearing up through the cellar opening.

I grab for it, jump, both too late. The ladder clatters to the floor above.

Another shuffle. Someone steps closer to the hole. A lone silhouette leaning over to peer down at me.

A woman.

I was right, I think. *Those kitten-pretty looks don't age well.*

I try another jump. Straight up, my hands stretching to find the edge. And again. A good foot short each time.

"You were always tall," Lisa Goodale says. "But not *that* tall."

She waits for me to collect my strength, to stand straight after resting my hands on my knees. At least I guess that's what she's waiting for. I'm wrong.

Another set of steps over the floorboards. Another figure coming to stand next to Lisa.

"Michelle?"

"Hiya, Danny."

"I thought—I saw you in the school theater."

"You did. But it turns out the show was *here* the whole time."

Neither of them make a move. Just look down as if politely waiting for me to ready myself for an already agreed-upon demonstration.

"You never turned around," I find myself saying. "You didn't call me on her birthday because you were worried where she might have gone. You knew."

"It wasn't *all* a lie, Danny," Michelle says.

"We *did* stop following her," Lisa says.

"Until we started following her again," Michelle says.

I look around. The cellar dark in the way of the bottom of the ocean, pressurized and frigid. Even if I could find my way through it there's no way out down here.

New sounds from above shoot my head back up. A third figure joins the other two, shadowing the hole so that their outline is all that can be seen.

"Long time no see, Danny," Winona says.

"Let me out of here."

"Why? I thought you wanted to find out about your sister. Well, your wish has come true."

The three of them inch closer together as if for warmth.

"So tell me," I say, trying to hold them there with words. "Tell me what happened."

"We stayed way back. She never looked around, not once," Michelle says. "And when we got to the corner, we saw her come in here. Waited five, maybe ten minutes, and came in after."

"Didn't she hear you?"

"We were quiet," Lisa says. "Quiet as mice."

"Mice wearing slippers," Winona says.

"And she was a little distracted," Michelle adds.

"By what?"

"Trying to stand up straight. Broke her ankle. Her foot swinging around, swollen up the size of a football," Winona says. "She must have fallen down there, landed where you are now. And she was trying to jump up or find a way out, just like you."

"Did you help her?"

"I think you know the answer to that one," Lisa says.

"Why not?"

"Couple reasons," Michelle says. "The gas, for one. The whole place was doused with it. Kind of hard to get a whole breath in."

"And the body," Winona says. "Meg. Lying at Ash's feet. All bashed up. You didn't have to score too high on the SAT to put it together."

"Oh Jesus. Oh *Christ*."

"You believe in that stuff, Danny?" Lisa says. "Your sister sure didn't."

"She murdered Meg Clemens?"

"See?" Michelle says. "You came to the same conclusion we did."

"How?"

"Smashed in her head with something hard, be my guess," Lisa says. "It was a mess."

"Why? Why did Ash kill Meg?"

"Who knows?" Winona answers with a shrug. "People said Mr. Malvo was fucking the two of them. Maybe she was jealous."

"Or maybe she just wanted to," Michelle says.

"For the hell of it," Lisa says.

"So to speak," Winona says.

"No. *No!*"

"That's what *she* said, come to think of it," Lisa says. "She looks up, sees us up here, figuring all her shit out. '*No!*' Like she knew what we were going to do before we did."

This stops me. The cold presses in hard so that it's a fight to get the next words out.

"What did you do?"

Winona lowers her eyes to me. Gives me the pitying look of the smart girl in class who has yet again underestimated how dumb other people can be.

"We put an end to it," she says.

In living time, Winona could only have joined the others two days ago. Yet the three of them stand together with the weird familiarity of sisters. It would be easy to read them wrong. To see them as harmless, the grins on their faces a signaling of fun about to be had.

And then, as I watch, they change.

The years drawn away from their skin, their bodies altering shape.

It's like a thousand layers are invisibly pulled off them until their real selves are revealed. Their sixteen-year-old selves.

"Which one of you started the fire?"

"I guess you could say we all did," Lisa says.

"And she knew it was you? She saw you do it?"

"Right in front of her fucking eyes," Lisa says.

"It's why we're here," Michelle says.

"Why we'll never leave," Winona says.

I almost pass out. Something about this place drains me of my capacity to move, to speak, to think. As if I'm melting into it, solidifying. Losing myself as I become the house. It's the same thing that's happened to the three of them up there, to Bob Malvo, to my mother, to everyone in the After who can't move beyond the borders of where they've been put. I'm a dead tree being planted in the last cellar on Alfred Street.

Ash didn't want me to come inside the house to find out who started the fire. She wanted me here, with her.

"You're killers just like her," I say finally.

"We thought we were putting an end to something. Teenage vigilantes. Protecting others, y'know?" Winona says, puffing her chest in self-mockery.

"Because of what she did to Meg."

"Because of who Ash *was*," Michelle corrects again. "You knew it better than anyone, Danny. She was just getting started. A murderer at sixteen. She was on her way."

"So how'd you do it?"

"She was going to burn this shit down," Lisa jumps in to answer, liking this part. "Gas *everywhere*, right? That was her plan. Destroying the evidence. Meg's body. God knows there's enough arsons in Detroit that nobody would dig around much. It didn't have to be *perfect*. The fire trucks would take an hour to even get here. Ash knew all that."

"Just like we did," Michelle points out.

"Just like we did," Lisa continues. "When I looked at Winona and

Michelle, I could tell they knew what I was about to do. I could tell they wouldn't stop me, that they would keep it a secret forever. It was as clear as if we'd said it all out loud. I was smoking back then—Newport menthols, remember them? How kids said they helped keep your breath fresh?—so I had a lighter with me."

"Oh, she was cool. Cool as a Newport," Winona says with a rehearsed laugh, the kind that comes after a frequently repeated joke.

"*Whoosh!*" Michelle says, making an exploding motion with her hands.

"That bitch was dead," Lisa says, nodding.

"And then you bicycled back up Woodward, but not as far as the pay phone at the zoo," I say. "That would have taken too long."

"Maybe you're not so dumb," Winona says.

"We used the phone at the Medical Center," Lisa says.

"My quarter," Michelle says.

"You used it to call me."

"Following orders," Lisa says.

"How do you mean?"

"It was the last thing she said to us from down there," Winona says. "The *only* thing she said."

"'*Get Danny!*'" Michelle screams, a perfect copy of Ash's voice. "'*Get my brother!*'"

"Isn't that fucked?" Lisa says, bringing her hands together in a single clap. "Not 'Help me' or 'Call 911.' She just asked for *you*."

I'm sufficiently distracted by this thought that, at first, I don't notice the fluid dripping down on me, splashing on the ground, a small waterfall around the edge of the opening in the floor above. Gasoline. I look up to see it pouring out of a can Lisa swings around, grinning.

"Why are you doing this?"

"Because you came back, Danny," Michelle says.

"And she said if you ever did, we should keep you here. Like you *should* have been kept here," Winona says. "Except you cheated. You went back."

"That sounds like something Ash would say."

"It *is* something she said," Lisa says, putting the can down when it's empty.

"You don't have to. You're free of her now."

"*Free?* She has more power here than she ever did when we were kids. She was always special," Winona says. "But here, her specialness is . . ."

"Fully realized," Michelle says, finishing the thought.

"That's why she can move around," I say, figuring it out as I speak. "Wander. Unlike the rest of them. Unlike you. She's not damned. She's a demon."

"I've never really used that word to describe her," Michelle says.

"Doesn't mean you're wrong, though," Winona says.

"Who cares what she is? We gotta do what we gotta do," Lisa says, and pulls her lighter out of her pocket.

And just like the last time, without a pause, she lights it with one turn of the flint and lets it drop.

42

I stumble out of the way of the falling flame. Get far enough that when the lighter splashes into a puddle of fuel and ignites, making the sound of a folded bedsheet snapped open to its full size, I don't go up with it, too.

The first flame shoots straight up through the hole, licking the sides, starting a new fire on the first floor. When it lowers it widens at the same time. Searches for something to connect itself to down here. Finds a pile of oily rags to the right, some ripped-up floorboards to the left. Ignites them both.

I can't see the three girls because of the smoke, even if they're there. Something tells me they're not. This is a house fire in Detroit. They likely wait outside, watching from the sidewalk the way others do on Devil's Night. Enjoying the show of destruction that people here always describe the same way.

It's cheaper than the movies.

The heat knocks me back into the corner. The cellar alive in dancing oranges and reds soon obscured by black fog. The smoke reaching down my throat. Writhing and heavy.

There's no way out by going forward. No way behind, either. Only a single window between two rafters, too high to reach and too small to fit through even if I could.

A figure steps toward me from out of the smoke.

A girl.

She's come to burn with me. Twins again.

Backlit by small explosions of fire so that her face is hard to see in detail, though there's light enough to see it isn't Ash. It's the girl she murdered. Meg Clemens. Clumps of soil wormed with small yellow roots clinging to her T-shirt and jogging shorts. Hair matted, skin bloodless and thin as a plastic corner store bag.

The dead, risen from the dead.

Though this isn't her place. Like Greg in the car lot, she's come here for me.

She raises her hand. I don't have the strength to resist her if she means to strike me or pull me close. So I watch. A finger stiffening straight to point directly behind me. Her eyes squinted closed as if against a blazing sun, but knowing where the cellar window is all the same.

"I can't reach it," I tell her. The words starting a painful series of coughs.

Meg comes closer without waiting for me to find my breath again. Locks the fingers of both hands together. Bends and lets the hands swing like a stirrup.

"I'm too heavy," I say.

Now, Danny.

It's Meg, but not her voice. That's been taken from her. It's her soul—there's no other word for it—that reaches me. A girl who liked working on the school paper and singing on a stage, someone who was blessed with a handful of talents but didn't use them to make others feel unlucky the way others born with good luck did. Meg Clemens wanted to *live*. And then she met Ashleigh Orchard and accepted her invitation to come to an abandoned house on Alfred Street—an offer of peace, a chance to *work things out*, to be *friends*—and found the end of that life in a part of Detroit she had never seen before that day.

Now.

I put my foot into the cup of Meg's hands. Her knees almost buckle at half the weight I put in them, but the fingers stay locked. They'll break apart when I stand on them and they have to lift me up a foot and a half for me to grip the window's ledge.

Yet that's just what she's doing.

Lifting me before I'm even ready for it. Strong and untouched by fire even as the first licks of flame stroke the backs of my legs and a howl dries to nothing in the superheated air.

Meg lifts me up until my head is even with the window, the glass missing though a few orange shards remain. There might be room for my head and shoulders to squeeze through but not enough leverage for hands to pull myself out.

I try. Prove myself right.

Nails biting into the hard ground of the house's backyard but getting nowhere. My head out, sipping the night's coldness, but the rest of me still hanging against the cellar wall.

Then I'm sliding forward. Pushed. Meg lifting my feet with both her hands, getting me out to below my ribs so that I have the leverage to claw the rest of myself onto the ground.

I end up rolled onto my back. Blinking up into the black of what, in life, is understood as sky, but here is just the end of things.

The house shrieks.

As the fire eats through the wood the foundation shifts, a grinding of materials that comes out as an utterance of grief. If I don't move soon the whole building will come down on me. But first I'm crawling back to the window. Looking through to find Meg still there. Her eyes open now, finding mine. The fire encircling her as if waiting for permission to proceed.

"Why?" I ask, though I mean only to thank her.

She's your twin. Not you.

The flames devour her all at once. She stands unmoving at their center like a wick. The light a cone rising up from her, yellow and high.

She isn't you.

The heat knocks me back. Followed by a tentacle of flame, reaching over the ground, pursuing me as I crab-walk away.

When I'm a hundred feet from the house I'm stopped by the low remains of a brick wall. Part of the original stables that were here when the house was first built, before motors and assembly lines. It lets me prop myself against it and watch the fire eat. Taking Meg along with every other memory connected to its walls and floors. The past itself burned to nothing.

Where are you, Sister?

Ash had no associations in life, only wants. As for love? She was incapable of feeling any herself, and there were only two people who she needed it from. She had mine, was born with it. But the other was denied her.

What place was forbidden to you? Where is the one door you most wished to open?

The baseball stadium's lights go on. An instant brightness that obliterates what was visible of the skyline a moment ago.

Except for the round towers.

Black and broad-shouldered. Holding high their two blue letters like a calling. Like an answer. Telling me where she is.

43

There's a small crowd on Alfred Street when I come around from the back of the house. I don't see Winona, Lisa, or Michelle among them, not that I study the faces, trying not to attract attention from where it's currently held by the fire.

Less than a hundred yards on, a deafening crash turns me around to see the house falling in upon itself. A tornado of sparks spiraling into the chalkboard night.

When I make it to Woodward, the cold has returned along with the shivering, even with the burns to the lower half of my body. The stadium's lights remain on, so the streets and structures of the city's core are glazed in tarnished silver, their shadows stretched miles to the west.

There's an underwater quiet as I cross the Fisher Freeway and enter downtown proper. My stride slowed as if pushing through denser matter. The air halfway to stone, to ice.

It didn't seem I would make it the thirteen miles from my Royal Oak bedroom to here, yet I have. The last mile to the black towers is a different matter, though. A distance made impossible not only by injury but the city itself. A resistance I can feel in the ground, grasping at my ankles with every step.

I will keep going for the ones I have come here for, their faces now erased along with their names.

For love.

Love was the only skill that lay beyond Ash's reach. But when it came to our father, she yearned for his attention with an intensity that was something akin to it. She didn't care about acting or ballet or piano or glittering report cards or any of the other things she was effortlessly good at. It gave her no pleasure to excel, not in itself. Yet she did all those things. She did them for him. So that he could see her superiority and she, in turn, could mistake his admiration (something she could grasp) for affection (something she could not).

The more she performed for him, the greater the distance he removed himself from her. He knew what she was before anyone else did. From the first moments of her life, after she was miraculously returned from near death and the nurses handed his baby daughter to him and he looked into her blue eyes and saw nothing, felt nothing, recognized her as nothing, he saw how she would be a thing to be contained. Failing that, a thing to be denied.

I know all this because he told me. In those years when there were only the two of us in the house on Farnum Avenue, he confessed to having knowledge of his child that he didn't know what to do with.

"She would have killed, Danny. She had a life of taking life ahead of her," he told me once at the kitchen table, dry-eyed. "I saw that while I changed her diapers or fed her stewed plums or held her on my knee. And I saw something else, too. How I would never be able to pretend I *hadn't* seen it."

At the time, I assumed Ash was only a secondary reason that explained why my father pulled away from his family. There was work, I thought. The diminishing sales of Made in America cars adding pressure to the upper-floor guys like my dad, looking for costs that might be cut, aware that their own jobs might be among them. Not to mention his wife's drinking, his cowering son, the whole midlife trap. But none of that pushed him to make a second home—his true home, however solitary—on the forty-second floor of GM's world headquarters in the Renaissance Center. That was Ash.

And Ash knew it.

That's where I have to go now. Up there behind the smoked glass of the tallest tower, the one that holds the blue letters for the whole underworld to see. It was where she longed to be more than anywhere else—not in our father's workplace, but with *him*, a partner to his secret thoughts, a daughter he would put his arm around and introduce as such instead of standing apart from her and letting his wife be the one to say her name aloud.

A COUPLE BLOCKS ON, WOODWARD OPENS UP INTO THE SEMICIRcle of Grand Circus Park. The windows of the buildings—the Broderick, the Kales—now close enough to see as a thousand opportunities for someone to look down at me. Me, the sole walker making his way past the patches of earth where trees once grew, the Edison Fountain now a rust-stained crater.

A light.

White and electric and strong, coming out from behind a parking facility on Broadway. Flying thirty feet above the ground.

A dragon.

This is the thought that comes first.

A beast of the air.

For a second the brightness falls directly on me and I'm blinded by it, held motionless like a forest animal crossing the road before it's struck.

When the light is thrown elsewhere I see it's followed by other, duller squares of illumination. Which makes it more snake than dragon. One that's ingested hundreds of humans, their faces looking out from along its length.

The People Mover monorail. Vacant in the living Detroit. Packed tight here.

The train glides into the Grand Circus station a couple stories over the sidewalk. The doors open.

Nobody gets off any of the cars. It is their place. Circling downtown, taking on new passengers from time to time—I watch one, a woman who drops her shopping bags on the platform and gets on—but none disembarking. With the passing of time there will only be more strangers to squeeze against, less air to breathe.

The doors close and the train starts away. Rounds southward again toward the river and is gone.

I'm expecting the appearance of the People Mover to lure others out from the shadows, but the plaza remains empty. But as I continue south, I'm more certain of being observed. The century-old office blocks of downtown, once the architectural pride of the nation and now little more than brick shells, leaning toward me as I walk. Trying to hear my thoughts.

And what would they hear if they could?

I'm coming for you. And when I find you, you're not going to like it.

It's only me trying to convince myself. Pushing the fear away with words.

It doesn't come close to working.

At the corner of Woodward and Grand River, I stop in front of the smashed-out window of Eastern Wig & Hair. I remember it from when I was a kid: the smooth plastic heads arranged on tiered displays, all wearing different curls and beehives and ponytails. On the rare occasions I walked this strip with my mother, I'd ask if I could "look at the heads," and she would bring me here, never asking what interested me about them. If she had, I would have said they looked like Ash to me. Not individually, but collectively. Sculpted faces adorned with different looks, different moods, different appeals.

The heads are still here, though the wigs they wear are filthy and balding. Behind the tiered display stand four female mannequins. A couple missing arms. All white. Alabaster ghouls.

I start on again.

But not before one of them moves.

When I check back to confirm it, I see that they're all moving now. And that they're not mannequins.

They fix their eyes on me.

I spin around too fast. Nearly lose my balance, recovering by diving forward and hoping my feet can catch up. The four of them twenty feet behind.

Cut right a block on and find myself on the street beyond the outfield wall of the ballpark. The lights still on.

If there's a way in, there may be somewhere to hide.

I duck into the nearest gate. Dance sideways through the turnstile, past the overturned concessions to the closest archway and out onto the concrete deck at the top of the rows of seats. Some of them occupied, I see now. Maybe a few hundred dotted throughout the stadium designed to accommodate forty thousand. All of them watching the events on the field.

I have to step forward and take a seat in the back row to see.

The white baselines and foul boundaries mostly obscured by dust, the grass brown. Only the pitcher's mound recognizably remains. A circle of pocked earth like an anthill.

There's a game going on. But it's not a baseball game.

People running. A quick count puts them at six. Some injured, dragging broken legs or holding hands against open wounds. As they try to find a place to hide in the wide-open diamond, they step around the bodies of the already fallen. One man halved so that one part lies in the left outfield, the other in the right.

At first I can't see what they run from. Then I do.

Red Eyes steps out from where home plate used to be. Lopes after the closest prey, a barefoot woman in a sweat suit. Brings its teeth down on her head, snaps her neck, and drops her.

Some of the people in the stands clap, a sparse and echoing *pock-pock-pock*, but most remain still in their seats. Watching the monster start after the man with the broken leg who is now pathetically scratching at the outfield wall.

I bend as low as I can and make my way along the row.

A shriek from the field.

Pock-pock-pock . . .

At the next aisle, I start up.

But Red Eyes hears. Swings around. Spots me.

It bounds across the field and leaps into the stands. Jumping off the backs of seats. A few sections over and slowed by the uneven surface, but coming fast nevertheless.

I run down the ramp and out through the gates. At Madison, a half block on, I check over my shoulder. See the tiger come out of the gates and spot me right away. Digs in and comes hard.

The floating lights appear again. The People Mover, coming in toward the Broadway station. The stairs up to the platform another twenty yards on.

I take them at a run, propelled up the first flight without feeling the steps under my feet. The second flight is the opposite: the steps doubled in height, both hands grabbing at the railing, hauling me up.

Above, the train stops at the platform. The doors slide open.

Wait for me.

Red Eyes slams into the base of the stairs. Squeezes through the frame and starts up. Its claws scratching at the concrete steps like knives on slate.

I make the platform. The train's brakes hiss as they're released. The cars filled with the dead looking out at me. Witnessing my dash for the doors, now sliding closed.

44

It almost works.

I'm halfway in when the doors catch me at the shoulder, sandwiching me down the spine. A second later, they open automatically. It gives me time to jam myself in.

It also gives the tiger time to burst out of the stairwell.

The doors close again. The train eases away as the creature skids on the platform, bumping against the side of my car. It considers leaping on top, but decides against it. Watches the train travel south. Its tail flicking in irritation.

It takes a second to find me through the window in the door. When it does its whole body stiffens. The mouth opens and its tongue comes out, polishing the length of its lower teeth. Then it starts down the stairs.

Not in defeat. Coming after the train.

The cars roll slightly as they pick up to their sluggish maximum speed.

Go, you piece of shit. Go! GO!

Wishing doesn't make the shattered buildings and bombed-out parking lots pass any quicker. And I can't spot Red Eyes on the streets below, either.

For the first time since I boarded I turn away from the glass and meet eyes with my fellow passengers. *All* of their eyes. Because they're looking at nothing but me.

A big guy toward the rear of the car with a bandana wrapped around a head missing both its ears muscles toward me, squeezing through the crowd. Others who are closer—a young woman wearing broken glasses, a teenaged boy with half his body clothed, the other black from burns—pressing in as well. A hundred in this car alone. Strangers locked in their own looping regrets and with nothing in common aside from having this circling of Detroit's financial district be their place in the After. Until I joined them.

I turn my back to them. It doesn't stop them from crushing in. And instead of keeping my elbows out and trying to hold the ground I have, I slip back into them.

Because the train is stopping at the Greektown station. The doors about to open. If I'm next to them I'll spill out and they won't let me back on.

The passengers don't seem to be expecting my voluntary backstep into their arms. They hold me up without putting their hands on me, as if I'm a carrier of disease.

The doors open. None get on, none get off. The doors close.

That's when the big guy with the missing ears finally reaches me.

He starts by trying to dig the eyes out of my head. One hand grabbing my hair and the other planted on my face, the thumb working for the leverage required to gouge in.

My scream startles them. Even the bandana guy pauses a moment to shake his head. It doesn't seem he'd be able to hear anything with those ear holes of his, but my voice reaches him. Not that it inspires any pity. Seconds later, he's at me again. His callused thumb pumping at the air in front of me.

This time, I don't let him get my hair. He takes out his frustration by punching me in the face. It seems to lighten his mood. Something like a smile moves his lips around.

Then he punches me again.

A glance out the windows shows the train making the corner that leads into the Renaissance Center station. My stop.

The doors only four feet away. But three rows of passengers between me and them.

I time it so that I crouch down and start plowing through just as the train eases to a stop. When I hit the ones between me and the doors they fall back into the ones behind them, some giving way as a result.

None of them shout or snarl or speak. It occurs to me as I break free of them and the doors close behind me that, for the whole time I was on the train, none made a single sound.

Except for me. My shouts. My blood-spitting breaths.

Which is all there is to hear in this place, too.

A concrete hallway the width of Woodward Avenue that leads to the Ren Cen's main atrium. On the walls, forty-foot-long photos of GM cars and trucks from over the years. A Sierra overlooking the Grand Canyon, a Corvette zipping across salt flats, a Cadillac emptying its tanned, tartan-slacked passengers at the front doors of a golf clubhouse. Images that have all been stabbed and slashed and smeared as if attacked by monkeys armed with knitting needles.

I remember this place when it was the future.

My father introduced it this way whenever we drove by, whenever the towers were pointed out by a rare visitor to our home or if he spotted them during the intro to the suppertime news.

"That's the future, right there," he'd say, with a hint of bitterness, as though with his pride came the anticlimax of knowing it wouldn't get any better than this, that his employer, his city, his driving-around-for-the-hell-of-it America had nowhere to go but into more and more acute realizations of how little time it had left.

To me, the Ren Cen looked like the future, too, though a cartoon version of it, the cylindrical, reflective structures like something a champagne glass spaceship would putter toward on *The Jetsons*. That was from the exterior. On the inside, it left a similar impression to the one I have now: too wide, too hard, too easily aged. Something built to be ahead of its time, which doomed it to be a monument to obsolescence.

After a time, the hallway slopes up and feeds into the atrium. An immense open space that, through a shattered window on the far opposite side, offers a glimpse of the frozen river, gray and snowless. From the level I'm on, the atrium plunges down to a concrete floor a hundred feet below. I take a look over the side. Before rearing back from vertigo I glimpse what's left of the display laid out on the basement exhibition floor: a scale model of Detroit made out of unpainted metal, CITY OF STEEL spelled out in a circle around it. The baseball stadium wide as a toilet bowl. The downtown buildings tall as a man.

Once the waves have subsided from my vision, I scan the space for a way up. Other than the stairs (wherever they might be), only one: the white column on the opposite side, an artery of elevator shafts rising up seventy-three stories.

Little chance the elevators would still be running. But it's worth a check.

I take a second to judge which is the best way—right or left—to get to where they are. The atrium is structured as a series of tiered balconies circling the building's core, multiple viewpoints from which employees and visitors were meant to admire the showroom of product, cars and trucks sitting on floating islands. I'm surprised to see that some of them are still here. A Chevy Volt furry with dust beneath a SOMEBODY HAS TO BE FIRST banner. Somewhat closer, a minivan directly across the abyss on the right even has passengers inside. A family. Dad behind the wheel, Mom next to him staring at the horizon, brother and sister visible through the open side door playing lifeless video games in the bench seat behind. Realistic wax statues fixed in expressions of middle-class boredom, the faraway stares and private thoughts of an interminable road trip.

They turn at the roar before I do.

The dad now slapping at the wheel, pumping the gas. The mom urging him on by saying the same thing, though not out loud—a *Harry!* or *Hurry!*—that I can lip-read. Trying to get the thing to *move*.

When it sees me, the beast roars again.

Red Eyes pauses at the bottom of the slope I'd just made my way up, a hundred feet away. Panting from the chase. The tail thrashing against the hallway's ceiling.

This time, it doesn't wait. Neither do I.

I head right. If I make it to the minivan I can close the doors, barricade myself inside the Dodge Caravan along with the terrified Midwesterners who probably died trapped in one and now call it their afterlife home.

Not that it will stop the tiger from ripping the roof off and flaying all five of us.

Not that I'll make it halfway there in the first place.

The monster bursts onto the concourse. I can hear its claws slide on the sheer, polished floor as it makes the turn. Bounds after me.

There are no exits or doors between me and the minivan. The only way out is over the side of the chest-high parapet to the floor below.

I try to scream but the cold steals it away the moment it passes my lips. Only the tiger is permitted a voice here, this close to the river, this close to the end of everything.

It's why, when I feel it, I say nothing.

A bubble of warmth I run through, brief and inexplicable as a pocket of heat that strokes your skin when swimming in a lake. It stops me. Not its strangeness, but the sensation it leaves me with. A wallop of thoughts and emotions, swirling and unreadable. The mark of the human.

A presence here that wasn't here a moment ago. Not meant to be here. One that, like me, has made the journey in the name of another.

45

The boy stands between me and the tiger.

Eddie's back to the beast, eyes on mine, at once finding strength in me and lending me strength of his own.

It's not the sight of him that returns his name to me. It's the memory of what he means, the commitment to something other than the self, the ungovernable mess love leaves behind.

I see the boy and I remember being alive.

Eddie knows the tiger will reach him in the next second or two, that it sees him and is deviating its course a single stride in order to strike him down, but he doesn't move. He has come here for this. He will let the beast take the moment required to cut him in half so that I might have a moment more.

Eddie!

I don't make a sound no matter how wide I open my mouth, no matter how hard I push the name out of me.

He climbs up onto the edge of the balustrade. It forces the tiger to skid hard to the left to reach him. The great back legs pushing the head up to sink its teeth into the boy when he jumps.

It could be a slip, a miscalculation, an accident that has an unimaginable result.

Except it isn't.

Eddie pushes himself off into the atrium's empty space just as the beast lunges at him. Its front-loaded weight carries the creature forward, the jaws still snatching as it, too, tumbles over the side.

For a sliver of time they are both suspended. The tiger awkward and flailing against the inevitability of its fall. Eddie still. Arms and legs extended as if ready to be met by water.

Then they're gone.

I rush to look over the side but it takes a while to get there. The nightmare slow motion that stretches out the most terrible revelations.

It takes a further moment to figure out the puzzle on the floor below.

Red Eyes is there. The tiger's body twisted in a way that makes it look like two or three tigers atop one another, one head visible, looking up. Dead. It's not the fall that's killed it, it's Detroit. The model CITY OF STEEL's towers speared through its rib cage, its neck. The enormous skull spilling its contents out after being smashed open on the miniature office buildings of Woodward Avenue.

Eddie is nowhere to be seen.

There's no way he could have walked away from the fall, so the only place he could be is under the tiger. Crushed. But maybe not. Maybe shielded by the struts of the Penobscot and Guardian Buildings.

I find the stairs beyond the minivan and fly down them, leaping four steps at a time and shouldering into the wall at every landing. At the basement level I fall, tripping on a pipe exposed through a hole in the foundation. It feels like something cracks in my leg, not that I hear it. Not that I hear anything but my speaking, beating heart.

Eddie . . . Eddie . . . Eddie . . .

More of the tiger's insides now spilled over the model city so that the streets are awash in its blood. The beast so heavy it has up-rooted many of the structures it fell upon, but not entirely flattened them, so that there is a space of three of four feet between it and the ground. This is where Eddie would be if he survived. Or if he didn't.

Either way, he's not here.

DING!

Across the atrium's floor, one of the glass elevators—missing all of its glass now—opens its doors. Nobody inside. Waiting for me.

Two thoughts, both arriving at the same time, both seemingly inarguable.

One, Ash sent the elevator for me. And if I step inside it will take me to her.

Two, I can't leave without finding Eddie first.

And then a follow-up consideration, less certain than the first two, but persuasive all the same.

I'll never find Eddie, not on this side. Because if he's dead, this isn't his place.

If he died in the hospital in Boston, he would have gone to a different place, the best day of his life, whatever that would be. Pushed on the swings by his mother in the playground in Marcellus. Playing soccer with his dad after he came home from a shift still wearing his uniform, the smooth leather holster, the shining badge. Something from the time before he met me and Ash was introduced to his life.

Which means he *willed* his way here.

Which means he did it for me.

I walk to the elevator and step inside.

46

I press the button for the forty-second floor but I don't have to, the doors closing on their own, the elevator rising before being told where to go. As I drift up, I watch the monster's body shrink on the floor below, its red eyes now lifeless and dark as buttons. Gone to a deeper hell where it will hunt again. Where it will exist for eternity as something worse.

The elevator passes through the atrium's roof and I'm knocked back by a blast of arctic air. Below, the river is gun-gray, its surface mottled by what looks like spattered paint—browns and blacks and whites—that I know to be the faces of the dead. The damned of the damned, staring up through the ice.

That's forever, Tiger.

It's like he knew. Like my father tried to tell me what every father tries to tell his children without frightening them, coming at the subject sideways. An effort to say that while there is an end, it only means we should live as hard as we can while we're here. *Not like me,* he was trying to say. *I want you to live better and more awake than me.*

I thought I didn't know what he meant when he said those things, yet I remembered them, cling to them still.

There's a border in the middle. An invisible line.

My mother left me a watch. My father a puzzle of words.

DING!

The doors open.

From the hallway, the stale smell of printer ink and recycled air. The perspiration that comes not from physical exertion but stress, the sourness of human worry left in the carpet, cleaved to the ceiling tiles.

As soon as I step out of the elevator the doors close behind me. I don't even try to throw my hand in to stop them. There is only here, the room I'm already starting toward. There's only the unmeasurable now.

It still looks like a corporate workplace—the interior modular desks, the exterior offices where the management worked their phones and screens—but one left in a hurry, an evacuation from which none returned. There's papers on the surfaces, computer keyboards, name tags fixed to the walls next to doors, calendars pinned to the sides of cubicles. All blank. Arranged as if by the hands of those who once came here every day, but all trace of their presence erased. Like they were ghosts even for the time they were alive.

My dad's office is second from the end. I remember that because his boss had the larger unit, a man whose first name I never knew as he was referred to exclusively as "Henley, the sonofabitch," though the two men golfed and drank and worked together for over twenty years.

Both my dad's and Henley's doors are closed. The only ones I've seen that are.

I open Henley's first.

His things are still here—the kidney-shaped desk, the view of the Ambassador Bridge, now collapsed—but no photos or personal items. The Detroit Tigers bat, signed by the entire 1987 American League East championship team, no longer stuck in the wood brackets screwed into the wall.

"Come on, Danny! You're keeping poor Dad waiting."

I can hear her.

Not just in my head anymore. I can hear her calling through the wall, six feet from where I stand.

"He's been so patient. Haven't you, Daddy?"

The voice takes me out into the hallway again. It's not my decision but hers, taking over things as easily as she'd ever done. Telling me to put my hand on the door handle, a ball of ice she urges me to turn. The door a slab of steel she suggests I might shoulder open.

Cold.

A single step onto the office's carpet and the air crystallizes, making it almost impossible to move through. It cramps every muscle, stutters the simplest thoughts. An equal slowing of body and mind.

It takes a moment to see my father.

He sits behind his desk. The chair turned around so that he looks out the window, the leather back obscuring all of him except the thinning hair of his head, the liver-spotted knuckles on the armrests.

One foot on the far side of the river and the other on your throat.

"Dad?"

He doesn't respond other than the slightest shifting in his seat, an involuntary twitch. Something about it suggests it is the outward expression of an internal struggle to be heard, to signal that a part of him still feels and hears, too.

"Go on, Danny. I'm sure Dad wants to sink his eyes into you."

Ash leans against a bookshelf of binders. Our father's lifework, the memos that weighed the chances of a certain engine or headrest or seat belt causing paralysis or dismemberment or death for those riding the open roads. She's no longer burned, but Ash the ugly-beautiful, radiant and blue-eyed and flushed, a masterful simulation of gratitude in her dimpled show of straight white teeth.

"Really. *Go on.*"

So I do. Side-step around the desk with my back to her—feel the septic breath she leans forward to blow against the back of my neck—and stand at my father's side.

"Say hello, Danny."

"Hi, Dad."

He twitches again.

His face a rictus of desperation, eyes swollen half spheres. The black nostril hairs flickering. He knows I'm here and it has brought on a new layer of whatever horror he's already been inflicted with. Whatever my sister has already done to him.

"See? Look how happy you've made him!" Ash squeals, coming around to press against me. "I haven't seen him this excited in, well, *forever*. He's positively *beaming!*"

A single finger touches my chin and turns my head to face her. The skin on the inside of her lips blue as something hanging in a meat locker.

"Have you missed me?" she says.

She opens her arms. Steps closer. Wraps them around me.

An embrace suffocating and dark as soil spilled onto a body thought to be dead but isn't. A hold my father will never escape. And now neither will I.

"You drowned her."

It's something less than a whisper, but the sound I make is so close to her ear she hears it. Her whole body hardening to stone.

"Why?" I say. "She was our *mother*."

"You *know* why," she says, tightening her hold. "She wanted to save our lives but she showed us the river instead. And I went through, Danny. I saved you but they took me down. They took my soul."

Just when I'm about to black out she lets me go.

"So I took hers," she says.

I try to back up toward the door but I can't. A wall of density, a charged force stops me whenever I move away from her. It forces me to stand where I am so I can take all of her in, admire the full realization of her perfection here, her home from the moment she was stillborn.

"Eddie," I manage.

"I'm sorry. Who?"

"The boy. Did you bring him here?"

"You saw him? That would be his doing if you did. I just pulled him away from his worried momma. Bait for you to come find me. It didn't matter to me what happened to him after that."

"He was here."

"Bad boy."

"Does it mean he's dead? If I saw him?"

Ash pouts in fake sympathy. Cocks her head to the side and her golden hair, shining without any light for it to reflect, makes a half moon of her face.

"I see that you *care*, Danny, but you'll stop soon enough," she says. "You'll forget. That tree stump of a woman you married, the runty boy you thought you could be a pretend dad to, that ridiculous bit of time where you let yourself think you were *free*—it'll all be gone. I promise you that."

She slides over to stand next to our father. Strokes his head with a manicured hand.

"You'll be just like Dad," she says. "The last of the Orchard men, reunited. And only with eyes for me."

Just being here with her draws the last vapors of life from me. Whatever I'd carried with me that allowed me to walk from place to place, the thing that infuriated the dead who saw or sensed or smelled it on me, is going. Soon Ash will steal the last of it and leave me like the man in the chair, encased within himself, tortured in ways of her design but unable even to scream.

She was always special.

"Why did you kill Meg Clemens?" I ask her, as much to test my ability to speak as for an answer. "She helped me, you know. When the friends who killed you tried to kill me. She got me out of that house."

She lifts her hand away from our father's head, the fingers stiffening a second before relaxing again. A tell of irritation she fails to wholly conceal.

"Meg the Good," she says. "May her spirit rot in heaven."

"She didn't deserve to die."

"We all die."

"Not like that."

"But we *could*," she says, and smiles, her "sweet face," a masterpiece of rehearsed authenticity. Then it drops. Circles appear below her eyes the color of an old banana peel. "Because you never know, do you?"

Dots of shadow explode before my eyes. The reverse fireworks that precede a blackout. I reach out and, as I stumble, find the wall. Clip my head against it and half the dots shoo away, though the rest still swim before me, binding and doubling like cells.

"Easy now," Ash says.

Not damned.

"Why is Dad here?" I fight to ask her, holding on to my voice like a rope tossed to a drowning man. "Why is this his place?"

A demon.

"You didn't figure it out yet? You didn't *guess*?"

A bright flash behind my eyes, the chalky taste of bleach at the back of my throat. Migraine symptoms. Never had one in my life, but talking with Ash—doing it here—is a new sickness, mutating and becoming more creative by the second.

"No," I manage.

"He was an accomplice to murder," she says. "He knew the most terrible things and this is where he'd let himself think about them. Look out this window and whisper all his secrets to himself."

That's forever.

"I don't—"

"He followed me. Two days before my birthday. *Our* birthday. Ever since Meg went missing he wondered if I might have been involved somehow, might have known something. So he went all private eye and saw me getting into Mr. Malvo's car after school and tracked us all the way to the house on Alfred Street. When the two of us went in Daddy sat behind the wheel and watched. Two minutes later poor Dean came running out, got in his car, and took off."

"Why? What happened?"

"I *showed* him Meg. I showed Mr. Malvo that I was the only girl for him. And he looked down into that cellar and saw her body and figured out a couple things in a hurry. One: I was in charge now, not him. And two: he couldn't tell anyone because he'd be the one who'd go to jail, the pervy teacher, not me, not a *girl*, not Meg's friend."

"So he left you there."

"Until Dad came in. Sneaky Daddy. Tiptoed up behind me and looked down just the way Dean did. It was like he was seeing something he half thought he'd end up seeing. He just sort of nodded— you know the way he would? That okay-so-that's-that nod of his? Turned around and made a funny kind of speedwalk for the door like he was trying not to throw up on the floor."

It's like she's reading my mind, which is nothing new. My father's fight not to be sick the same as mine.

"Dad *knew*?"

"Don't you remember the way he was acting around that time? How weird he was? I tried to talk to him about it but for two days all he would say is 'Let me think.' He was twisted up tight as could be. 'Let me *think* about this, Ashleigh.' And then it was the night before my birthday—*our* birthday, there I go again!—and he opens my bedroom door and whispers, 'Meet me at the house tomorrow.' I heard that and I knew he'd never tell. I was his daughter and he had a duty to me. That's the kind of man he was, right? The funny part, the sweet part, was my killing Meg brought me and Dad closer than anything."

A dry spit. Nothing in my stomach to throw up. Nothing inside of me at all but a churning nausea, edged with clawing pain.

"So you weren't meeting Malvo the day of the fire," I get out. "You were meeting Dad."

"It was my Sweet Sixteen! I deserved a special party! You thought Daddy went to work, remember? So I asked the girls—Michelle, Lisa, Winona, remember those bitches?—to come along with me. Promised to show them something. A surprise. And they *would* have been surprised, wouldn't they? Seeing Meg. Watching my dad make Ash's mess go away. And they would never tell, either."

"Why?"

"Because I told them they couldn't."

The floor undulating under my feet now. Not swaying in the way of a ship at sea, but bending unpredictably, knees buckling, like trying to walk across a trampoline. Except I'm not walking.

"It was going to be fun," Ash says. "But then the girls chickened out and I kept going on my own. When I got to the house, Dad was there. The place dripping and stinking with the gas he poured all over. He told me what I already knew: he wasn't going to the police, he was going to cover things up with me. *He was my father.* It was really quite beautiful, Danny. It was so *worth it*, you know? But then he said something I *wasn't* expecting. 'But this is the end of that,' he said. 'Once this is done, you'll be nothing to me. This is the last act I will perform as your father. From this point on, *you're not mine.*'"

Ash laughs. It's like the screech of tires. The helpless moment before impact.

"But you would never let him go," I say.

"Clever Danny."

"So what did you do to him?"

"I kissed him."

Ash turns her head to look out the window. Scans the grey, undefined horizon as if words were written there.

"A *real* kiss. A grown-up kiss, a fuck-me kiss, a this-is-going-to-be-so-good kiss," she says. "I started loosening his belt with one hand, the other on his back. I just wanted to keep him there. So I could let him know that he could do whatever he wanted. I was still *his.* I wanted to be his. I wouldn't tell because that's the kind of girl I was. The kind of girl every boy wants because you can do things with them that nobody else would let you get away with."

She turns to me again and the shadow-dots race and cloud. I have to blink hard to stop them from claiming all of the light that's left.

"What did he do?"

"He pushed me away," she says, taking a step closer. "He understood exactly what I was offering and it disgusted him. I disgusted him. He kind of threw his hands into my shoulders. Pushed me. Hard. I stepped back, lost my balance a little. And then I'm falling. Went through the hole in the floor and landed weird, broke my ankle, and I'm screaming for him to get me out of there. But he just looks down at me. Not angry. It was hatred, Danny. Hate isn't a feeling, it's the absence of feeling. And that's what he felt toward me: absolutely fuckall."

Her arms rise at her sides, readying. Coming at me slow but filling the space of the room until there is nothing but her.

"He just walked away," she says. "I'm guessing he was going to find a ladder somewhere or something, because I don't think, even after all that, he'd leave me to starve down there with a dead body, that he'd let me die. But I'll never know for sure. Because the next thing is those three cunts are standing there and they're lighting the place on fire."

Dad jolts in his chair. His lips tremble, but nothing comes out. His hands gripped to the armrests as though fighting to stay upright.

"And you're screaming for me," I say. "Not for Dad, not for them to call the cops. Me."

"There *was* only you, Brother," she whispers. "Useless, unwanted you."

I look back at her and Ash is inches from me. Her fingertips on my eyelids, drawing them closed.

The darkness is a weight. Like falling into water wearing a parka and jeans and boots. The struggle to the surface a hopeless shifting that only takes you deeper.

But there is something down here with me.

The vague notion of a past. Something found and cherished and lost, though I can't see it or think of its name.

Come, Danny.

Ash pulls me down to where the water hardens into stone. Holding me in place.

Come . . .

And I do.

Not toward her, but into her.

The thing with me in the darkness—the warm thing, unnamed,

alive—tells me to open my eyes. And when I see my sister I push forward.

Wrap my arms around her like a drunk. Use my height, my long legs, to set her off balance. Backstepping.

What are you doing?

I'm thrashing at air. Drowning in darkness. Eyes closed against it for the same reason I refused to open my eyes when swimming underwater: there may be something there, something unexpected and monstrous. Except this time I know if I were to look there would be an immense nothingness, and it would be more terrifying than any imagined creature.

But I'm kicking at it anyway. Cutting the dark with my fingernails. Resisting.

Danny?

Because there's another down here with me that isn't Ash. A something to her nothing.

Look at me, Brother.

I squeeze my eyes tighter until they hurt. Two entry points where knitting needles have found a way through, a pair of probes looking for a brain. To deny them, to deny her, I try to summon the unnamed thing I remembered a moment ago.

I thought of it as something. But really it was *things*. Voices, faces. The way they speak and laugh and touch.

People.

There were people in the past, and they're there now, in the present. Two in particular. Summoning me just as I summon them. Some call it prayer. And as with all prayers, it comes down to either asking someone else to fight for you, or asking yourself to fight.

Stop it, Danny. Stop it now!

Ash's voice is the pain in my head. It's the knitting needles. It's a disease of the bone marrow, malignant and enflamed.

But that's not what's important now.

What's important is to not stop. To push deeper into my twin, the space inside her, thrash and kick at her borders.

Look at ME!

The shattering glass sounds like rain. A downpour that attacks every surface, a symphony of concussions.

We're through the office window, the two of us cycling and tumbling. The rain replaced by the howling rush of air.

LOOK!

I look.

And there is my twin, tumbling away faster than me, as if her density exceeds mine. As if the earth wants her more.

Danny!

The same voice, the exact same pleading as when I looked down at her in the house's burning cellar.

DON'T LEAVE ME HERE!

Now, just as then, I reach for her. And now, just as then, she's too far.

I reach down to my sister, and she reaches up. But the only thing we touch is air.

DANNY!

They look like stars.

Behind Ash's spinning form the ice is a night sky buckshot with points of light. The river a Milky Way of distant systems, summoning from an uncrossable distance.

But they are only the faces of the dead. Coming into detail as we hurtle toward them. They see us, too. Fingers scratching at the ice's rough underside, desperate to be the first to pull us down.

They aren't people under there. Not spirits or souls, either. They are a collection of all the horrors they have created in others and themselves, nameless and distilled. A bottomless current of fear.

The ice swings up fast. In the next breath we'll hit it. We'll be through.

I find Ash's face and see how this was the vision she had when she died the moment she was born. It terrifies her. But she resists it even now. Does her best to appear defiant, even calm.

Don't leave . . .

She does it for me.

My sister, offering comfort. Shushing away a nightmare from her bed across from mine when we were kids even when my nightmare was of her. Telling me she will always be here, there is nothing to be scared of other than being without her, that no matter what, in life or death or the places other than these I have yet to see but she knows awaits us, she will never let me go.

PART 4

Within the Flames Are Spirits

47

My eyes open and I'm certain of two things.
I'm alive.

And someone else's heart is inside me.

As soon as I can make my mouth work right I ask one of the nurses the same thing over and over as she sponges my crotch, changes the sheets from under me. A nurse with strong, expert arms covered with dark hair and moles that someone should probably take a look at.

"Whose heart?"

"You'll have to speak up a bit, sunshine. These ears aren't what they were."

"Whose *heart* did I get?"

"Oh, we're not supposed to talk about—"

"I won't tell."

She neatly folds the end of the sheet over my chest, smooths it flat. It gives her the time to decide to break the rules.

"Car accident," she says. "Brain injury we couldn't do anything about, but the rest of her barely even scratched. What we call an ideal donor."

"Her?"

"It was a girl," she says, the smile dropping, the big teeth smothered by big, downy lips. "A sixteen-year-old girl."

WILLA HAS TAKEN TO RELIGION. IT WAS ALL THE PRAYING SHE DID in the hospital chapel, asking for her son and husband to be returned to her. The promises she made if they were.

"Never was much of a churchy girl," she says. "But I guess I've got to be *now*, right? A deal's a deal."

I tell her we can go every Sunday, every day of the week if she wants. Anything she wants to do, we'll do.

"I want to go home and be normal for a while," she says when I ask.

"That's it?"

"Have you been following current events around here, Danny? That's a *lot*."

She wheels Eddie in to see me on the second or third day after I came back. I ask her to give us a moment alone together and she raises her eyebrows but slips out without any questions.

"We can talk about it all you want, or we never have to talk about it again," I say. "But I need you to know that you were there with me on the other side. You saved me. Do you remember any of that?"

Eddie glances over his shoulder, confirms we're alone in the room. "I asked, but the doctors said you can't dream in a coma."

"This wasn't a dream."

"I know *that*. I'm just saying nobody else will believe us."

"Nobody else matters."

He doesn't remember everything, but he remembers enough.

Searching for me through an empty city, knowing I was alone and needed help, following my voice. And when he found me there was something after me, something he knew if he looked at he wouldn't be able to move or think, so he looked at me instead. Let the thing come after him so I could get away.

"I'm so sorry I let her do that to you, Eddie. It was wrong for me to get you involved at all. I should have stayed alone."

"You didn't do anything wrong. She did. And nobody should be alone. Besides, you took care of her, right?"

"Yeah, I did."

"Was it bad? For her, I mean. Did it hurt?"

"It was bad for her. And it hurt something awful."

"Good," Eddie says, not needing to hear anything more than this. "Then we're even."

THE CARDIAC SURGEON I LIKE IS THE ONE WHO LED THE TEAM that did the transplant procedure on me. Not that I was aware of it as it happened, but knowing it was him removing my dud of a ticker and ladling a stranger's heart into the space it left behind is an immense reassurance, as if the intimacy of these elements—my heart, her heart, our two fist-sized slaves to life—is most appropriately handled by friends.

"Well, well. Seems you've got another book to write, Mr. Orchard," he says the first time I'm conscious when he comes by my bed.

"Don't think so. This time, the secret stays with me."

"That good, was it? Don't want the wife knowing about all the heavenly virgins offering themselves to you up there?"

"Something like that."

He checks my pulse, blood pressure, reads the chart. Shakes his head.

"You're in unbelievable shape, aside from looking a little hungover," he says.

"You look a little hungover yourself."

"That's because I *am*."

I thank him. It takes a while. Trying to tell him all the ways what he's done for me will change not just my life but others, as many as I can help in as many ways as I can. How it may not mean anything to him but I promise I won't squander the extra time I've been given. I ask what his first name is—Steven—and assure him that if Willa and

I have a child together, if we give Eddie a dog, if I ever buy a boat, we're naming it after him. He grins at all this, having seen versions of it before. The magical outcomes that come along among the more usual disappointments, the inability to make any difference, the fadings away.

"I'm just the mechanic around here," he says. "You found a way back, Danny, not me."

"What can I say? I like it here."

"You should. Here is pretty damned good, most of the time," he says, and steps closer, lowers his voice to a more serious register. "So let me ask you this. If you're so attached to this mortal coil, why'd you take a sprint into the Public Garden? Some guy with a knife after you? Trying to make last call at the Four Seasons?"

I don't want to lie to this man. And something tells me that, if I told him the truth, he would get it, or at least see that I believed it even if he didn't. But how far do you go in telling a story like mine? Too little, and it won't make sense. Too much, and he might sign me up for a psych ward evaluation.

"I had something to take care of over there," I say in the end.

"I take it you mean over *there* there, and not over there on Boylston Street."

"If it was Boylston Street, I would've taken a cab."

He seems halfway satisfied by this. He doesn't ask anything more about it in any case. Just shakes his head again in that agreeably baffled way of his and steps away from the side of the bed, signaling the serious moment has passed.

When I ask him when he thinks I might be getting out of here, he makes a face of mock gravity.

"Well, we have at least one other test to run," he says. "Rather unpleasant, I'm afraid."

"Okay. What is it?"

"Rectal exam."

"Why?"

"To see if we can find the horseshoe you've got stuck up there."

◆ ◆ ◆

Eventually, once they get permission from her parents, a hospital administrator tells me the name of the girl who was in the car accident, the one whose heart now beats inside me.

Nadine.

For the rest of my time in recovery I write a letter addressed to Nadine's mother and father and family "and All Who Loved Her." History's most inadequate thank-you note. But I include a postscript that I hope might provide real comfort. The promise that wherever Nadine is now, it's a good place. The best day of her life forever.

When it's finished I fold the pages and, along with a copy of *The After*, lay them in the bottom of a FedEx box. Before I seal the flaps and give it to Willa to send to the address they gave me, I take the Omega off my wrist and slip it in.

I lied to the cardiac doctor when I told him I had no plans to write another book.

The fact is, after only two months at home, I'm deep into something new. An account of the After from the perspective of someone who's been to the place we worry might exist, that might be where we end up if it does. The place Violet Grieg spoke of and that Lyle Kirk said made her an Underworlder. Which means I'm an Underworlder now, too.

It's about what happened to my mother and father, about a burning house, about Ash. It's about the fates we're born with and the ones we make for ourselves. A true story that tells of solitude and hauntings and finding unexpected ways to be happy even when happiness seems to lie on the other side of an uncrossable river.

I'm calling it *The Damned*.

The tricky part is going to be the ending.

There are some questions I don't know the answer to, as there always are about the future. Willa and Eddie and the lives I wish them to have. How long Nadine's heart will carry on with its duties in its new home. Whether Ash will ever come back or not.

But you know what I know and you hold as close to the present as you can. Keep your eye on what's certain.

Ash went through the ice and I didn't.

She's somewhere lower than Detroit, a place where she's fixed in water hard as stone. A place so distant from the world of light it would be impossible to rise up and find me in it, though she'll try.

She's something else now, something I hope to never see, but she'll always be my sister.

Which means she'll never stop trying.

Acknowledgments

First, thanks to my editor, Sarah Knight, who has talked me off ledges and pushed me to the edge of some of those same ledges, always brilliantly and productively. My gratitude also to all at Simon & Schuster, Simon & Schuster Canada, and Orion who've had their hands on this book: Carolyn Reidy, Jonathan Karp, Marysue Rucci, Richard Rhorer, Kevin Hanson, Alison Clarke, David Millar, Kate Gales, Molly Lindley, Elina Vaysbeyn, Amy Jacobson, Amy Cormier, Michelle Blackwell, Jonathan Evans, Joshua Cohen, Lewelin Polanco, Jason Heuer, Jon Wood, Kate Mills, Jemima Forrester, Gaby Young, and Graeme Williams. Additional thanks to Anne McDermid, Stephanie Cabot, Peter Robinson, Jackie Levine, Howard Sanders, Sally Riley, Monica Pacheco, Martha Magor, Chris Bucci, Jason Richman, and Danny Hertz.

In researching *The Damned*, I read many books about Detroit, but would like to acknowledge in particular the excellent *Made in Detroit* by Paul Clemens, *Detroit: A Biography* by Scott Martelle, and *Detroit: An American Autopsy*, by Charlie LeDuff.

Finally, thanks to my wife, Heidi. There's no one I love being caught in a brainstorm with more than you.

About the Author

ANDREW PYPER is previously the author of six novels, most recently *The Demonologist,* a #1 bestseller in his native Canada and winner of the International Thriller Writers Award. His other novels include *Lost Girls* (winner of the Arthur Ellis Award and a *New York Times* bestseller), *The Killing Circle* (a *New York Times* Crime Novel of the Year), and *The Guardians* (a *Globe and Mail* Best Book). *The Demonologist* is currently being developed for feature film by Oscar-winning producer and director Robert Zemeckis and Universal Pictures. He lives in Toronto. Visit him at www.andrewpyper.com.